Midnight Oil

Stories to Fuel Your Nightmares

A WordCrafter Midnight Anthology, vol. 3

Edited by Kaye Lynne Booth

WordCrafter Press

Introduction by Kaye Lynne Booth

Compiled and edited by Kaye Lynne Booth

Cover design by DL Mullan of *Sonoran Dawn Studios*

WordCrafter Press

Table of Contents

Editor's Note

The language used in this book may offend some readers. My goal is to use all the tools at an author's disposal and all the tools in my author's tool kit to create as exacting a sensory experience for the reader and to be as accurate and authentic to the story as possible. Sometimes that means language or situations which may offend some are used to create such discerning imagery.

I have worked hard to make this anthology the best it can be, but I am human. Please be forgiving if you happen upon typos or other errors, and please, call them to my attention to help make my work better in the future.

This is a diverse global anthology with contributing authors from several countries. Authors from abroad may use European spellings, while North American authors may use American English. They are not misspellings, but simple differences found when you bring together a varied mixture of voices.

Characters, events, places and things described or depicted in this work are fictitious. Any similarity to actual persons, events, places, or things are purely coincidental.

Introduction

Midnight Oil is book 3 in the Midnight Anthology Series from *WordCrafter Press.* It brings you 16 deliciously dark tales from 14 different authors which will tantalize the tastebuds of dark fiction connoisseurs. It includes the winning story in the *2025 WordCrafter Dark Fiction Contest*, by Denise Aparo, "The Vanishing".

Each year, *WordCrafter Press* receives submissions for the annual short fiction contest, but in 2025, all submissions came from previous *WordCrafter* authors. These talented authors have provided a selection of original dark tales, which I'm sure you will enjoy.

These are tales which will make you ponder the unknown and have you returning, hungry for more. There's a little something for all dark fiction lovers in this collection as we bring you evil bat-gods, magical beauty spells, carrion eating beetles, South African voodoo magic, or tales of misery and grief. Pull up a chair and get comfortable as we burn the Midnight Oil and settle in for a spine-tingling tale or two, or three. Once you begin, *Midnight Oil: Stories to Fuel Your Nightmares* you may not be able to put it down until the last drops of darkness are absorbed.

Villa's Gold

Mario Acevedo

The Mayan bat-god Camazotz snacked on the dismembered remains of his human prey. Grasping a femur between the claws at the front of his enormous wings, he gnawed bloody flesh off the bone.

A faint glow illuminated the cave entrance, alerting him that dawn was about to break. Reluctantly, Camazotz dropped his meal and retreated deeper into the cave, scrambling to hide from the morning sun and its deadly, agonizing rays.

Urbano Quezada wrote in his journal:

22 April 1924

It's been almost a year since that son-of-a-bitch Pancho Villa died. Shot full of holes like a tin can used for target practice. I was his faithful soldier, one of his Dorados. But with the "Revolution" over, I am left with nothing but regrets and an empty belly.

Which brings me to this journey. In search of Pancho Villa's hidden treasure, what I—as one of his tax collectors—looted from banks and haciendas. We're told Villa's gold is a myth, but what betrays that lie are the caches unearthed in Chihuahua, Torreon, Cuauhtémoc, El Paso, and San Antonio.

I paid a santero to sacrifice a rooster and read its entrails, and he divined this premonition leading me to the Sierra Madre Occidental west of Durango. I hired as my guide, Nestor Marquez, a Tepehuán with a strong back who knows his place. What amazes me is his lack of curiosity about Villa's treasure, which explains why these indio peasants remain peasants, poor and perpetually underfoot.

Once out of the llano, the trail snaked up narrow draws, so steep and punishing they left me laboring for breath and questioning my judgement. At the instant I damned myself a fool for trusting that guajiro witch doctor, I found by my feet a 1-peso gold coin, worth five Yankee dollars! So encouraged, I continue on my quest for Villa's gold.

Camazotz crept to the mouth of the cave and gazed upon the rocky terrain illuminated by a starry night. The atmosphere in these desert mountains was so clean, so sparse, so sterile. How he missed the humid, jungle smells of his Yucatan home.

The great Kukulcán —the Feathered Serpent Supreme God—had banished Camazotz for doing nothing to save his sister, a bat-god like himself, from being incinerated by the morning sun. They had been stalking prey in the jungle and lost track of time when the dawn broke. In panic, Camazotz raced ahead to safety. When in the cave, he looked back as the morning sun's illumination tore into his sister. She fell, writhing, burning, screaming in agony. Her incinerated corpse crumbled into black ash, to be scattered by a sudden breeze, as if Kukulcán himself was whisking away the last of her remains.

The Feathered Serpent God then accused Camazotz of cowardice because he had shirked his duty to protect his sister. Besides banishment, he forbade Camazotz from consuming prey beyond his lair. Camazotz could range the grounds outside, but he had to lure his victims to his cave before eating them.

Camazotz had been exiled to the rugged mountains of western Mexico. Forbidden from hunting outside his lair, he had come close to perishing from starvation. He trapped mice to catch roving predators, but these meals were too infrequent. So, he built a cistern inside the mouth of his cave to gather rainwater and thus attract armadillo and deer.

But the best meal was the succulent flesh of humans. Those who ventured into this mountain canyon were little different from the humans he had stalked in the Mayan wilderness. When he pounced upon them, their shrieks of terror were almost as satisfying as their warm, fresh meat.

23 April 1924

My second day on the trail. My horse and mule plod beside me, the path too steep to risk riding the horse, the mule laden with our supplies. I trudge for hours on this accursed incline, my feet and heart aching. But the moment I'm ready to surrender to good sense, a piece of gold appears in the dirt. Yesterday, it had been another 1-peso coin. This morning, a Yankee golden eagle. It's as if Providence sees the need to goad me forward.

Seven cycles of the moon ago, Camazotz praised his luck when a hard rain drove a pair of humans into his lair. He'd clung to the high ceiling, his coarse skin blending with the rock, watching, waiting to strike, confident his prey would not look up until too late. He'd learned to keep his cave tidy, else the bones, bits of rotting flesh, and remnants of pelts or clothing from his meals would spook new victims.

The man and a woman seemed fascinated by the pool of water contained within a circle of rocks just inside the cave.

He studied the two, listening to them speak a different tongue than that of the Mayan people. From their guttural sounds and by reading their auras, Camazotz learned enough to understand most of what they communicated. He guessed they were a mating couple and, from her rich scent, that she was pregnant. Such a meal she and her little one would make.

They built a small fire within the cave. Its yellow light stung Camazotz's eyes and the acrid smoke chafed his throat. By the light of a torch, they explored the cave. The woman pried the remains of a human skull from the dirt. Camazotz had forgotten to get rid of this one. Strangely, she acted surprised, but not afraid. "*Dios mío*, what happened to him?"

The man: "Perhaps he had been dragged in here and shot. There was a war, remember? Or maybe a bear got him."

She wrinkled her nose. "Explains the stink. What else died in here?"

No longer interested in the skull, they turned their attention to a crevice in the back wall. Camazotz knew what was there, for he had already explored the inside of the mountain, discovering the spoils of what other humans had left behind. Mostly piles of yellow metal coins.

After reassuring the woman that he'd be careful, the man slipped through the crevice, the glow from his torch shrinking as he crept away.

Camazotz focused on the woman. She returned to the fire and with a stick, poked at the flames, lost in thought.

Quiet as a spider, Camazotz moved across the ceiling.

Slowly, he uncurled himself, clawed feet locked within a rocky crevasse, and dangled over his prey, ready to reveal himself in a horrific flash of wings and fangs.

23 April 1924

I write this by the light of our campfire. As with every day on the climb, when the going gets at its most trying, I find gold. Today it was another 1-peso coin. Almost like crumbs leading me to the banquet.

Urbano relaxed close to the campfire. Sparks floated upward, losing themselves in the night's stars. He and Nestor were on a circular shelf on the trail, the path up the mountain seeming to go forever. The day had been long, leaving his muscles limp with fatigue.

On the other side of the flames, Nestor's eyes glowed red, the flickering light animating the chiseled contours of his indigenous face. He sat cross-legged with a machete balanced on his knees and ran a stone across the blade's edge.

Skritch. Skritch. Skritch.

He carried no firearms, as with the war over, *indios* like him were no longer needed as soldiers and therefore not trusted with guns.

Needing to entertain himself, Urbano withdrew two stogies from a bag. He threw one at Nestor.

"*Gracias, jefe.*"

Both men pulled smoldering sticks from the campfire to light their smokes.

Urbano puffed. "You have family?"

Nestor exhaled a long plume. "I do, *señor.*"

"Tell me about them."

"I lost my first wife and our three children to cholera and the war."

"My condolences."

"My fortunes changed. I now have a new wife and a daughter."

"A daughter? Her name?"

"Kismet."

"Interesting. As if you're not sure what to expect from her."

"Let fate decide," Nestor replied.

"With a name like that?"

Nestor changed the subject. "And you, *señor*?"

"Two wives. Actually, a wife and an *amante.* As if getting nagged by one woman isn't enough. What's that look on your face? You disapprove?"

"It is not for me to approve or disapprove." The *indio* pointed to the sky with his cigar. "That is up to the Almighty."

"You believe in God?"

Nestor didn't answer.

"You know religion is nothing but fairy tales meant to oppress us?"

"Many things oppress us, *señor* Quezada."

"Such as?"

"Misfortune. War. Taxes. The government."

For an uneducated man, Nestor could be rather on point.

"One more thing," Urbano said. "If you know about this gold, why haven't you come before and collected it?"

Nestor knit his brow as if he'd never considered the question. "I have no horse or mule of my own to carry it. As you can see, this mountain is no easy climb. How many trips would I have to make?"

"One pocketful of gold pesos is more than you'll ever make as a campesino."

Nestor shrugged as if that didn't matter. Typical *indio*.

Urbano yawned. He tossed the butt of his cigar into the campfire then stretched on his bed of pine needles and fluffed a blanket over himself. "*Mañana, pues.*" For a pillow, he used his chore coat, where in one pocket he stashed the gold coins. Under the coat, he kept his revolver, just in case.

Urbano felt prepared for anything.

Camazotz readied himself to snatch the woman. He was reaching for her when the man's voice echoed from the crevice. "Esperanza! Esperanza! Look what I have found!"

The light of his torch flashed within the crevice. Camazotz retracted against the ceiling, frustrated that he'd lost this chance for an easy kill.

The woman hopped to her feet to greet the man as he wiggled through the crevice. Holding his torch aloft, he offered his other hand, which he opened to display several of the yellow metal coins.

"I found it!" he exclaimed. "Villa's gold!"

The woman took the coins, inspecting them.

He gestured to the crevice. "Three casks. Filled with gold coins."

Camazotz watched, puzzled how to continue. His belly grumbled from hunger. But he had to plan his attack wisely. If he sprang upon the man first, he risked losing the woman should she flee out the entrance.

But if he attacked her first, the man could burn him with the torch.

Camazotz decided to drop and block the entrance, shock them with his presence, then swipe their legs, hobbling them to dine upon on their flesh at his leisure.

Using his feet and wing claws, he crept upside down across the ceiling to the entrance, slowly as to not attract attention. Once in position, he turned to face them and floated to the ground. At last, noticing him, the two humans cringed in terror. Camazotz rose to full height, bared his fangs, and spread his wings as he emitted his horrific howl.

The man pushed the woman aside and defiantly waved the torch.

Camazotz shook his wings and again, emitting that dreadful scream.

But the man didn't cower nor retreat.

Camazotz realized the mortal creature must have been an experienced soldier. If Camazotz made one mistake, it could be fatal. Or equally bad, if Kukulcán found out that the bat-god had been bested by a human, it would mean yet more punishment and humiliation.

Man and monster glared at each other.

Camazotz pondered what to do. He couldn't let the humans go, as he was hungry. And there was his pride as a deity, albeit a lesser one. Mortals should pay dearly for defying the gods.

He spotted the gold coins the woman had let fall to the ground. The torch light reflecting across their surface brought an idea. Humans so valued this metal, even killing one another for it. Why eat these two humans if he could use their greed to betray others?

He looked at the woman and softened his expression. "You have a name?"

The man and woman grimaced in astonishment.

She blinked. "You speak?"

"You understand me, do you not, Esperanza?"

The woman gaped, wide-eyed. "How is it you know my name?"

Camazotz pointed at the man. "Isn't that what he called you?"

"Yes, my name is Esperanza," she said. "My husband's name is Nestor."

"Esperanza. Nestor." The monster tipped his head. "Camazotz." He gestured with a wing's claw to the gold coins. "You want?"

"You're going to give us the gold?"

"Not quite. Let us arrange a deal."

Nestor shook the torch. "Don't trust him."

Camazotz showed his dagger-like fangs. "You don't have much choice."

Esperanza placed a hand on Nestor's arm. "What is your deal?"

"I'll release you and let you take those coins."

Nestor: "That's the deal?"

Camazotz was enjoying this game. Seldom did he use his intellectual cunning. "I've noticed how you humans lust for this yellow metal, which you treasure as much as life itself. Take those coins and spend some on yourselves. Esperanza is with child..."

She covered her belly and retreated a step.

Camazotz continued, "...and you deserve to live free of want. But you must use what remains as bait to bring others to me."

Esperanza: "Why don't you hunt your victims on your own?"

The bat-god felt a pinch of irritation at having to explain himself. "There are reasons I cannot hunt and eat outside this cave. That is why you need to help me."

Nestor: "Why should I do such a thing?"

"You have enemies, no? Powerful men who have stolen from you. Made you suffer."

A sudden gloss in Nestor's eyes told Camazotz that his words had found purchase.

Esperanza raised on tiptoes to whisper into her husband's ear, who then narrowed his eyes at Camazotz. "Why should we trust you?"

Camazotz side-stepped from the mouth of the cave. "There, go. You are free to leave." He paused a beat. "Without the gold."

Neither of the humans moved. Esperanza's gaze swiveled to the coins. He sensed their auras quiver in temptation.

"You want us to bring you victims," she said. "We'd be monsters like you to do such a thing."

"But you will have gold. That will make your life as monsters more comfortable."

Their auras trembled with indecision. Then abruptly, Esperanza bent over and with both hands, raked the coins into her fingers. "We have a deal."

Nestor nodded but kept the torch at the ready.

Camazotz motioned with one wing to the entrance. "Go." As the humans crept out, he warned, "In taking those coins, we have made a pact. I give you a half cycle of the moon to bring me my first meal." In the meantime, he would satisfy his hunger with mountain critters. "But remember, cheat me and I will hunt you down. The night is mine. I cannot pursue my meals outside this cave, but nothing prevents me from killing you both. And your baby."

24 April 1924

I found more gold on the trail. Nestor uncovered the piece with his big feet, but he didn't even notice. A small coin to be sure, but enough to whet my appetite in that I will soon find Villa's horde.

I try not to lose myself in fanciful speculation, daydreams about the rancho I will purchase, the fine horse and splendid saddle I will ride. What horse? I will buy an automobile. And hire a chauffeur. I will live as the rich man I deserve to be.

Though my joints creak and my muscles ache from exertion, my certain hopes drive me forward. How much gold will I find? I wonder if our horse and mule will be able to carry it all.

Nestor halted ahead on the trail and pulled the animals into the adjacent shade. He planted his sandaled feet on a large, flat rock beneath the trees, where he crouched, the sheathed machete draped at his side.

Nestor looked over his shoulder up the trail. The crest of the mountain loomed over the tree line, appearing tantalizingly close. "We've made good time. The cave is nearby."

The announcement surprised Urbano. "When you say nearby, what do you mean?"

The *indio* squinted toward the sun. "We should reach it by late this afternoon."

Villa's gold! Urbano could feel the heavy coins bounce in his hands. The aches in his joints vanished as if soothed by a *curandera's* herbal balm.

Two weeks after Nestor and Esperanza left his lair, Camazotz heard men outside.

One spoke gruffly. "Quite the ordeal reaching this place. Smells like animals have been using this cave as a shitter."

True to his word, Nestor brought the first victim on time. An older, rough-looking type, but a good meal.

When Camazotz had lunged upon the man, Nestor stepped outside. The winged monster flipped his victim over, tore open the throat, and lapped at the torrent of blood. Slashing the victim's garments to ribbons, Camazotz broke apart the ribcage and scooped out handfuls of bloody organs. So warm. So delicious.

At last satiated, Camazotz rested on his haunches on the cave floor, surrounded by bones and scraps of gore, the dirt clotted with blood. He folded his claws over his belly, distended and round with its bounty of human flesh.

Nestor returned but didn't advance beyond the threshold of the cave entrance.

Camazotz picked his teeth with a sliver of bone. "Yes?"

"I'm here for the gold."

Camazotz waved him forward. "Come get it."

"I prefer that you toss the coins."

"You do not trust me?"

Nestor scanned the butchered remains littered about. "I trust that you will remain true to your nature."

Camazotz resented having to move. Reaching uncomfortably for the bloody tattered clothing of his victims, he ran the fabric through his claws until he found the coins, then ripped them loose. He pitched them toward Nestor, who recovered the coins from the dirt.

"What about my gold?"

"What do you mean?"

"This gold is the bait. I need my gold, my revenue from this venture."

Camazotz chuckled. *This venture? Meaning this cruel deception whereby you bring your fellow humans to their deaths?*

The bat-god glanced to the crevice. The thought of getting up and squeezing through the narrow crack spoiled his good mood. "How about you come back tomorrow? I will leave"—he waved a claw—"one large coin buried in the rocks outside the cave."

"Very well. And in the future, have my coins ready when I arrive."

Camazotz chafed at taking orders, let alone from a puny mortal. As Nestor turned to leave, the bat-god asked, "I'm curious, who was this victim?"

"The man who murdered my first wife and burned my home."

"Are there are other such men on your list?"

"Many," Nestor answered.

So, it continued for fifteen more cycles of the moon. And always, the victims acted surprised by Nestor's generosity, how graciously he had forgiven them for their offenses against him, lured by the tempting promise of gold.

After receiving these dinners of human flesh, Camazotz would hand over only a few coins from the casks, meaning this arrangement would last for years. But after the gold was depleted? What would happen to this deal then?

Camazotz put the thought aside. That was a small worry for a distant future.

25 April 1924

We arrived, just as Nestor predicted, by late afternoon at the mouth of the cave. Though inside I'm trembling with excitement, I've decided to jot these notes, to preserve these moments for posterity. I know that once we find the gold, it will be a race down the mountain because as they say, the wind has ears, and I don't want company.

Nestor stopped occasionally to check his bearings. Upon verifying their position, he veered off the trail to follow a narrow animal path, the horse and mule trampling the weeds. After about thirty paces, he and Urbano reached a wall of *pino* and *romerillo*. Nestor led them to a gap in the thicket, which opened to a tiny clearing set against a rocky knoll.

One side of the rock had cracked open, forming an entrance large enough for a man to walk through. Various animal tracks—deer, coyote, armadillo—funneled into the cave. But no human footprints.

Urbano studied the cave's murky void. *Was this finally it? Villa's treasure?*

"Are you sure this is the place, Nestor?"

The *indio* remained blasé about the discovery. "I am certain, *señor*."

"You act as if you've been here before. The way you track signs."

"I'm only following the legend."

Urbano scoped out the area, the immediate carpet of flora, the side of the mountain extending up and up, the bowl of trees surrounding them. Now that he was here, the cave was obvious, but imagining this one fissure in this one mountain, this one mountain among so many in the Sierra Madre Occidental, he was awed by his presence in such a vast landscape, and that fortune had indeed smiled upon him.

"If you are correct, we will be rich."

"Perhaps," Nestor replied.

"What do you mean, perhaps?" Urbano asked. "I thought you said this is the place."

"It is, *jefe*. If the legend says the gold is here, it is here."

Urbano imagined Pancho Villa and his circle of thieves making this trek, searching for the perfect spot to hide the loot. Then after stashing the gold—well, dead men tell no tales.

He averted his eyes from the *indio* and let guilt wash through and out of him. Gold made men do crazy, wicked things and after they found the treasure, who knew when Nestor would use that machete of his to keep the riches for himself.

Using his most sympathetic voice, Urbano said, "I don't understand you, Nestor. Why the apathy? We are on the brink of being wealthy. From this day forward, you will want for nothing."

Nestor tugged at the horse's reins. "Shall I make camp?"

Urbano noticed the dulling of colors in the late afternoon light. "Not now. So, it gets dark, it'll be dark inside the cave. With luck, we'll find the gold right away. If that's the case, we'll load the animals and get down the mountain as fast as we can."

"Very well." Nestor tied the horse and mule to a stump. He reached to pull Urbano's rifle from its saddle scabbard.

Urbano said, "Leave it. I have my *pistola*."

Nestor retrieved a miner's lamp from the mule's pack.

Urbano thought, *when to do the deed?* He might need Nestor's help to load the gold on the animals. Then again, he figured that as the gold should be in coin, he could carry them by the handful to the mule's pack and the horse's saddlebags. Going down the mountain would not be as arduous as the climb up and he was certain that by the day after tomorrow, he'd be in Durango. Plus, he would rest easier knowing that Nestor could no longer decapitate him in his sleep. Right after we find the gold then. *Sorry, my trusting indio friend, but business is business.*

"*Listo*," Nestor announced, waving the lantern. In the accumulating twilight, the lantern's flame shimmered a golden yellow, as if to foreshadow the treasure awaiting them.

He led their way into the cave, the lantern throwing an arc of light before them. Stepping inside, an intense stink made Urbano's eyes water.

To the left, just within the cave, rocks had been fashioned about a round depression, forming a primitive basin of sorts, surrounded by animal tracks.

"Someone made this," Urbano said.

"*Si jefe*, so it would seem."

"Who? Why?"

Nestor shrugged.

Urbano scanned the inside of the cave, seeing only dirt floor and rock walls. But no gold. He dragged a boot across the ground, hoping to see the flash of a coin turning over.

Nothing.

The back of his throat tightened, the first rumblings that his quest had been a fool's journey, that Villa's gold remained a myth. His gaze panned the back wall, where he saw it, a black gash in the darkness...a crevasse. One wide enough for a man to wedge through.

Urbano heard himself whisper, "The gold." He pivoted toward the crevasse, heart beating to the chant, *Villa's gold! Villa's gold!*

He grabbed for Nestor. "Give me the lamp."

But Nestor didn't move, his eyes fixed on something behind Urbano. In the dim light, the *indio's* eyes showed danger. Carefully, Urbano let his hand creep toward his revolver while he very slowly turned around.

Not two paces from him stood an enormous bat-monster, wings extending the width of the cave. Eyes like polished obsidian glared above an open snout displaying teeth long and sharp as daggers.

Urbano's thoughts stammered as his mind oscillated between disbelief and terror.

At the instant when his thoughts snapped into a reaction, (*Fight back, grab your gun. Shoot! Shoot! Shoot!*), this infernal thing swiped its wings forward, claws seizing his shoulders. Skin and bone, and hard muscle enveloped his arms and torso. Fangs sank into his neck.

A pain like fire burned through Urbano. Blinding agony dropped a shroud of darkness between himself and the monster. A scream echoed in his skull. Iron-hard claws ripped into his chest and hot blood gushed over his skin.

Camazotz crouched on the cave floor to tear the heart from his prey. The bat-god chomped on the knot of muscle, relishing every squirt of blood. This meal was worth the wait. "You are good at this, Nestor, this betrayal."

Hearing no answer, the bat-god stopped in mid-chew. Usually, Nestor eased out of the cave to avoid witnessing a fellow human dismembered so savagely. This time, Camazotz hadn't seen Nestor leave and sensed he was still behind him.

Then, an intense pain cleaved across the bat-god's upper back and spine. He jerked and fell on top of his victim.

Though he tried, nothing moved below his neck. Struggling to turn his head, he caught the lantern's glint on the blood of Nestor's up-raised machete.

"Yes, I am good at betrayal." Nestor planted his sandal on Camazotz's head to stretch the bat-god's neck. "Let me show you what the revolution taught me. That this is Mexico, and when it comes to gold, you can't trust anybody."

With a grunt, Nestor heaved downwards.

In that brief moment, Camazotz prayed to Kukulcán. *Master, please grant me one last wish: Curse this cave's gold with the same treachery that Nestor brought upon me.*

Camazotz waited for an answer, but all he heard was a *Whack!*

The cave's interior swirled about him as his severed head tumbled through the dirt, then rolled to a stop. His eyes fixed with Nestor's triumphant gaze until this world went dark.

Nestor brought his family north and settled in Tucson. He smuggled the remainder of Villa's gold across the border and buried it in the nearby mountains, carefully spending his loot one coin at a time to avoid attention.

His daughter Kismet grew into a winsome young woman, though as enigmatic as she was beautiful. Growing up, she obsessed about two things: the gold coins and collecting wild desert herbs to brew what she called "magical potions."

Nestor wrote in his journal:

8 June 1940

I traveled north to the land of gringos, to put safe distance between myself and the treachery of my homeland.

Last year, my darling Esperanza took mysteriously ill and passed on, leaving me heartbroken. At the funeral, our only child, Kismet, asked for her share of the family secret, our stash of Villa's gold.

I told her she must wait until I am old and die.

Then I became ill. Now I lay on my deathbed. Kismet stands beside me, her eyes glowing with betrayal, like those of a vengeful bat-god monster.

Jeremiah

(A Tale of the Northern Clan)

Joseph Carrabis

There is a scene in the movie *Jesus Christ Superstar*, when Jesus is surrounded by lepers and cripples and all kinds of sick sons-a-bitches. They're all reaching out for him to heal them.

Only they're not waiting for him to heal them. They're a mob dying of thirst seeing a glass of water. They're a panicking crowd seeing a doorway out of a burning house. They're a swarm of bottle flies descending on a wounded moose.

He has something they want and they're going to get it, and fuck anybody who gets in their way. It's not "Help me, Jesus," it's "Get out of my way, motherfucker."

In the movie, he's engulfed by them, like he's a single-celled animal being devoured by this amoeba of humanity. Right before he's totally devoured, he cries out, "Stop! There are too many of you!" And he's pleading because he can't stop them. There are too many, and because there are too many, he can't help a one of them.

But they don't. It's I'll get mine and screw the next guy.

I remember watching that scene in awe, whispering my revelation because I understood. "He doesn't know who he is."

My date leaned towards me. "What?"

"He doesn't know the difference between *he* and *they*."

Some guy behind me '*shhh'ed*. I stared at the screen. "He can't Shield. He doesn't know how to Shield himself."

Shhh.

A shooting pain in my head forced my eyes open. A man stared down at me, one hand gently lifted my head, the other held a canteen to my lips and eased water down my throat.

My tongue pushed past loose teeth and rasped over brittle blood clots on my lips. I got out "Who..." then coughed up a mucousy gob of lung.

"Shhh. Tom. My name's Tom." He wiped my face.

I looked around and blinked at the sunlight. The pain centered on the sides of my head, behind my eyes.

"Don't move. Somebody did a good job loosening your brains. And you have several knife wounds. Must have pissed somebody off right well."

I inhaled the best I could. Forest scents. Pine, mostly. Oak pollen. Birch. "Where?"

"The Taconics. Mount Greylock to be exact, on the eastern face. Morning. You've been here overnight." He closed his eyes and turned his head away from me. "People are coming. You should sleep."

"Hello?"

No answer.

I lay on a cot, one of two placed toe-to-toe along a shorter wall of a single room cabin, maybe 25x40. Spartan from what I could see except for the four windows, either stained glass or pieces of glass glazed together, and clear enough to show it was light out. A big woodstove sat in the center with radiator wings coming off towards the long ends of the room. The wall opposite me had a shelf half the wall's length with an upside-down basin, an old fashioned well pump, pots and pans neatly stacked, dishes and cups on a higher shelf, and between the two, a fine looking set of butchery knives. Diagonally, opposite me a door, hinged to open out, not in, and closed.

One long wall held drying plants, herbs, slabs of bark - a regular pharmacopoeia. I didn't recognize any of it. Nothing sellable, anyway. Sealed mason jars lined the floor under the herbs. I didn't want to look too close at what they held. Somebody's dead mongoloid baby or a floating eyeball. Didn't want that. Whatever they held, I couldn't smell formaldehyde, so maybe somebody canned their own food?

The remaining wall had a small kitchen-ish table and two chairs. A kerosene lantern and sewing supplies lay on the table.

I stood and the room swirled. My legs gave out and I fell backwards onto the cot.

The door opened and Tom walked in with a rack of split wood in his arms. "Ah, you're standing. You feel much better."

I reached for my blade, then realized I wasn't wearing my own clothes anymore. What I had on fit tight and long, and I guessed they were his.

"It's over there." He pointed with his chin. "By the basin on the shelf."

He was older than me. Fifteen, maybe twenty years. Tall and lean, but something told me he was wiry strong. And quick.

He started towards the stove, and I moved towards my blade. It didn't look like he was carrying anything.

"Where's my sheath?"

He set the wood down quietly. When he rose, he looked larger than before. Still wiry, just bigger. He turned to me, and I could've sworn his eyes got wider. Not bigger, just further apart on his face.

Then he walked to the table and picked my sheath up in his hand. "The stitches were pretty poor on one side. I mended them. Hope you don't mind."

"Toss it here."

He did. It sailed directly into my hand, like Spiderman webbing a handgun before the crook pulls the trigger.

"I whet your knife, too. It had some serious nicks in it."

I put the knife back in its sheath and settled them both in the small of my back. "What's the game?"

He leaned back against the table. "Game?"

"What are the rules? You patched me up. I remember ten, twelve guys taking their turns with me, knives, fists, and feet. What do you want? How long have I been here?"

He looked down and to the side and shook his head. "Rules. Do what I say, and you'll be safe here? Is that an acceptable rule to you?" He turned to face the table. "You've been here about a day. You slept most of that."

He opened a drawer I didn't know the table had and reached in.

I let my blade fly.

It got a foot away from him, *thwang*ed and clattered to the floor. But it didn't hit anything. There was nothing for it to hit.

Unless Tom slapped it down. I'd heard about guys like that. Special Service and Black Ops vets who couldn't be around people anymore and knew sixty million ways to kill you with a thumbtack and a Hershey bar.

"Hey, I don't want any trouble." Stupid thing to say after you just threw down on somebody who could smoke you before you blinked.

His hand came out of the drawer with a pack of cards. "Do you play cards?"

"Okay. I got it now. Whoever draws high card wins? Except I wouldn't stand a chance against you. I draw high card, and you let me go?"

"I'd hoped you'd stay for dinner, Jeremiah, but - "

"That's not my name." One time, must've been ten, fifteen years ago, I'm walking through an airport picking up a friend and this little, tiny woman, couldn't've been more than five feet tall, thin like a whip, and wrinkly old with frosty white hair, a walking Q-tip, moves through the crowd towards me.

Except she's not walking through the crowd. She's making a beeline for me and the crowd's separating around her, getting out of her way without realizing they're doing it, like she had some kind of bow wake that's moving people aside. Except for me. I couldn't get out of her way. Her eyes were on me, and they locked my legs to the floor.

She walks right up to me and her bow wake envelopes me. I can't move, but now the whole universe is just this little old woman and me. We're not in the airport anymore, we're in something thick and milky, like a ball of hot wax, and I must work to breathe. She looks up into my eyes and pokes me in the chest, except her finger feels like a bullet breaking through my ribcage. "Lower, Center, Relax, Breathe," she says. "You're name's Jeremiah. Remember that." And she's gone. I turn around, but I can't see her. Whatever bow wake she had isn't working anymore because everybody's walking and milling and there's no ancient Q-tip anywhere.

I stared at Tom and checked for my blade with my peripheral vision. "How d'you know that name? I talk in my sleep?"

Okay. This time his eyes definitely went wide. They got further apart on his face and his ears got pointy.

"No, you don't talk in your sleep. Jeremiah is the name Sade gave you a while ago. It's your real name. Jim's not your real name. That's her gift, to know the real." He held out his hand. "My real name's Ezekiel. Among our Kind. Straights know me as Tom."

Our Kind? Straight?

He laughed. "Same words, different culture."

He knows what I think?

He knows what I think?

"I just want to get my blade and leave. I won't tell anybody about you. I swear. Okay?"

"You are free to leave. You are not free to hurt me in leaving." He tilted his head back and his nostrils flared. "You may not want to leave just yet though. Someone's looking for you. Smells like the same people who left you before I found you." He moved his head in an arc like a dog pinpointing a sound. "A few minutes downhill from here. Ten men? No, twelve men." He sniffed again, eyes closed. "Ethnic Chinese. One Honduran. And a mixed blood?" He opened his eyes and stared at me. "Sorry, can't be sure like this."

"Like what?"

He shoved off the table and faced me. "Like this." His hands fluttered down his front like he was dusting crumbs off his shirt. "Not like this." Tom disappeared. A small sun took his place. I turned my head and shielded my eyes, sure the heat would singe my skin.

Then Tom stood in front of me again.

"What the - "

He shuffled the cards overhand. "You'll learn." He shuffled the cards in a weave. "In time." He riffle shuffled. "If you're smart enough to survive." He spread his hands apart, waist height in front of him, cards in his left hand. They flew up in an arc and dropped into his right hand. They flew up again making a circle with his smiling face in the center, a life size cameo framed in Bicycle-brand playing cards. Circles and figure eights and towers, and houses, and dragons flicking their tails replaced the frame and finally, a fifty-two Bicycle whirlwind grew in front of him before falling neatly back into his hands, twenty-six cards in each. "Are you smart enough to survive, Jeremiah?"

The people Tom-Ezekiel sensed were Kam and members of the Bear Tong. Halcón brought up the rear because Halcón paid The Chinaman to have me done. The Chinaman assigned Kam and the Bears to the task, only the message got screwed up; they were supposed to hurt me bad, but bring me back, so Halcón could finish the job. Hurt me bad they did, but they thought they were supposed to kill me. They thought they had and, believing I was dead, dropped me in a secluded spot far from prying eyes.

Which is where Tom-Ezekiel found me.

Halcón refused to pay The Chinaman until he had proof something was done and even so, only half because he wanted me barely alive and they left me fully dead. The Chinaman ordered Kam to take the Bears and Halcón to wherever they left me and either find me or my body, and don't fuck up again or they'd find themselves on the side of a mountain far from prying eyes.

Which brings us back to Tom-Ezekiel shuffling cards, my blade on the floor between us, and him asking me if I'm smart enough to survive.

Wait a second. Kam and The Bears left me with enough knife wounds to be a sieve and more broken than unbroken bones.

But Tom-Ezekiel said I'd only been with him a day?

I heard voices yelling in half a dozen languages I didn't understand getting close.

"What do I have to do?"

"Your part is easy: Lower, Center, Relax, Breathe."

The voices grew quiet and now I'm hearing footsteps outside the door.

"Better hurry."

No way I could relax with Kam and the Bears outside the door, I didn't know what lower or center meant, so I breathed.

The cards flew over Tom-Ezekiel's shoulder and landed neatly on the table. He stepped towards me, and I felt the bow wake from years before. Next thing I know, he's standing beside me inside the milky white ball of wax, and he grabs my wrist. "Good start."

He looks at me. His eyes are so far apart I think they've come off his face. *Relax.*

My muscles. I feel them going soft. Not so much soft, as pliable. Liquid. And the sounds of Kam and the Bears outside the door? I feel them like percussions against my skin, soft featherings like gentle, concentrated winds. And I'm still inside the ball of wax.

Lower.

Everything I am turns into a river cascading down a mountain that stops and collects somewhere right behind my balls.

Center.

The pool becomes an ocean and pulls back further. Something, some part of my skeleton - do I still have a skeleton? - tingles and lights a fire, a brilliant spark, a tungsten bulb igniting, and I'm glowing like the sun.

Breathe.

One long, slow, breath, the ball of wax melts away and so do we. I feel Tom-Ezekiel's hand still on my arm, but there's nothing there. We're invisible.

Shhh.

The door opened and a SPAS 12 muzzle, Kam's chosen weapon when he wasn't pushing a butterfly-knife into someone's vitals, followed. "Hello? Anybody home?"

Kam came in and The Bears followed with their 44 Desert Eagles.

One walked up to us, looked around, walked through us and stopped. "Anybody feel that? Got hot in here for a second."

Kam went to the door. "Nobody here."

I heard Halcón's voice, smelled him, felt his steps nearing Tom-Ezekiel's cabin. "Look again."

Wah, The Chinaman himself, said, "If Bears say not here, not here."

Halcón again. "I paid for property, Wah. I want property, or proof of property, or proof there is no property, or word will be on the street that you're no longer reliable. You want that, Wah?"

"Qù kàn kàn. Nòng chū diǎn shēngxiǎng ràng zhège húndàn bì zuǐ. Rúguǒ nǐ néng dài gěi wǒ tā de shītǐ." *Go look. Make some noise and shut this bastard up. Bring me a body if you can.*

My blade. Still on the floor. I moved towards it.

No, Little Brother! Stop!

One of The Bears stops and looks right at me. "Nǐ kàn dàole ma?" *Did you see that?*

Halcón came in and picked up my blade. "This is Jimmy's. He's here or been here."

Wah called from outside, "Zěnme huí shì?" *What's going on?*

Tom-Ezekiel closed his eyes and flared his nostrils.

"What are you doing?"

He smiled at me. He had fangs. *Calling for backup*.

The woods were filled with grunts and the sounds of heavy things loping and running.

"*Xióng!*" The Bears screamed followed by growls and roars. I heard their weapons drop to the ground.

The Bears bolted in all directions. Mostly downhill.

Then quiet.

Tom-Ezekiel backed away from me, leaving me in a kind of afterglow. "What happened?"

"Come. Time to say thank you."

Ten large black bears grubbed the earth. I pulled back into the cabin. The afterglow faded. The bears focused on me.

"Wait." Tom-Ezekiel closed his eyes. The afterglow returned. The bears returned to grubbing. "Best wear that for a while. Until you know who you are."

"I know who I am."

"No, Jeremiah. You don't. Not yet. But you're learning." He walked amongst the bears, patting their heads as if they were pet dogs. One grunted and licked his arm. "You want some honey? Okay, I'll get you some honey." He looked up at me. "It's okay. They're friends. Reinforcements. Backup. Our visitors call themselves Bear Tong thinking they could claim Bear-like power." He laughed. "Most Straights have no idea what power really is."

Something nudged me in the back, pushing me outside the cabin. A jar of honey floated past me towards Tom-Ezekiel.

"Time you learned, though."

We stood outside the cabin cording firewood, the two of us naked from the waist up and slick with sweat, steam rising from us in the cool, Autumn morning. He stopped, canted his head, smiled.

"It's time, Jeremiah."

"Time for what?"

"Time for you to go, find other teachers."

"Six months? That's all I get? Six months?"

"Time for other teachers."

"But - "

We don't argue. We do.

"I still don't know anything about myself, what I can do, who I am. How'm I supposed to find other teachers?"

Tom-Ezekiel repeated, "Time for other teachers, Jeremiah. You'll find them. Or they'll find you. You'll know when they're near."

"What is this, *Highlander*? The Quickening?"

He laughed.

"How about you? Can you teach me to do what you can do?"

"You don't want my gift."

"Come on. We've been working together six months, and I still don't know what you do exactly. You've taught me lots of stuff, but not what I do. Not what you do."

"You don't want my gift."

"Why not? What's your gift? What makes you so special you can't share your gift with me?"

His eyes captured light, reflected it, like an animal's at night. "As you wish."

He was beside me before I could move, a beautiful, double-bladed Butterfly knife in his hand. He snapped it open faster than I could follow and buried it between my ribs, back and forth, up and down. I could feel it knicking bone, slicing organs.

He smiled. *Last lesson, Little Brother.*

He pulled it out with a twisting motion so the wound wouldn't close, couldn't seal. I'd bleed out before I fell.

Watch.

A hole formed on his left side, between his ribs, a perfect mirror to the knife wound in me. Blood erupted. He clutched his side, groaned.

I rasped, "Jesus Christ fuck. The two of us have to die?"

Watch.

The hole grew. I saw a piece of rib, some internal organ, probably lung. The ground's collecting our blood into one thick puddle between us.

Except I'm not bleeding any more.

He screamed. God awful how he screamed. The trees shook with his scream. The sun went dark, then light again. Holy Jesus Fuck.

Watch.

The hole in his side began closing. Mine closed with it. Less than a minute later there wasn't a mark on him.

Or me.

He put a hand on my shoulder to steady himself.

"I'm a Healer."

"Jesus Christ Fuck."

"I take on other people's illnesses, diseases. Even psychological and emotional problems, if necessary. My body, my mind, soul, learns what the problem is, comes up with ways to cure it, stop it. Then my body teaches the other person's body how to heal. Or their mind. Or their spirit."

"Holy Jesus Fuck."

So, Little Brother, do you still want my gift?

"My name is Eleanor."

I found her two days after leaving Ezekiel. I left with my knife, its sheath, two days' change of clothes, and some cans of beans and meatballs in my pack. He gave me a walking stick, a pack of cards, a pat on the back and a direction.

The walking stick had been an elm branch, slightly taller than me and tapered. From waist to chest, it was thick enough to provide a solid grip. The bark was nibbled off from the base to three-quarters of the way up. In its place were what looked like little chisel marks, but I couldn't imagine someone doing that fine a work, or that much of it, and then putting it aside never to return.

It's a beaver-stick. Maker energy. Use it wisely.

"The cards?"

Practice. Remember, a juggler never walks with his hands in his pockets.

"So, I'm a juggler? Wait. What's a juggler?"

He shook his head and gave me a nudge down the mountain.

Shuffling the cards while holding the stick didn't work well. I tightened my grip on the stick and tossed the cards up in front of me, letting their own energy catch them and lift them. Easy. I'd done this with Ezekiel many times. Bicycle laden dragons, and castles, and knights on horseback jousting each other, and landscapes on other worlds.

Sometimes the stick got caught in their movement and gave me a shock like electricity moving through a line.

I laughed. "A juggler never walks with his hands in his pockets? You wanted me to learn the next piece; a juggler always keeps his hands free."

I hit the earth with the stick, like Thor grounding his hammer. It flew up and danced with the cards becoming a knight's lance, a serpent's tooth, a dragon's wing, a beam of sunlight, a -

Help!

The stick and the cards fell to the ground.

Something grew up around me, walls built of bricks of air forming something like a castle chess piece with me at its center. I had a sense of weight, mass, like I got heavier, but then I realized I wasn't getting heavier, I was drawing earth energy up through my legs, they were turning into tree trunks and their roots spread deep.

I touched the castle wall. Cool, not cold.

I laughed. Cool like the air on an Autumn day. Solidified air, not solid because of some super cold technology, solid at room temperature, another form of matter.

Then it wisped away.

Help!

I remembered Ezekiel's teaching: *You have more than one sense. Use them all.*

My body filled with her scent. Hurt. Pain. Broken bones, unmending. Open wounds flowing.

What was it Ezekiel said? Like everything else, scents have gradients. Follow the gradients. Know the gradient, find the source.

I laugh remembering Ezekiel's teachings: *Go to where the scent originates. Follow it back to find yourself.*

Two miles further on the trail. I could sense her, not see her.

I'm coming!

Hurry. I don't have much time left.

I lifted myself the way Ezekiel taught me, but couldn't manifest. The more I wanted to lift, the more my legs locked to the earth.

Was someone blocking me?

Ezekiel told me we were like everything else: good and bad and some in the middle. *How did we come about? No one knows. We've always been around. Long-lived children of forgotten gods, perhaps? Or unintentional accidents. Stray gamma rays turning a DNA sequence right instead of left? Does it matter?*

Was someone blocking me from answering a call for help?

I ran. Up ahead, on the side of the trail, a woman in a blood-streaked mink coat lay balled up on the ground, tucked into a fetal position, protecting herself.

"You okay?"

Help.

I looked around, let my senses roam. Was whoever did this still around?

"Oh, Christ, Lady. Limbs don't make those angles unless they're no longer attached."

Long blonde, blood-clotted hair fell away from a face so badly swollen I couldn't figure out what she normally looked like. I opened her coat as gently as possible.

She wore nothing but black, fine-silk underwear, a matching lace bra, and a body length patchwork of black-and-blues. One CFM was spiked into a pine about ten feet away, its strap broken.

And knife wounds. Lots of knife wounds. Bear Tong knife wounds.

Two of which closed up as I watched.

You're a Healer!

I need time. Can you get me somewhere safe?

I had no trouble lifting her. It almost seemed she lifted herself. Perhaps she knew how young I was, caught me in her wake.

But it wasn't her doing the lifting, it was her coat. And it wasn't mink. It disguised itself as mink.

So, nobody would know what it really was? Mink wouldn't have been my choice for a disguise.

But considering what she wore under it, maybe mink fit in best with her line of work?

And clothing can be our Kind? Ezekiel never told me about anything like this.

The bruises around her mouth receded. Split, broken lips mended. "My name is Eleanor."

"Nice to meet you, Eleanor."

I awoke before she did. I felt bad because I must have pulled her coat over me while we slept. I looked over at her. She looked lots better. All healed, in fact, and still wearing only her bra and panties.

I got up to close the window and took in the view. Her apartment was on the top floor of Park South. Impressive.

"Hello, Jim." She sat up and put on fire engine red lipstick with a little mirror. Her eyes never left the mirror. She smacked her lips, and it felt like she smacked my face. "My fur looks good on you."

I looked down at myself. "Oh, sorry. Hey, how did you know my name?" I reached for buttons or hooks. There were none.

"Keep it. It'll help me track you."

"Huh?"

She laughed.

I tugged a sleeve. It felt like I was ripping my skin off. "Hey, what is this?"

She patted my impression on the bed. "Come here. I haven't said thank you yet."

"That's o - " That's as far as I got. The fur-coat-thing had wrapped itself around my legs and made me walk to the bed, lay down, spread my legs. The fur, which I now realized had covered everything except my head, my hands and my feet, parted and spread open like a fat man's zipper, bursting apart.

I screamed. She put one hand over my mouth. The other hand grabbed me. She began slow, with her nails walking along my dick like a spider making a web.

I don't know how long she kept me there. I left Ezekiel's with a six-pack and now I couldn't see ribs.

She stood at the foot of the bed. The black lace underwear and bra must have been part of her. She never took them off and they never got in the way of what she wanted. "No, I think there's some life in you yet."

She got on the bed and straddled me, taking me in her hands until my dick swelled like a third arm and eased me into her.

I cried. It hurt.

She leaned over me, her breasts heavy on my chest, and backhanded me. "Fuck me."

I swear my teeth loosened in my jaw.

"Fuck me!"

I thrust as hard as I could. Something snapped. Pain I'd never known before.

"Good. That's good. You're ready. Halcón won't have any trouble with you now."

My eyes, tearing, opened wide. "Halcón?"

She got off of me and laughed. "Hold."

The coat tightened on me.

She pulled a black leather coat out of her closet and adjusted the straps on her CFMs. "Don't wait up for me, Darling. I'll be home late." She gave me a peck on the cheek and left.

"Hold"?

Not "Stop," "Guard," "Restrain," "Secure," or "Control."

Hold. It tightened around me. It held me.

It didn't do anything when I opened the window, stood on the sill, and leapt, hoping I had enough strength to lift myself to the ground.

I didn't care if I dropped to my death.

I woke up on a cot in a green room with a single window, barred on the outside and overlooking an alley. An overflowing dumpster sat square under the window. A handful of winos and addicts lay on the cracked pavement around it, some of them in puddles of their own filth.

At least I hoped it was their own filth.

A breeze blew a dirty ocean scent into the room. I hadn't showered since the coat-thing claimed me, and I didn't smell much better.

Somebody knocked on the door.

"Yeah?"

A guy with blonde hair and glasses poked his head in. "Hi. I'm Alan. Okay if I come in?"

"Where am I and how did I get here?"

His eyes went a little wide. He *path*ed and spoke simultaneously. *A brother, Jedidiah, the Lifter in our Clan, brought you here.* "This is the Rescue Mission. New York City."

My head shook. *Hearing* and hearing. I collapsed on my cot.

"You alright?"

"Jedidiah? Clan?"

That's for later. If there's a need.

"Can I get a shower? And some food?"

There was a problem in the shower. "Alan, I can't get this coat off."

He reached out and his hand stopped. "Hmm..." He moved like a mime, making believe he's running his hands along a wall. "Did you have a lot of wounds when she gave you this?" *Mind if I call for help?*

Before I could answer, I heard voices in my head, felt unseen hands moving around me.

The coat tightened on me.

A voice, deep, reverberating. *Ariel, what do you see?*

Alan's eyes grew wide. *It is alive. Or close to. Has Our touch but not of Us.*

Like Tom-Ezekiel, Alan was Alan-Ariel?

A familiar voice. Ezekiel's? *This is Other work. Malachi, can you get to him?*

Something touched me inside. In my chest, then my gut, moving my internal organs around. It moved from my inside out and began lifting the coat from my skin. I screamed. The coat flayed me as it lifted. Blood flowed through the coat's fur. My blood.

Another voice, quiet. *He doesn't know who he is yet.*

One more voice. *Ha. Do any of us, truly?*

Some chuckling. *I'm goddamn dying, and you people think it's a joke?* I didn't realize what I did.

This time, Ezekiel. I was sure of it. *Easy, Little Brother. We've all been where you are. Differently, and the same.*

So, what am I supposed to do?

Remember what you've been taught. Learn more.

A chorus of celestial *Yeses.*

The voices quieted. "Do I call you Ariel or Alan?"

"Depends what you need from me."

"How did you know I got this from a woman?"

Because, Jeremiah, I can see.

That outbreak of Jersey Devil sightings a while ago? That was me. The Pine Barrens afforded me time to decide what to do, aside from scare people away from their camps, so I could go through their supplies or steal supplies from backyards.

Funny that nobody's dogs ever bothered me. Maybe they thought I was one of them.

Each time I stole or scared people, the coat tightened, merging more and more with my skin until I looked like a real hairy bastard unless you looked real close.

Summer came early and strong. I left the Barrens for the coast and worked the docks north. Nobody cared what you looked like, only how much you could lift. I planned to get to Canada, go far north, get lost in the New Brunswick or Quebec woodlands, maybe the western end of Nova Scotia. Heard stories of people going in there and never coming out again.

I lorried at the Groton Shipyards for a month, then left Long Island Sound and headed up the curve of Rhode Island, hoping to sign onto a Pt. Judith trawler and sign off in Sakonnet. I got as far as Charlestown Beach, on the landward side of Block Island, on the hottest, muggiest day of the year. Even people without body-welded coats were sweating oceans into the sea.

Voices drifted over the dunes of a long grotto, jutting half a mile inland from the coast. More than voices, laughter.

About a hundred yards from the water line a tall, skinny guy, wearing nothing but Raybans, red Speedos, and heavy work boots is standing up wrestling with...nothing. Nothing I can see, anyway.

His darkly tanned skin and black hair glistened in the sun and glared off the water. All I could think of was, he was using two hands to wind up the propeller on a rubber-band powered airplane the size of a bus. Down at the waterline stood a lone wooden dock pole, a half-height telephone pole, but no wires or identifiers of any kind. Every time Speedos wrestled whatever it was, the dock pole jigged just a little. Could've been just a trick of the water and the heat. Might not have moved at all.

College students watched him from blankets on the seaside of the dunes. On every few blankets were white Styrofoam coolers with blue lids. A guy on the blanket next to me popped a Lowenbrau. "Want a beer? Watch the show?"

I shook my head and pointed at the skinny guy. "What's going on?"

"He's here a lot. Not every time we come, but often enough we look forward to it. We got plenty of beers. Sure you don't want one?"

"What's he doing?"

Simultaneously, and in two different voices: the guy on the blanket, "I have no idea," and not the guy on the blanket, *They can't see, Jeremiah. Borrow from Ariel. See!*

"Huh?"

"I asked if you wanted a beer. We got plenty."

Speedos' body bulged with muscles he didn't have a minute ago. He grunted and wrenched whatever he held hard. The sky darkened.

Blanket said, "Oh, Christ. It's going to rain again. Happens every time this guy's on the beach."

Help me, Jeremiah. Borrow from Ariel the way I just borrowed from Jedidiah.

It's so hot I'm standing seven inches from the noonday sun, and I shake with a chill. How many of these people - *Our Kind* - are there?

Not enough sometimes.

And if everyone around you is insane, your best bet is to gibber along with them. What the hell, right?

Ariel? Could you help me See?

Ariel's voice, just like at the mission. *Of course. All you have to do is ask.*

Something shimmered. Whatever Speedos held, it shimmered. From his hands down to the dock pole at the waterline, it shimmered.

Speedos' voice. *See!*

Ariel. *See!*

Something snapped. I heard it, inside me, like cracking a knuckle, but all of me lining up, straightening. I touched the sides of my head, ran my fingers over my face.

My eyes were further apart.

A huge white towel, as if a cloud became cloth, colored with sea and sky, held in Speedos' hands, down to the dock pole and back. With every twist, clouds gathered. With every twist, the towel grew darker and darker. With every twist, moisture sheened the outside of the towel and a few drops fell to the sand underneath.

Help me, Jeremiah.

I stood beside him. I felt myself pass through a membrane, a slight solidification of the air. It enveloped me, allowed me to enter it, and once inside things changed. It wasn't a towel. It was an ocean of cloud. The moisture that fell from it created a river of sand.

I grabbed hold.

Twist.

I cranked. Thunder. Muffled by the thin veil of air and still recognizably thunder.

Again.

I clutched the ocean in my hands and torqued. Lightning, far out at sea, and thunder a moment after.

One more will do it.

The ocean resisted. I bent over the cloud, using my weight to wrench the moisture from it. The cloud in my hands turned black.

Lightning blasted overhead. Raindrops the size of mortar shells fell in all directions as far as I could see.

And a moment later it was gone, the ocean-towel-cloud was white and puffy, and dry, and the sky cleared.

Have you ever wondered why some horrible storms just fade away before they ever happen? Why what starts out as a tornado ends up as just a bit of wind? Why some tidal waves never make it to shore?

The towel fell from our hands and unwound like a hurricane falling into the sea.

You wrung moisture out of the air?

We did. You and me. With a little help from Jedidiah.

"Who are you?"

It had the feel of a mocking pout. *You don't remember me.*

"Should I?"

I was back in the mission. Alan-Ariel called for help. Someone *pathed*, *He doesn't know who he is yet.* Then I was back on the beach, Speedos stared me in the eye.

You're...

Work it out. There are four basic things we all must learn to do. Thinking is one of them.

Ezekiel, I know, and Ariel. You borrowed from Jedidiah, and my name is Jeremiah, so Jedidiah's not here. Not that I know of, anyway.

Ezekiel spoke to Malachi, and yours was the next voice I... I hesitated... *heard?*

Go on, you're doing fine.

So, you're Malachi?

At your service. He shook my hand. *One more thing: Nice pathing.*

I didn't realize I had.

That's what makes it work. Until it's natural, it's not you doing it.

I counted on my fingers. *Jedidiah, who I haven't met yet, is a Lifter, meaning he can move things, some kind of levitation. Ezekiel is a Healer. Ariel Sees.*

Malachi corrected me. *Visioner, what ancients called a Sees-Far, and it's not levitation. You'll figure it out when you meet him.*

What do you do?

I do this. Malachi stood there, and he didn't. I could see him. I could feel him. I could hear him. But he wasn't there.

Go ahead. Touch me.

My hand passed through him. My hand touched nothing, like waving your hand through a hologram.

Watch.

He walked through me before I could move. I felt a vibration when our surfaces met in front, and when he walked out my back. Otherwise, I didn't feel a thing. I wracked my brain making sense of it.

I Move, as in, I move through things.

"What was that vibration I felt?"

His eyes narrowed on his face as he reached out to me. "That coat you wear. It defines who you are." He shook his head. *No, that's not correct. It lets someone else define who you are, set your limits.*

"Yeah, my dick."

We all suffer heats. Some suffer less than others. "You've had that coat on half a year now, correct?"

"Something like, yes."

He touched the coat. I couldn't tell if he put his hand into it, or it swarmed around his hand. "It signals. Someone put some of their essence, their life, into it. It calls out to them, so they can find you."

"A homing beacon?"

He mimicked my words and nodded, his hand still exploring the weave of the coat. *Something like, yes. They did so to restrain you, confine you. Weaken you.* "Never let someone else define who you are."

"Tell me about it."

His brow furrowed. *But this raises another question; The coat sends a signal, but it goes unanswered. The signal is blocked. The beacon is masked, covered.*

"The question is?"

"Who's keeping you hid?"

Ever been with someone you know knows something important, but isn't telling you because they want you to figure it out? A real "What do you know that I should?" situation?

And the look on their face says, "Come on. This is simple. Figure it out."

That describes my time with Malachi. He showed me how to *move* and always there was the un*path*ed *This isn't your talent, but we all can do a little of what the others can do.*

So, he taught me how to *move*. Much of *moving* is recognizing what you are, and what you are not. Learn to keep the two separate and you can *move* through anything. People are taught to think of what they are as their physical body. That's true, as far as it goes, but once you get that, what you are is a bunch of interacting particles, smaller and smaller until you can feel the universes inside you. You can learn to twist and turn those little bits to avoid something else's little bits, and there you go, you're *moving*, and that's just your physical body. Get all your bodies lined up and you can move through anything. That's Malachi's gift. Or talent. Or core. Whatever you want to call it.

I got good enough I could even *move* through the coat.

But it was always surrounding me when I got back. Truth be told, mid-Fall on the Rhode Island coast, a fur coat's a nice thing to have.

My last night with him, we sat on the dunes down a ways from his shack. He listened to something I couldn't hear, having a conversation I wasn't privy to, and kept shaking his head or nodding to whatever some others said. I lay back, my hands behind my head, feeling the roughness of the dune grass on my hands and feet.

"Awful lot of meteors tonight."

Those aren't meteors, Jeremiah. Those are your brothers and sisters.

"They are?"

A bunch flew across the sky, twisted and turned like kids playing tag, spelled my name in fiery starlight, then went away.

"Two questions - "

Only if they were meant to. Yes.

"How can you do that? Get inside my head and know what I'm thinking when I'm not *pathing*?"

He stared at me. *The answer is in your question. All answers are in the questions asked.*

"'How can you do that?'?"

Continue.

"'Get inside my head and - '"

Slow down.

I remembered an episode of *Taxi* where Reverend Jim is taking the taxi test, and asks one of the other cabbies, "What does a yellow light mean?" They answer, "Slow down," and Reverend Jim responds "What... does... a... yellow... light... mean?"

Okay, do that. It might help.

I laughed. "Fine. Get... inside - " and that's as far as I got.

Malachi's laughter shook the tide.

You Moved. You literally got inside my head!

Very good. He picked up a smooth stone and skimmed it across the incoming waves. *Won't be able to much longer.*

He stopped. He was going to share more but stopped. But there was a flavor, a taste, a scent on the wind, of what he wanted to say.

Something about my talent, my core, my gift. You've known all along and not told me. Neither did Ezekiel or Ariel.

Because you've known all along. Or parts of you have. The Deep parts, waiting to rise up into awareness.

He paused. His eyes went wider than I'd ever seen before. *Self-awareness. But we're through protecting you, Jeremiah. Time for you to realize who you are, what you can do.*

You've been protecting me? You, Ezekiel, Ariel, and how many others? Are you the ones keeping me hidden from Eleanor? She put this coat on me.

Not us, Jeremiah. You've been keeping yourself hid.

The wind brought voices across the dunes. The meteors slowed and gathered in the heavens.

It's time for you to rise.

The voices. Halcón. Kam. The Chinaman. Some Bears.

And Eleanor. *Lilith*. "He's over this way. Follow me."

Malachi *moved* into the sand, his body shifting, each bit of him knowing what he was and what he was not, not displacing the sand so much as filling the empty spaces around it, cozying up to each grain. *You are too valuable a prize, Jeremiah, to decide your fate unaware.* "But now you must decide."

Decide what?

A mouth disappearing into the sand whispered, "Better hurry."

The air grew hot, then bright.

Eleanor-Lilith came over the dune wearing a fur coat similar to mine. She shrugged, it fell, and my breath steamed in the cool, Fall night. Black lace panties and a bra supporting breasts so full and proud they needed no support. She bent one leg at the knee, raising it slowly behind her until that foot's CFM came within reach. She pulled it off, held it and repeated the exercise with her other leg.

Is flexibility your gift?

If she heard me, she didn't respond. Instead, she spread her legs slightly, one arm under her breasts, lifting them and I swear for a second her aureolae were irises, her nipples pupils, and they were winning the stare-down contest like it was nobody's business.

She twirled her CFMs by their straps in front of her, spinning them around her index finger until little sand devils rose around her. *Oh, Jeremiah. What am I to do with you.*

The sand devils gathered around me, around the coat I still wore, her coat, and it tightened on me.

Lilith tossed her CFMs on the sand in front of me. *Come on, now. Be a good little boy. Pick Mommy's shoes up and let's go home.*

The wind brought her scent towards me, covering me like a warm blanket.

Wouldn't it be good to sleep in Mommy's arms. Come home now. I have something special waiting for you, sweet boy.

I reared my head. This is not who I am. "This is not who I am." *This is not who I am.*

She cupped a hand under each breast, lifting them, offering them. *Oh, yes, it is. Don't you remember?*

I remember. Everything. Healing. Wounding. Lifting. Seeing. Moving. Animals do not fear me. Elements work with me.

I stared at her. Her cheeks sagged, her breasts flattened. Her hard, yielding stomach paunched. Her hips flared from too many childbirths. Veins appeared on her legs, arms, and hands.

I remember. I draw from the earth. Earth. Not the planet, all that the planet is. All it ever has been and will be.

"I can't hold him. He's yours."

I remember. The air growing solid around me. Walls of energy separating me from what I am and what I am not.

Malachi! This is the lesson. What I am. What I am not.

Eleanor-Lilith yelled. "Hurry!"

The brightening air collected around me.

The brightening air was me.

The air around me erupts into flames hotter than the sun. They reached into the coat, into its fibers, crisping it to ash. A dust devil grew up behind me, devoured all those Lilith sent to me, gathered itself around me, blew the ash away.

The coat was gone. It was not me. It was gone.

Kam led the Bears over the rise. Halcón and The Chinamen walked side-by-side, casually, two good friends followed by their spouses, all walking towards their cars after a dinner out.

The Bears rushed around Lilith. She shimmered, glowed, her features reforming as they passed, then returning to reveal her true shape and form.

Halcón came up behind her, bent her over, unzipped his pants and thrust himself in. "Oh, Jimmy, she is so sweet like this. You can have her, if you return to me. A gift. And you can do what you want with her." A knife, my knife, flashed up in his hand and he raised it over her, Zeus preparing a lightning bolt. "You can repay her for what she did." He traced my initials on her back with the tip of the blade. "See? Branded. Just for you. No one else will touch her. Ever. My promise."

Eleanor-Lilith shimmered, her breasts firming with each thrust. She spread her legs and placed her palms on the sand for support. Blood trickled down her back, into her hair, down her arms, into the sand.

"Oh, Jimmy. She is so good. Wouldn't you like?"

He distracted me. She distracted me. The Bears circled me. Butterflies snapped open. They rushed me.

Think, Jeremiah, think. Quick. What to do?

Ezekiel, quiet yet strong. *Think too much about what you do and all you do is think about it.*

A voice from long ago, almost forgotten, heard in an airport. A tiny, dark-skinned, wrinkled woman, Sade, hovers before me, except she is young and beautiful, and lifted by reptile wings. *Thinking is only one part of you. Use all parts of you to* do.

A butterfly cuts the air before me. I block without thinking.

Use all that I am.

All that I *am.*

What is me and what is not me.

I *push.*

Kam orders his men, "Shāle tā! Ràng tā shòukǔ!"

Ezekiel again. *Listen. To them. Not the words, to them.*

"Kill him! Make him hurt!"

If I am to become a sun, so be it. PUSH!

The air around me solidifies, another state of matter, it surrounds me, and moves out like an exploding sun...

And stops before touching them.

Except they couldn't get to me, either. Like long ago, in Ezekiel's cabin, when my blade hit a wall and fell to the floor, something stopped them.

"Lǎobǎn, zhège shì shénme?" "Lǎobǎn, wǒ zhēn de bù xǐhuān zhège."

"*What is this, Boss?*" "*I don't like this, Boss.*"

The Chinaman barked, "Jiějué tā!"

"*Finish him!*"

One of the bears flashed his butterfly over the sphere of air. An appendage forms, grows around him, envelops him, an amoeba and its prey.

He drops his knife, grabs his throat, his chest collapses, his face turns blue.

He falls; the appendage recedes. He rolls, gasping for breath.

One of Kam's other men backs away. "Lǎobǎn?"

"*Boss?*"

Kam pushed his men out of the way and brought his own blade up. "Bié shuōhuà!"

"*Shut up!*"

The sun grew, its horizon caressing the sand, leaving the grasses unharmed, and driving Kam and his men back, back, further back.

It stopped at the fallen man, still gasping for breath.

I stopped it at the fallen man, still gasping for breath.

"Pick up your man."

Kam nodded to his men. They grabbed their brother's arms and dragged him over the dune.

The sphere became a wall driving them back. They hurried past Halcón and The Chinamen. They fell back before the wall reached them.

But not Lilith. Nor did it drive her back.

It ripped away her facade. What remained crawled over the dunes, caught in the starlight, a thing of hopes and whispers, its body bloated where desires had eaten away at her, leaving flowing, mottled flesh.

I fell to my knees, retching, sobbing. I was inside that.

The walls of the sun came rushing back. A hand rested on my shoulder.

I bolted up, spinning, wishing I had my blade.

Ezekiel held it in his hand. *Here. You won't need it anymore, and here it is, if you want it.*

Malachi stood beside him. *A memento.*

Ariel came up behind them. *A memory, perhaps.*

What am I?

Ezekiel handed me a pack of cards. *Here. More fun, perhaps. What are you? What did you do?*

I guarded.

The word didn't feel right.

I protected.

No, not right, either.

Ariel closed his eyes. *Stop thinking.* See.

What is me. What is not me.

Shield!

I am the Shield.

Malachi nodded. "Through whom nothing can pass."

Ezekiel brushed sand off me. "You are the 'why' that brings the 'all' of us together. Without you, none of us can exist."

Ariel opened his eyes. "Which is why Lilith worked so hard to bind you. You are too powerful a prize. For either side."

"She... It... works with Straights?"

"Her abilities lie in deceit, blinding people to what is, making them believe their desire is this over that, fulfilling their wants while denying their needs."

"Shouldn't her name be Helen?"

They laughed.

I have much to learn.

And so, it begins.

So, Christ could not Shield. Or maybe he didn't know what he was doing. Maybe he didn't know the difference between *he* and *they*.

You know what? I'll bet it was something completely different. I'll bet he just couldn't deal with what he was doing and believed what everybody else was saying about him. I've been down that path, too. Lots of us have. It's just learning not to make it your own. That's the hard part.

(Thanks to Gina Martin for sharing her knowledge of what women wear to seduce men)

The Stairs

Jon Shannon

I can hear voices whispering. They are somewhere above me, but also around me. There are at least five, but possibly as many as ten. They don't all whisper at the same time. I don't know what they are saying. The whispers aren't clear enough for that. I only know that this is the end for me. Death is next, and it's not going to be pretty.

It started a few hours ago when my car got a flat tire. My stupid mistake for not having AAA or another road service to come and help me. My spare was also flat, so that wasn't an option. I know how to change a tire. That's one of the first things my dad taught me when I first got my driver's license.

"A man needs to know how to change his own oil and replace a flat tire," he said to me, more than once.

He was right. On more than one occasion, I would have been stranded on the side of the road thanks to the cheap tires I kept buying for my old Honda Civic. Cheap car, great gas mileage. Those were the two most important things. It didn't help that half of my time on the road was in areas with no cell service, so calling for help wasn't even an option. I go where the work takes me, and these back roads in northern Maine are where I do all my pickups and drop-offs.

I have no idea what I'm picking up or dropping off. I don't ask questions. They pay me well, and it's worth not knowing. It's not worth a lot since I can't afford decent tires, now that I think about it. I don't even know why I'm thinking about this as I lie on the dirt cellar floor, listening to the weird whispers around me. It's almost like a chant or something, rhythmic words and phrases connected in a sing-songy way.

My day started ordinarily enough with breakfast at the diner on Washburn Road near the Aroostook River. The food is decent, and the staff is polite. Some days, that's all you can ask for. I had my Delorme Gazetteer map laid out on the table, highlighting the route I would be driving, when the waitress asked me the standard "Warm your coffee?" question.

"No, thanks," I said, knowing there was no place to piss between here and my destination, besides a few thousand pine trees along the road. It didn't matter, anyway. I pissed myself when the stairs collapsed, and I hit the dirt floor in this old cellar. I don't think I broke any bones, but I was scared shitless to move after I started hearing them.

The whispers come from the left and right, and from above. The wooden stairs are in front of me, and I can't see anything behind me. It can't be much different than any other direction, I figure. Like I said, nothing seems broken. But oddly enough, I'm not able to move. Not a single muscle. I'm completely paralyzed from head to foot. I'm more damaged than I think, I guess. Maybe I busted my back.

Reversing in my thoughts, I was driving down the road and minding my own business. That's always the best plan when you've got a job like mine. Eyes straight ahead, no questions, take the cash at the end. Like a lady of the evening, if you get my drift. I'm just a delivery man. Then, the cheap tire blew out.

The Civic started to fishtail, which was no surprise, considering I was going 70 miles an hour on this old back road that didn't deserve any speed over 45. I ended up sideways in a ditch, clipping the "moose crossing" sign as I went off the road. One tire flat, two tires on the passenger side deep in the mud. The leftover mud from all the spring rain wasn't doing me any favors. There was no way I was getting out of this hole without a tow, even if I could change the flat. The deflated spare in my trunk was about as useless as a screen door on a submarine.

I don't know why I chose the direction I walked in. It seemed random. Maybe something pulled me that way. Staring up at the back-ass ends of the floorboards above me, I can't help but wonder how much better off I would be if I had just walked the other way.

The whispers are closer now. They're chanting something. There are so many of them.

I can feel the dampness of the dirt floor soaking into my hair and clothes.

When I saw the dirt driveway a ways into my walk, I was happy. It meant a house would be at the other end of it. Down the long, wide dirt path, I only found an old timber-frame building with no signs of being lived in for decades. They must like it that way.

What are those words they keep repeating, anyway?

There's a rhythmic metallic sound now, over and over again. Clang, scrape. Clang, scrape.

Only darkness around me. A little bit of daylight pokes through the gaps in the floorboards above, otherwise there's nothing but black.

Curiosity got the best of me at the old building. I'm an explorer at heart. There's something about abandoned buildings that makes me want to explore. I poked around the rooms on the single floor, noting what looked like an old kitchen and living area. It was a mix of isolation, abandonment, and an odd stack of leather-bound books on the table. The books were old, but they weren't covered in dust, like someone had been reading them recently.

When I saw the partially open door leading to the basement, it seemed logical to swing it wider and look.

"Hello, anybody there?" I asked into the darkness.

The whispers came back to me. Surprised to hear a voice, I stepped forward to ask again.

"Is someone there?"

Then, the bottom of my world dropped out.

Whispers, even louder and closer now.

I don't know what they're planning. But that scraping sound is the same as when I sharpen my knife before cleaning a deer during hunting season.

The whispers stopped, replaced by footsteps, soft and deliberate, circling around me in the dirt. Hooded figures emerged from the shadows. Men and women from their outlines, their faces hidden, their movements well-practiced. This wasn't the first time they had performed this ... ceremony. I knew it now.

They formed a ring around me. As one kneeled close, I felt a softly gloved hand on my face, almost caressing my cheek like a lover. The others began to chant again, steady and low, the words unfamiliar and unknowable, but the intent unmistakable.

From the darkness behind them, a figure stepped forward holding something long and thin. The metallic rasp I'd heard echoed again as the blade caught a stray shaft of light through the floorboards above as it was being sharpened. A knife. Sharpened for me.

It all clicked. The flat tire. The path through the woods. I wasn't lost. I was led here. I had become ensnared in their trap, like countless others may have been. This was not their first time.

The circle of robed figures around me tightened, closing in as the chant rose in intensity. I understood too late what I am, what I was brought here to be.

The knife lifted, gleaming in the meager light.

I am the sacrifice.

The last thing I saw was the blade dropping toward me as the chanting roared to a climax, and then the cellar went silent.

The Price of Beauty

Rebecca M. Senese

Tanya leaned closer to the bathroom mirror, peering at her chin. There, just to the right, she could see the reddening skin of irritation, the slight swelling compared to the left side. The beginning stages of yet another pimple.

Dear lord, she was thirty-two and still dealing with acne. In what world was that fair?

She patted on some makeup, but even that wouldn't last long, she knew. The swelling would soon intensify, the reddening would deepen, and she would be stuck with a huge pimple on her chin.

So embarrassing.

And she had that big presentation with her boss late this afternoon. Just in time for the pimple to blossom. She wanted people to pay attention to her ideas in the presentation, not to the damn pimple on her chin. Sure, she'd heard people say no one would notice, but that was a lie. She'd had enough blemishes to catch the surreptitious glances, the grimaces, the outright stares.

It had nothing to do with what she ate. She ate very healthy, hardly any sugar, it was just her damn skin.

Something had to be done before the presentation. It didn't start until four. She could take the morning off to deal with this mark.

She turned away from the mirror to grab her cell phone and leave a message for her boss.

Tanya had tried all manner of spas treatments for her skin. None worked for long. She had gone through most of the places in the city, but there had to be somewhere she hadn't tried yet. Somewhere she could get in this morning, as an emergency.

And that led her here.

Callis Spa and Life Enhancement was in an old strip mall off the main road out of the city. Sunlight sparkled on the grey asphalt of the parking lot, encouraging the weeds that sprouted out of cracks crisscrossing the lot.

A single car was parked at the far end, in front of a liquor store, leaving Tanya with her choice of spots. She parked one slot over from the front door to the spa. As she turned off her car, she swept her gaze over the place. The spa took up four windows worth of the strip mall. The windows covered over with dark green paper patterned with diagonal stripes, were probably designed to protect the privacy of their clientele.

The air smelled of exhaust and mulch as she stepped out. Traffic rumbled in a constant hum, just loud enough to be irritating. She hoped they had decent sound proofing inside the spa. She didn't want to be listening to the traffic the whole time.

But who knew? The place didn't look like much and this location... How did they do any business in such a dingy-looking strip mall?

Too late to back out now. It was either this, or cake on makeup on her chin and hope it didn't drip off during the presentation.

She sighed. Give it a shot.

The glass door squeaked when she opened it. A plain wood podium stood alone in a small entry way. Dark green fabric hung from the wall. Silver threads were spung through it, dissolving into patterns the more she looked at it. The glass door swung closed behind her and to her relief, cut off any sound of traffic.

Silence settled. Tanya relaxed a little. Then she noticed the slight sound of trickling water. There was a fountain somewhere.

A dark green curtain to her right opened and a woman stepped through. She was dressed in a light purple smock over purple pants. Although her face was unlined, she had grey hair pulled back into a bun on the back of her head. She smiled, tiny crow's feet deepening at the corners of her eyes.

"Welcome to Callis," she said. "May I help you?"

Tanya swallowed and cleared her throat. "Ah, yes, I made an appointment online this morning. I need to deal with this."

She pointed at her chin.

The woman leaned forward, studying the blemish on Tanya's chin.

"I have an important presentation this afternoon," Tanya continued. "I didn't want to just slather on makeup. Can you help make it a little less noticeable?"

The woman's eyes narrowed as she studied Tanya's chin. She reached out, lifting Tanya's face so she could study it more. Finally, she nodded.

"I can take care of this," she said. "I can do enough so it doesn't mar your presentation, or..." She raised her eyebrows. "I can get rid of it completely. That is more time. More intense." She smiled. "And it will never come back."

That sounded like quite the claim.

"Acne always come back for me," Tanya said.

The woman let out a snort. "Is good thing you came to me. I can stop that. If you truly desire it."

Desire it? Tanya would kill for it. Clean skin, never having to worry about it, never stressing about having enough concealer, or if it would run or drip off.

Settle down. She couldn't let herself get too excited.

"Take care of the chin first," she said. "Then I'll see about the rest."

The woman nodded. "Agreed. You will be happy."

The treatment room was dimly lit. A cot was set up in the center, a dark blue blanket draped over it. A flat looking pillow lay at the head. Two small cabinets holding various bottles and jars sat on either side of the cot near the head. Dark fabric draped across the walls, creating more shadows.

"Take off your shoes and lie down," the woman instructed.

Tanya complied, leaving her shoes near the door. Her feet sank into the plush area rug as she crossed to the side of the cot. Even that cushiony feel made her more relaxed.

When she turned to the cot, the attendant was already there, pulling the sheet back. Tanya slid underneath. Instead of the hardness she expected, the cot molded to her body, cradling her.

She was going to have to be careful not to fall asleep. She had to be alert for the presentation.

Even the thought of it made her tense again.

"Relax," the woman's voice came from beyond Tanya's head.

Cool fingers touched Tanya's cheeks. A moment later, the woman wiped Tanya's entire face with soft, damp cloths. Next, she rubbed lotion into Tanya's cheeks.

But nothing near her chin.

Tanya wanted to say something, remind the woman she was here because of the blemish, but her face felt slack. Her body was heavy. Her breathing slowed. It was hard to keep her eyes open, to focus on the dim room around her.

She closed her eyes.

Darkness.

Dreaming.

The warm smell of linen tickled her nose. Her body felt cushioned, cradled, cocooned. The urgency of the presentation melted away. All stresses, all cares dissolved. Her body felt heavy, yet light at the same time. She felt like she was floating, as if her body drifted up from the cot and hovered in the air.

The feel of her clothes dissolved, but she didn't feel naked. Something wound around her body, stretching, tightening, but more in a supportive way than constrictive. She could feel it winding around her torso, her limbs, bringing along the scent of linen and other scents she couldn't identify. Musky, oily, herbal, with a hint of floral. Light, refreshing and soothing all at the same time.

She relaxed deeper until she couldn't feel anything anymore, just the lingering smell of spices tickling her nose.

"There now."

The voice tugged at her consciousness. She didn't want to respond, wanted to stay submerged.

"There you go."

Now she felt fingers pat her cheek, became aware of her cheek. Of her head, her body. The cot underneath her. Her eyes were closed. She fluttered them open, then closed them again. Even the dim lighting seemed overly bright.

After a moment, she tried again, and this time was able to focus. The suggestion of walls around her and above her, the unlined, young-looking face of the attendant with grey hair.

The woman smiled at her.

"You have nice dream, yes?"

Tanya breathed in. She felt her chest expand, but as it did so, it felt like something tightened around it, something wound around her, pressing against her skin, her flesh. She shifted on the cot. The feeling vanished. It was just her clothes. Just their usual constriction.

She sat up, expecting some dizziness, but instead she felt alert and refreshed. Energized in a way she'd never felt after a spa session.

She was going to comment on it, but then she remembered why she was here. The blemish on her chin.

"Do you have a mirror? I want to check my chin."

The woman smiled. "Of course." She turned to the counter beside her, retrieving a squarish mirror with a plastic handle. She handed it to Tanya.

Tanya held it up. Her face, her skin looked rejuvenated. Vibrant.

And not a mark on her chin.

But that was here in this room with the dim lighting. What about in full daylight?

She swung her legs off the cot and stood up. Momentary dizziness made her pause. She remembered the restriction she'd felt on her torso and on her limbs. Something wound around her, tying her down.

Just an illusion, a fragment of dream. She didn't have anything on her than her own blouse and skirt.

She shook the thoughts away and held the mirror up.

"I'd like to look at my chin in full daylight."

"Certainly." The woman stood up and crossed the room, moving in a smooth, gliding motion. Overhead, florescent lights bloomed on, filling the room with white light. In the brightness, Tanya could see the fabrics on the walls looked a bit dingy. The paint poking out between them was streaked and muddy. The cabinets looked scuffed and off-white, yellowing with age.

The dim lighting hadn't been only for atmosphere.

But one look in the mirror and Tanya didn't care. Her face looked smooth and clear. Her skin had a glow to it that she'd never been able to achieve herself. And her chin...

Clear.

Not a hint of redness. Not a slight puffiness of swelling.

Smooth and clean.

A miracle.

She touched her chin, trying to feel any hint of irritation, but there was nothing. Not even a hint of the blemish. Not even a trace that it would return.

She grinned at the woman. "This is perfect!"

The woman smiled and bowed her head. "The treatment will last a few days, but you need regular treatments to keep it up."

Tanya glanced once more at her face, taking in the smooth, clear, vibrant skin.

"Let's make another appointment," she said.

That evening, reveling in the success of her presentation, Tanya pulled out the two small bottles the woman at the spa had given her. She shed her business attire and wrapped herself in a soft, white, microfiber robe. She shoved her feet into fluffy white slippers and shuffled into the bathroom, clutching the two bottles.

Not even the harsh, white, makeup bulbs lining the bathroom mirror took away the smooth, clear, shine of her face, although it did look a little less smooth after a full day. The shine was a little bit duller, her cheeks a little bit puffier.

Fortunately, her chin still looked clear. The esthetician's promise had held.

But to keep the rest of the look, Tanya had to follow the woman's directions.

She set the two small bottles down beside the sink. They were both black, the dark glass impossible to see through, with gold markings etched onto them. There were no manufacturer labels, the woman had told her she bottled the ingredients herself.

Tanya was very particular about what she put on her skin or into her body. She was always sure to check labels. Using something and not knowing anything about it wasn't something she did.

Or at least, it wasn't something she had done before.

But the woman had done an amazing job, saved Tanya's presentation. She knew if that blemish had remained on her chin, she would have been distracted the whole time, even if it hadn't erupted. Not having to worry about it at all was worth a leap of faith.

Tanya opened the bottle.

The fragrance was faint, a little musky, with a hint of cloves. She tipped it into her fingers and a thick, viscos fluid flowed onto her fingertips. Her skin tingled where she rubbed it in. In a circular motion, sweeping up from the chin, up her cheeks and up, across her forehead, as the esthetician had instructed.

With each motion, her skin tingled and warmed, then the warmth faded to nothing, leaving her skin feeling numb. By the third sweep across her forehead, her eyelids were fluttering. She was so tired. The stress of the day pressed down on her. All she wanted to do was sleep.

But it was way too early, barely six thirty. She couldn't go to bed now.

Maybe a little nap though. Just twenty minutes and then she could have something to eat.

Her fingers fumbled with the bottle, but she finally managed to screw the lid back on.

Then she shuffled into the bedroom, barely managing to make it before falling sideways across the bed.

She dreamed.

Lying on her back, floating in the air. A cool breeze brushed against her skin. Long, flowing strips of fabric, smelling of honey and cloves, wound around her body. Pulling tight, but not too tight. Still tight enough to feel like they were sinking into her flesh, becoming part of her.

Her arms stretched out, forming a T, and she felt the strips again winding around them. Her legs split apart. More strips wound around her thighs, encasing her, winding, winding.

She was being encased, enclosed, cocooned. Her legs came together, then her arms folded over her chest, each hand toward the other shoulder. The strips had wound around her entire body. It should be finished now.

But it wasn't.

She felt more strips wrapping around her, thickening the layer. This time, it was thicker, harder. Her legs were bound together, heavy and unbending. Then her torso, trapping her arms where they crossed, until she couldn't move her hands or twitch a finger.

Encased, enclosed.

Entombed.

She tried to struggle, tried to wiggle her body, but the strips held fast. She was no longer floating. She felt the hard press of earth on her back.

With effort, she managed to lift her head. Around her, walls of earth stretched upward. They were all around her.

She was inside a hole.

Buried alive.

She started to open her mouth to scream, but a strip of fabric slapped across her face, blocking her mouth.

She jerked.

Jerked awake.

Thrashing, twisting, she jerked into a sitting position even as she slapped at the mattress. Disoriented, confused. What was happening? Where was she?

She blinked at the forms around her as they conformed to the contours of her bedroom furniture. The C-shaped nightstand with a lamp on top and two books on the bottom. Her dresser, two sets of four drawers, painted a dark, rich green with the stencil of an old piece of art showing faded flowers applied on the front, the edges jagged and rough, as if the green paint had been scraped aside to reveal the image instead of the image applied after the fact. It had been one of her artsy purchases, one that always made her smile.

She didn't feel like smiling now, but at least her heart rate steadied.

A dream. Just a dream.

But it felt so real.

Except she didn't have any fabric wound around her. She was still wearing her robe, impossibly rumpled and twisted around her.

That was probably where the wound feeling had come from. She had moved in her sleep, and her clothing constricted her. Her sleeping brain interpreted and incorporated it into her dream.

That had to be it.

She sagged with relief. Just a silly dream after all.

She shook her head. Details faded. After a moment, she couldn't remember any of it.

With a grunt, she heaved herself off the bed and headed for the kitchen for something to eat. She was starving.

The lotions in the dark bottles lasted less than two weeks. That was longer than Tanya had expected. The esthetician said they were samples.

The first taste was always free.

She had already set up another appointment, but it was still two weeks away. Although her skin felt clear and looked refreshed, she knew any progress would be diluted without the lotions. She had to get in sooner.

She called at lunch and when the esthetician said she had an appointment at four fifteen, Tanya took it. It meant she had to leave work a little early to get there on time, but she was still riding high on the successful presentation.

It was a cloudy, overcast afternoon when she reached the strip mall. The dull light made the place look even dingier than the first time. As before, the parking lot was empty, and Tanya had her pick of spots.

She parked right in front of the spa.

Stepping out of the car, she thought that this clinic could be anywhere and command exclusive pricing. She didn't understand why they stayed in such a low-end location.

She breathed deeply when she entered, taking in the soothing aroma. This time she could smell a touch of eucalyptus. As she let out her breath, her entire body relaxed.

She originally thought every six weeks would be a good pace, but maybe she should come more often. Maybe once a month.

Or once a week.

Easy does it there. She didn't want to overdo it, either for her skin or her bank account.

The same woman stepped out, unlined face and grey hair pulled back into a bun. She looked the same as the first time Tanya had seen her, even wearing the same smock. Tanya had noted a pen mark on the corner of the breast pocket and there it was.

"Thanks for fitting me in," Tanya said. "I've run out of my lotions." She held out the bottles.

The woman took them. She sniffed at the tops, nodding.

"The first few months you'll use a lot of this, but after a while, you'll barely need a few drops," she said. She tilted her head. "Did you wish to just replenish them? Or you want treatment?"

It hadn't occurred to Tanya that she could just replenish them, but of course she could. She could do that and be out in moments.

But the lure of a treatment tugged at her.

"Treatment, too," she said.

The woman smiled. "Of course. Follow."

Same room, same cot. Even as Tanya laid down, her body relaxed even more. She closed her eyes against the dim light.

It was going to be so nice.

At first, it felt so. The esthetician's fingers on her cheeks soothed muscles Tanya hadn't even realized were sore. Spicy aromas filled her nostrils. Then she felt the woman applying something thick to her face. Was that mud?

The feeling of pressure spread down the sides of her neck to her shoulders, then across her torso. Her limbs felt heavy, constricted. Something was wrapping around them. Tight, limiting her mobility.

Unless at another's command.

She tried to shake off the feeling, but her body felt sluggish. Even her mind felt like it was functioning too slow. Taking forever to realize a problem.

And there was a problem.

Wasn't there?

She couldn't move. Couldn't think. Everything felt heavy. Bound down. Tight. She felt it, that sensation of something wrapping around her limbs, around her torso, binding her.

Then a voice, murmuring in her ears. Staccato, clipped words in a high, sing-song tone. A strange, foreign voice, speaking words she didn't understand, but strange sensations started in her body. Muscles quivering, clenching. Her arms lifting, hands moving.

Not of her will, but in response to the words.

How? What?

She focused on her right arm, right hand. Felt it lifting, her hand moving as if it was holding a pen.

Stop it, put it back down.

But her hand didn't obey. Her arm stayed up.

Her heart began to pound. Sweat broke out on her skin. She could feel it prickling her forehead. Her stomach clenched.

Afraid. She was afraid.

She couldn't move her arm. Couldn't control it.

Couldn't control anything.

Her body was no longer her own. She wanted to open her mouth and scream, but couldn't even loosen her jaw.

What was happening?

Her eyes opened. A face filled her vision. The esthetician's face. Smooth skin, now glistening with perspiration on her cheeks and forehead. Her face looking almost flushed and feverish. Loose strands of grey hair, freed from the bun, stuck out, looking almost as if she had stuck a finger in an electrical socket and shocked herself.

A smile spread across the woman's face, but it wasn't a pleasant smile. Instead it was gloating, triumphant.

"You are ready now, yes?" she said. "Ready."

Tanya wanted to reply, but couldn't move, couldn't even blink her eyes.

Ready? Ready for what?

She felt a dull sensation on her shoulders. Her body moved. She sat up on the cot.

The esthetician said something in that foreign language and Tanya swung her legs over the side. She stood up in a rigid, halting fashion.

The woman spoke again, and Tanya moved. Lifting her arms up and back, side to side. Moving her legs. Walking forward and back, then around the room. Responding to the woman's strange, lilting language, even as Tanya tried to stop herself.

Nothing worked. She grunted with the effort to be still, but her legs moved, first halting, and then smoother. Her arms were the same, first jerking, and then moving easily.

As if the woman was gaining better control over Tanya.

Tanya wanted to cry out in protest, in fear, but a bare grunt was all she could manage.

Finally, the woman waved her back toward the cot. Tanya's body obeyed, first sitting, and then lying down. The woman moved out of view and Tanya felt a slight pressure on her cheeks, stroking, smoothing, wiping the mud or whatever it was from her face. With every swipe, Tanya felt herself sinking down, relaxing, letting go.

Drowsy.

She closed her eyes.

There was only darkness.

Her eyes opened. She felt disoriented. What had happened? Where was she?

A moment later, the esthetician's face appeared, looking down at her. The face blurred in her vision.

The esthetician clucked her teeth as she lifted a cloth. Tanya felt it wipe the edges of her eyes. The blurriness went away.

"Hush now, no need for tears," the woman said. "It won't hurt anymore. You are now ready for the transference."

The what?

Tanya heard the door open and the shuffling sound of someone entering. The esthetician's murmuring voice instructed the new person to the second cot.

Tanya tried to move her head, turn it even an inch to see who was lying beside her, but she still couldn't move. The best she could do was move her eyes, but even then, she only caught a shadow of movement.

A slight creak sounded, and she felt a presence lying behind her.

The esthetician laid her hand on Tanya's forehead. At first the touch was cool, then the woman's palm began to warm on Tanya's skin. The warmth deepened, grew hotter, and the warmth began to spread, flowing across her face and down her neck. Tanya felt herself relaxing in the warmth. She felt drowsy again, as if she was floating. The sensations of her body began to melt away. The pressure from the cot, the smells in the room, the light hum from the ventilation, all fell away.

Tanya drifted in nothingness.

Then she became aware of the rise and fall of her chest as she breathed. The soft whistling through her congested nostrils. A low, dull ache in her back.

Weird, her back had never ached before. Maybe lying on the cot was affecting her.

Slowly, she became aware of her body. It felt stiffer, more sore than she'd ever felt before. The esthetician's hand pulled away from her forehead, and in that moment, Tanya felt herself regain control of her body.

She wiggled her fingers and felt them move for her, but even as they moved, they ached. Probably residual effect from whatever the esthetician had done to her.

Well, she was going to deal with this. She was going to sue this woman.

She tried to lunge up, but barely managed to shift her weight. She had to push herself upright.

Movement on the cot beside her caught her attention.

Tanya looked over...

at herself.

It was her body sitting upright, straight and tall, a huge smile blooming on her face. Her head turned toward the esthetician, nodding in pleasure at the woman.

What the hell?

That was her body, right in front of her. But if that was hers, what was this?

Tanya lifted the hands supporting her on the cot. Thick knuckled, bloated fingers. Discolored age spots on the backs of the hands.

Not her hands. Not her body.

As she watched, her body got up from the cot and walked to the door. Her body paused, looking back at her. Someone new reflected in her eyes. She smiled at Tanya with Tanya's smile, waved with Tanya's hand, and then turned and walked out.

With Tanya's body.

"Nooo." The lips she used felt odd, the jaw shifting in a strange way. Then she felt the weight of a hand settle onto her shoulder, making her aware of its stooped nature and the ache between the shoulder blades.

"It is done," the esthetician said. "It cannot be undone. You will have to accept that." She cocked her head as she regarded Tanya in this new body. "But now you can be someone new."

She raised an eyebrow in challenge at Tanya. And Tanya realized that was what had happened before.

This woman was swapping bodies for people and what did she gain? Money, influence, power. No wonder she kept her spa hidden in a nondescript strip mall. Better not to draw attention as she implemented her plans.

After the switch, did she have some kind of hold over them? Probably. They probably had to return for regular treatments, probably to keep the personality anchored into the body.

Tanya could break that cycle, break the swap right here. All she had to do was refuse the switch.

But as she thought of it, she felt herself sinking deeper into this body, felt the arthritic pain. The stiffness, the soreness, the tiredness. This body felt old and used up. Close to the end.

Was that what Tanya wanted? To live the rest of her days in this husk?

She looked at the esthetician's waiting face.

"What do I have to do?" Tanya asked. The voice croaked from her dry throat.

"Whatever I tell you to do," the woman said.

Tanya bowed her head. She knew she would agree. Anything to get out of this old, decaying form.

To think she had complained bitterly about a pimple on her chin.

She wished that was her only problem.

She sighed. "I will do it," she said, and the esthetician smiled.

The Initiation

DL Mullan

With a smack, graded papers slapped the foyer table. The top page had an "F" written and encircled by the thick red ink of a permanent marker. A young woman stood with her hands on her hips. Next to the front door, she gazed at herself in the mirror on the wall.

She shook her red tresses. "I'm never going to pass this course."

"Never say never, sis." A twenty-something youth moseyed down the hallway by the kitchen. His slouchy clothes appeared creased. He tossed a ripe apple at her. "The forbidden fruit of knowledge to match the color of your hair."

The young woman yawned as she caught the fruit in her hands. "Thanks, it's more vibrant than the dull color of my locks."

She rubbed her tired eyes. How would she be able to live up to her parents' legacy, if she could not live up to her own expectations? The daughter of the reality hackers, John and Ellenor Chisum, yet could not pass a science course.

"Ever since you did that group meditation focused on the Great Pyramid in Giza, Eliza, you haven't slept well." The man with sandy-colored hair, green eyes, and a gangly stature leaned against a nearby wall. "Something I can do to help?"

"Unless you can get the creepy guy with the Ibis tattoo in the third row of my "Intro to Physics" class to stop ogling me, Sam, then probably not." Once again, she gazed at her reflection. Her blue eyes were puffy against the pale of her freckled skin. "Plus, these dark circles aren't from meditation or hyperspace accelerants. Although, the visions were incredibly clear. I went to Egypt without having to pay for a flight or book a room, but the astral jet lag is a killer."

As he stepped to her side, he peaked at her grade. "Too bad, it won't help you write an acceptable paper."

"Oh, shut up, Mr. straight "A" student. Not everyone can do a research paper in three days, not study, pass exams, and get degrees." Eliza glared at him. "Some of us have to work at it."

With a sidestep, he stood behind her. His height allowed him to looked at their reflections over her head. "Mirror, mirror on the wall, who is the most insufferable stick in the mud of them all?"

"Hilarious. Unless, *bro*, you can make my professor see reason, but his facts are supposedly indisputable, and they don't care about my feelings." She crossed her arms over her stomach. "I am destined to flunk out my first year of college."

"Come, dear sister." He put his hands on her shoulders and maneuvered her into the living room.

"What are you doing?"

"Now, sit. Tell Samuel all about it."

Both sat on either end of a camel brown couch.

"Here it comes..." she said with a tease to her voice, "my big brother is in peptalk mode. What wisdom will you impart on me today, Sammie?"

She bit a chunk of apple and waited. He liked to amuse himself with protocol. Talk about insufferable...

After he closed his eyes, he breathed in, then out, as if to relax himself. When he opened his eyes, he yelled: "Stop trying to convince people that you are right!"

She jerked, not expecting his ruse. Then, Second, she threw the apple at him, bouncing it off his chest. Finally, Eliza furrowed her brow and in a calm voice uttered: "But I am right. After I returned from my global meditation months ago, ideas, information, and imagery came to me about the workings of the universe. I am right. The textbooks are wrong."

"I know that. You know that, but people who have been in the physical realm all their lives will never know anything else." He shrugged, tossing the apple back to her. "You can be right all you want, but to them, you will always be wrong."

"What do I do?" She harnessed the apple in her fingers. "Just let them drive the rest of us over the edge of a cliff?"

"Unfortunately, that is the way their world works."

"And, *our* world?" With a light dusting of the skin with her fingers, she bit the fruit again.

"We were lucky. Our parents understood consciousness as a vehicle to fathom the complexities of ourselves, our world, and everything in it. Unless other humans do DMT or ayahuasca, they have no clue about what is really out there beyond their five senses."

"My hypothesis about how dimensions work is revolutionary. It will help us understand the quantum realm, the space-time continuum, and consciousness itself. It would unlock so many mysteries."

"Mundanes don't care about the unknown. Your professor is stuck in first order thinking, while you are thinking fourth dimensionally." He stared at her. "You might as well write it in a fiction novel. It is where all good science ends up being accepted and eventually proven."

"*After* I am dead."

"Do a cost-benefit analysis. You'll discover there is a cost to being right." He stood.

She tilted her head upward. "Where are you going?"

"For my morning run."

"It's noon." Her nose wrinkled. "Did you sleep in those clothes?"

"I have levels of clean, Eliza, and twenty minutes left." He mussed her hair and laughed as he passed her, jogging to the front door. "Catch you later, alligator."

"Boys." She rolled her eyes as the door slammed. With a growing resentment about the world, she finished off her apple. If the world were a cartoon, steam would rise from her ears. "Cost-benefit analysis, my ass."

"Another F?" Her older brother scoffed, as he came in from the kitchen to the front door. "You cannot pass your theories off in class. The professors are going to demand a psych evaluation."

With a sarcastic voice, she turned to him. "Gee, thanks, James. Are you going to give me a bro talk too? Samuel just yelled at me."

"Well, you probably deserved it." Her oldest brother stood in front of the foyer mirror and fixed his tie. He combed his auburn bangs with his fingers and smiled through his gray irises. "What is it this time?"

"I figured out how dimensions work." She stood up and paced around him. With a toss, the remnants of her apple swished into a trash can near the kitchen. "Three points!"

"Good job."

"I wish." She wiped her juicy fingers on her jeans. "No one will listen, because I don't have a doctorate, particle accelerator, or both."

"I'll listen." He picked up her paper and handed the stapled pages to her. "Enlighten me."

"Seriously?" Uncertain, she peered at her brother. "Or, are you just going to make fun of me?"

"I have an hour before I am due at the office for a government project funding meeting. So, you have fifteen minutes. Read me what you believe is true." He walked over and sat in a sage green recliner.

"Okay." She retraced her path and sat down on the couch. She brought her knees up. "How Dimensional Definitions Lack Cohesive Realities. In accepted sciences, the fourth dimension constitutes light. What if this is an error? The first dimension is dark, uninhabitable. Yet, light survives in the most remote reaches of the Earth, even sea creatures at the bottom of the ocean have bioluminescence. Therefore, this natural illumination calls into question of light being only a fourth-dimension phenomenon."

"I can see why he failed you." James chuckled. "Go on. Tell me what you believe the right order of the dimensions are."

"Dimensions are nothing but microcosmic layers of energy, frequency, and vibration- geometric building blocks stacked one on top of another to create the physical world. I postulate that the first dimension *is* light. Light is energy. It illuminates. It denotes speed: going in every direction. It is also time. If the first dimension is a straight line, back and forth, side to side, and right or left, then light creates this linear path. In this dimension, any organic mechanism can see, move from side to side at any rate of speed, as well as move in time. Light confers past, present, and future tenses. In addition, light bends, reflects, and refracts. In space, light curves back onto itself, creating a loop of time and distance in space. This is why light is the first dimensional aspect to the physical realm."

"That is an interesting concept. How about the second dimension?" Samuel reclined in his seat. He appeared interested in her thesis.

Eliza scratched her head. "The second dimension is frequency. Frequency gives color and tone to light. The second dimension constitutes right and left, plus up and down. A flat box is created with which to occupy."

"The third?"

"The third dimension is a cube. Inhabitants can move right to left, up and down, as well as: in and out. Vibration is the energy of this dimension as light becomes manipulatable sound. Whereas in the second-dimension light's frequency was channeled upon wavelengths. The third dimension allows speech and music to be produced external to a light source."

"The fourth?"

"The fourth dimension is consciousness."

James made a confused face. "Did you say: consciousness?"

"Yes, did I stutter?" She winked at him, and then he smiled. "Consciousness is the fourth dimension, because how else can fourth dimensional beings live in the third dimension? The third dimension is in and out. This allows for the energy, or universal life force, to enter into physical bodies housed in the lower dimension."

"You've really thought this thesis through."

"Nikola Tesla did help a little bit." She made a small measurement between her index finger and thumb. "But that is my understanding of the universe, and why my professor keeps on flunking me."

"The way Samuel and I navigated higher education with our parent's expert knowledge was to just regurgitate what the professors fed us, ignoring it once we graduated. It's why I own ten patents the Pentagon wants." As he jumped to his feet, he smoothed the fabric of his olive suit jacket. "I suggest you do the same."

"So, you think my hypothesis is bunk, too?" She felt her heart sink to the bottom of her stomach.

"It's not physics, Eliza; it's quantum consciousness. Your instructor will never understand. Remember, education is for left brain thinkers. They cannot see outside their two-dimensional logic box. Creatives, like artists, are right brain thinkers. They cannot see outside the box they painted themselves into. Balanced brained thinkers, like yourself, see that the box is a tesseract: full of infinite possibilities, known and unknown."

"So, copy and paste like all those before me..."

"And receive a passing grade. Mom and dad died to keep us safe. If others believed that we know what they knew, then we are all in danger."

"You don't believe their deaths were just a car accident either, do you?" She saw her emotions of doubt and anger reflected in James' eyes.

"There is reasonable doubt to question the official narrative, I won't lie, so for safety's sake, we hide in plain sight."

Eliza slumped her shoulders in understanding and defeat. "Fine. I will become a copy and paste fanatic. No one will ever confuse me with having an independent thought ever again."

"Good, girl, then you will come to work for me. Sam signed a contract for next summer." He checked his watch. "Just rewrite it. It's bullshit. Speaking of bullshit, I have a meeting with a general. So, I do know about keeping up pretenses."

"And write a fiction novel like Samuel suggested." She made goofy body movements.

"Something like that." He leaned over and kissed the top of her head. "At least, you'll be alive."

James departed, shutting and locking the door behind him.

"It'll take centuries for the 'intellectuals' copying off each other's papers to realize there's a typo." Eliza tossed her paper onto the coffee table, then yawned again. This time she could not excuse her tiredness.

With a sluggish push onto her feet, she retreated. Her body slumped as she moved forward. She dragged her feet, every motion becoming heavier than the one before it.

After changing into her loungewear, she slipped into her bed. Her morning at college had exhausted her. With her head on a pillow and body under the covers, she stared at the ceiling. She breathed herself into a meditative state. In moments, her thoughts faded into the darkness of her mind's eye.

Smoke and dust filled the air as violent shaking and loud rumblings made the city unsafe. Buildings fell in heaps. Streets opened into chasms. People ran everywhere to avoid being killed.

"Neferidawen, take off!" A male voice boomed over the warning sounds of her ship's bridge, as well as the explosions coming over the communications link.

"I'm trying." As she stood at a neon-illuminated console, she swiped different colors until the engines of the ship ignited in red. The structure shimmied and shook. She glanced at the video images of the destruction outside. "Ready!"

With a final gesture, she waved a purple color across the keys. "Are you aboard?"

"Leave. You must rebuild our world. Go toward the blue planet, it's the only one close enough which sustains life." Again, the same male voice flooded the interior of the bridge as she held onto her console for stability. "Take the Arkieum, who you have rescued, and depart."

"No! Thothiemus, grab the last of our people and secure yourselves in the docking bay. The land is steadier here. I can wait a little longer before taking off."

"Not safe-" His voice became digitized as another wave of energy destabilized the ground and interfered with their radio communications, then the link went dead.

Tears flooded her brown eyes and ran down her red-tinted face. She grabbed her braided brown hair to ground her impatience. She needed hope.

The pods. They must all make it into the pods. In their status units, they could heal to survive the journey.

"Come on!" She screamed at her console.

As she heard the docking bay door shut over the airwaves, Thothiemus exhaled in exhaustion. "We're in, Commander. Take us to our new home."

With a sigh of relief, Neferidawen swiped the purple communications frequency into a yellowish-orange hue. The quantum repulsion engines created an energy field and the ship catapulted into the living stream of the universe. "Will do."

As the ship disappeared into the energy matrix, the red planet below exploded one final time. On her scanners, she witnessed a rush of organic materials breaking free from the planet. Soil, plant, and animal life spun in a glob. In mere days, the remnants of her home world would collide into the atmosphere and ignite the outer edges of the unaware orb.

Neferidawen watched from the safety of her piloting kiosk.

"It seems like a piece of home will always be with us." Thothiemus spoke in her ear.

With a grin, she turned to him. His reddish skin was splattered with dirt and blood. She threw her arms around his neck and kissed him. "You're safe."

"It was irresponsible of you to wait for us...*for me*." He embraced her small, curvy figure, but his purple irises conveyed a tender appreciation of her bravery.

"Everyone who could be saved needed to be saved, including you, my love."

"Only you and I alone will know about what happened on Atlantis."

"You're wiping their memories?"

"This blue sphere," he pointed to the image, "is called Orthe. The Council of Nine, who caused the nuclear war, withheld this knowledge of our sister world. Those elders are dead. Our battles must not touch the inhabitants, or their civilization will end in a holocaust too. We will rebuild. We will instill knowledge, wisdom, and discernment. Our way of life will live again, this time, through right action."

"The system has us waking before the others." Her gestures played with the colors on the screens. "There. It's done."

He took her by the hand. "Come, my lady. Our future awaits."

Eliza's mind rebounded into her human self. She remembered being in a pod, where Thothiemus placed her. As she watched, her former self closed her eyes and let the frequency encapsulate her body in living energy.

Next, fear rose in her throat. Neferidawen never woke up. All Eliza saw was darkness.

An inner scream of desperation rattled her being. Her raw emotions reverberated around her until the dream took on a life of its own. When Eliza opened her eyes, she was lying flat. She slid from a slab in an apparent blackout. Her bare feet touched the floor. There was no sense of time, space, temperature, or dimension.

"Hello? Is anyone there?"

A guttural growl emanated from the shadows. Next, two guards in Ancient Egyptian garb flanked an opening with lit torches in their hands. She walked to the archway. As she entered, the guards each took one of her arms and escorted her to another chamber.

Once there, the sentries shoved her inside and shut the passageway behind her. Torches illuminated the dark spaces around the room. Radiance from a skylight encircled the middle.

A snarl echoed off the stones. The source stood on the other side of the spotlight. The shadowy figure's silhouette outlined a monstrosity. A tall, muscular human body stood a yard taller than she. His red eyes glowed from his canine features and ebony skin. He was adorned with gold tattoos and gemstone adornments.

Eliza understood this was a test. "I am not afraid of you. I am a seeker of knowledge. I know about Thothiemus and Atlantis. I am the reincarnated soul of Neferidawen. I demand to see him at once."

The creature bowed his head and gestured her to follow him. With a grasp of her bicep, he phased them through solid wall after wall, as they travelled through the structure. She recognized it as the Great Pyramid of Giza from her group meditation.

He escorted Eliza into an underground cavern system that connected to an elevator. Inside, the doors closed, and both descended beneath the edifice above the sand. Once the elevator halted, the doors slid apart. The dog-man ushered her through a long stone hallway and swung two large wooden doors open. In the middle of an artifact-laden library with scrolls, statues, pottery, and adornments, the computer console from her dreams appeared.

"It's not a dream, Eliza."

In awe, she turned to see the man she once knew. "Thothiemus?"

"Neferidawen." He stepped closer.

Both were confused on protocol. Do they hug? Do they kiss?

Eliza's human body was a third of the size of his Atlantean construct. "What happened?"

He titled his head. "We remained in hyperspace for a cycle before we crash landed on Earth. The ship had been damaged in hyperspace, prolonging our status. Atlantis, what humans call Mars, became unhabitable."

"How is this possible?" She gestured to him and back to herself.

"In an Atlantean's mind, all things are possible." He closed his eyes, inhaled, and his size reduced to match hers, save for being larger and taller as a male.

Eliza smiled at his consolidated stature.

"And him?" She gestured to her escort.

"Anubis? You've won him over. He'll protect your consciousness forever."

She viewed him. "I feel like I still know you."

"And I, you, but we have more pressing matters to attend to at the moment."

"If only my parents were alive-" Her earlier resentment bubbled up.

"John and Elleanor Chisum are the subject of our meeting, as well as your ability to channel Atlantean knowledge."

"I don't channel. I only deal with the tangible."

He tapped his head. "Every human with Atlantean ancestry has extrasensory abilities. Psychics. Mediums. Channels. You stepped through that gateway process, remember?"

"Damnit." She glanced around the room. "How long have you survived down here?"

"Not just here, I have lived amongst humans in my various avatars for sixteen thousand Earth years."

"Then you died?"

"I have never slept, been ill, or perished. I simply disappeared. I walked the Earth for millennium. Once I could no longer blend into the background, I returned to my pod to regenerate."

"So, none of this is real?" Eliza pointed around them.

"Real in our minds." He held her shoulders. "We are as we are. I am in my pod. You are in your bed. Our consciousnesses are communicating on a deeper level. I have waited for this moment for twenty thousand years."

"Then, join me." She grabbed his arms. "The world needs you."

"No, my love. It needs *you*."

"How? I'm nothing. Look at me."

A single tear jetted from his eye. "You died in childbirth two thousand years in. Our technology failed to save you, and you have been incarnating ever since. I am unable to intervene as I have never had my heart weighed."

"But we had a child?"

"A daughter named Ruth. I raised her until she followed others into the desert. I figured she was safer away from me."

"And, now?"

"Your group meditation opened that doorway in your mind, which created a portal where we can interact."

"Portal? I thought my parents closed all the portals."

"They did, but their deaths opened a new paradox, shattering quantum time into millions of threads."

"They weren't supposed to die. I knew it." Someone stole her parents from her.

"They were killed by Special Access Project operatives. Your parents worked for the private contractor: Advance. Their handler was Agent Abigail Isham. Since your father blackmailed her with information he stole from the Hall of Records, she had quantum skippers delete them."

With a grunt, she punched her fist into her opposite palm.

"Knowledge leads to action." He showed her the images and history on his computer screen. "Quantum skippers are time pirates. Most know their place, but a corrupt few meddle where they should not. I need you to reverse the damage and reestablish a cohesive flow."

Eliza furrowed her brow. "Back up. I'm still in intro to physics."

"Would you like to save your family?"

"More than anything."

"Good. Hold onto that sentiment." He inputted some intricate spacial equations into the computer console. "It's your theory about how quantum dimensionality works relative to theoretical physics."

"But I just thought of the idea and received a failing grade."

"Be patient, eventually you will change the course of humanity."

"With Atlantean knowledge?"

"Your birthright." Thothiemus waved his hand and the inside of their ship appeared around them. "The Hall of Records that holds all human thought, emotion, and consciousness together is the energetic mirror realm of our ship. I hold true history. I know when the timeline was shifted. I waited for your consciousness to surface in relation."

With anguish in her eyes, she stared at him. "Why do you care about Earth and humanity at all? It seems we failed you."

"We lost many in the wars on Atlantis. Humans are on a similar path. One day, I will take our ship into the quantum universe, return before the destruction, and save us from annihilation, but I haven't perfected the science. But you, my love, don't need science."

"Because my parents are the inflection point and my consciousness will bridge the gap. I'll do anything to get them back. What happens, if I can't undo what has been done?"

"Human life as you know it will cease to exist as the quantum paradox pulls gravity in on itself, and reality disappears forever."

"Why is my parent's death so important to the universe?"

"When John and Elleanor Chisum reversed the consciousness paradox and set the timeline back on its natural course, their lives became a stitch in the fabric of consciousness. Others, who crave full-spectrum dominance, failed to realize that without them as an anchor, reality would unravel."

"Bastards."

"Here's your chance to right a wrong, Eliza."

"It's strange to hear you call me that, but avenge accepted."

He chuckled. "It's strange to see you as a fair-skinned, red head."

"I miss you."

"As I, you, but know that I am never far away. My avatars roam." Thothiemus waved his hand and the wavelengths turned into a neon blue and white combination. A doorway opened on the other side of the kiosk. A circular stream of light revolved, moving faster as time reversed. In the middle, pictures from different timelines and parallel universes morphed through the ages. "When you see a memory right before your parent's death, step through the event horizon. You will enter your younger self's physical manifestation."

"Then what?"

"You'll know what to do."

Eliza grabbed Thothiemus's hand and squeezed. He tightened his grip around her fingers until she released his hand. She stepped toward the time stream.

When she saw her thirteen-year-old self, she passed through the doorway. As Thothiemus stated, Eliza's consciousness morphed into her younger self.

With a song in her heart, she skipped down her driveway toward her childhood home in Scottland. Her parents exited from a side door. That is when Eliza sprinted.

The missing pieces of her life walked toward her. How she never grasped the void in her soul until she confronted the one event that destroyed her. She had buried her feelings with their deaths. Now, she met the past, present, and future at once.

Out of breath from running toward her heartache, she stood in front of their car's passenger side door. "You cannot go."

"Honey, we have a meeting." Her mother pulled her by the hand.

Eliza pressed her back against the car door. "No, you don't understand."

As the overwhelming fear and anger welled up inside her, Eliza phased from that reality into her former one. She drifted in and out of images until she recognized Samuel on his trail run in the Sonoran Desert. She pulled herself toward him while her brother spoke with an army recruiter. She eavesdropped, hoping to get his attention.

"Sorry, I'm not interested in the military, Major Mallory." Samuel handed a brochure back to the uniformed officer. "I have a signed offer with my brother's company, the Cornerstone, after I graduate. Thank you, anyway."

"I knew your parents, John and Elleanor Chisum, on a Special Access Project at Advance. I would love to see you revolutionize the world with their work."

"My parents never spoke about their field research with us kids. We were too young. I'm afraid they took all their secrets to the grave. Have a nice day." Samuel walked away.

Major Mallory gestured and two military police officers arrived from their posts in the bushes. The two guards grabbed Samuel and threw him into the back of their black sports utility vehicle. He fought them, but they punished him with several punches to the abdomen.

"Samuel!" Eliza screamed, but no one heard her panic.

"Hey, what the hell is this? Let go of me! Major!" Samuel shouted as he was being kidnapped.

Major Mallory commanded his underlings. "Tase him."

Samuel screamed in pain, then silence.

"No! Stop it!" She threw herself into the middle of the men, grabbing, scratching, punching, but her gestures were fruitless. She had no mass. All she could do was witness in horror with tears streaming down her face.

In an instant, the doors were shut. The major, military police, and Samuel disappeared. As the vehicle drove off, Eliza's strong emotions yanked her back into the energy stream.

"Wait!" Again, she reached for Samuel, but that reality sifted through her fingers and disappeared into darkness. Her disheveled feelings caused the next shift to pop into focus as misaligned pieces of a jigsaw puzzle, creating the inside of an office building.

Her anxiety was quelled, as she heard a familiar male voice. "James?"

In her ethereal college body, she rounded a corner to see James speaking with an older, bald service man. The duo stood in a conference room with the door shut. She phased through the doors and into the chamber.

"I told you Brigadier General Price, none of us children were privy to our parents scientific work." James tried to walk past the other man. "They destroyed it all."

"You own ten patents," the general stepped in the way, "but you argue John and Elleanor Chisum left nothing of their work?"

"I have three doctorates in engineering. Now, if you'll excuse me, I do have a business to run."

"You will be leaving with me, and you won't make a fuss." General Price pointed at her brother. "I have your brother Samuel at one of our facilities. Another team is picking up Eliza at your shared domicile. Unless you come with me presently, then I cannot guarantee their safety."

"You have no right, general." James retreated around a chair and dialed a number on the conference table's landline phone. "Hello, security-"

The general ripped the phone from Jame's grasp and smashed the device into a wall. "You have no choice, James C. Chisum. Under the state secrets and intelligence laws, you are under arrest until such time that we deem you and your siblings harmless."

"You're crazy."

With a wave of his hand, two military police personnel entered the space. Each took James by an arm. One punched the unarmed brother in the solar plexus.

"What the hell are you doing?!" Eliza shouted, but she knew she was helpless. Her sentiments again spun out of control from anger, hate, resentment, to revenge.

Red in the face, James sputtered. "No crime has been committed, except for yours."

Brigadier General Price grinned. "You haven't read Eliza's paper on the nature of the quantum universe and her ideas about dimensions. It's quite an interesting read, especially if you have a security clearance twenty floors above the president."

"Fiction." James spit blood on the floor. "She wants to write fiction."

"Let's see if her fiction is right." The general turned on his heel. "Bring him."

Eliza's heart sank. "This is all my fault." She put her hand to her mouth as she watched James, too, be abducted by the military. She sobbed in her palms as the men passed through her.

In that moment of desperation, she felt her world after years of denials. Her concealed emotions about the past exploded into her spirit. Each memory revealed the inner fight she waged against the outside world. Her life had been hijacked with the death of her parents. Again, the same scenario played out with the kidnapping of her brothers.

Her helplessness turned into energetic rage that shook quantum time itself.

A quiet voice entered her thoughts as a salve. It was Thothiemus. "To save them, use your positive emotions. They'll return you where you're supposed to be."

Her apparition ceased further motion. As she calmed her mind, she realized that the actions of the military men attracted her darker feelings. When she felt love and hope, she phased to her teenage years when her parents were still alive.

She closed her eyes. With several deep meditative breaths, she remembered her family. Eliza's consciousness flooded with hope, love, and gratitude for her mother, father, and brothers. She envisioned her parents at the car. In an instant, she returned. In glee, she grabbed the Earth keyring with her father's car keys out of his hand.

"Eliza!" John Chisum shouted in shock. "Give me back my keys!"

"I won't lose you again!" Her younger self ran from the car, down the driveway, and onto the sidewalk. She held the miniature Earth to her chest while the attached metal instruments clanked together. As she dashed from her house, she giggled until the afternoon changed to dusk.

She never felt so free.

When night fell, a portal appeared. She burst through the event horizon. Thothiemus awaited her. In her adult hand, she held her father's car keys.

This time tears of joy flooded her eyes. "How is quantum time?"

After the kiosk turned purple, he nodded. "Stable. Now, it is time for you to return to yours."

"No. I want to stay here with you." She clung to him.

He held her in his arms. "If you do not, then the alterations you made will only be temporary."

She wept. "There was never going to be a time for us, was there?"

He smirked as he pulled her chin up with his finger. "Depends on how you define time."

The two kissed.

"I will be with you." His thumb pressed hard into her shoulder. An imprint of an Ibis outline marked her skin, then faded away. "*Always*. Look for my avatars. They're looking for you."

"I will."

When he kissed her forehead, the room went black. No lights. No torches. Eliza's mind struggled to make sense of the endless sea of nothingness.

As she traveled back, a woman's face appeared in the distance, as light grew from a speck to a spotlight. Soon, both stood in the glow.

"Who are you?"

"My name is Sarah Mitchell. I understand what you did and why you did it, but there are consequences." The woman glanced behind her. "He'll be coming for you."

"Who?"

"This isn't over, Eliza Chisum. You have closed one door and opened another into a realm beyond your deepest nightmares, where Thoth and Anubis cannot venture."

"I don't understand." Her attention was diverted by a rapping. Was that her bedroom door? The knock came again. She turned to see no one.

In her sheets and comforter, she roused. She blinked her eyes open. She was still in her bedroom.

"Hey, Eliza, you're going to be late for your physics class." A familiar man's voice stated.

Was that her father? John Chisum? She bolted from her bed and threw open the door. John Chisum stood there with gray hair and his golf attire on. "Daddy!" She hugged him.

"Nice to see you too, sweetheart," he patted her back. "You have fifteen minutes and your mother is waiting in the car already."

He disengaged from their hug and walked away.

Eliza shut the door behind her and did a silent, congratulatory dance. "Yes! I fixed quantum time!"

After realizing she was in her reality again, she rushed around to find clothes, her satchel, her homework, and shoes. Before she exited, she pulled up the covers on her bed. As she did so, an Earth globe keychain with keys fell on the floor. She grabbed them. The keys were from the day she saved her parents' lives. She slammed them into her knapsack.

No one ever needed to know.

No one.

As she rushed to class, she dumped the decades-old car keys in a trash can. The disposal was in a high traffic area, which was dumped twice per day. No evidence. No crime.

When she entered her class, the professor handed back her graded paper. This time a red "A" was circled, instead of a failing mark. She read through her typed words as the professor made his way around the room. Copy and paste had been deployed for success.

Afterward, the weird kid from the third row came up to her. "An exceptional grade again."

Eliza shrugged. "Yeah, feeding them back their bullshit gets high marks in college."

The young man laughed. "Hi. I'm Aiden. Aiden Tott."

"Eliza Chisum." She noticed a tattoo on his arm of an Ibis-headed Egyptian god. "Interesting tattoo."

"You should see his." He waved for a taller man with rich dark skin to come over to them. "Ryder!"

The youth stepped to the duo. "What, Aiden?"

"Show her your Anubis tattoo."

Eliza then realized that the conscious energies of Thothiemus and Anubis were indeed in her sphere. For the moment, she felt safe with their avatars. As the class started, she sat next to her new friends.

The professor introduced their speaker for the class. "Please welcome Brigadier General Price and his second in command Major Mallory. They are here to introduce us to our university's collaborative project with Advance."

"What are the odds." Eliza squirmed down in her seat.

Anonymity disappeared once she saw her father's old key chain Earth bauble dangling from the major's left pants pocket, and in his hands a rolled-up stack of papers with a big fat red "F" bleeding through the cotton fiber. "Oh, shit."

Sarah Mitchell's warning revealed itself. She panicked. A darkness grew in her chest. She felt her heartbeat go arrhythmic. Her breathing became labored.

As Eliza slipped into unconsciousness, a door opened in her mind.

He waited for her in the frigid darkness.

Darkness Tolls

Zack Ellafy

"Some things that happen in the dark should stay there" – an excerpt from the dairy of Ofson Evans

The city lights bounded off the nighttime clouds, causing a subtle glow in the sky. I smiled as I looked up. The air smelled crisp, cool, and clean, and I could actually smell the tar from the highway nearby. The field I walked through had once been nice, and was now full of plastic, cans, bottles and who knows what else. I found my way towards this underpass my client had told me about. She wasn't keen on going herself, but I had to confirm if the rumors were true - disappearances, murders, overdoses, all around a specific underpass, in the not-so-great part of town. The carnage was so frequent that even the people on the street stayed away. A couple people in nearby camps gave me quiet warnings.

"I hope you aren't heading that way, sweetie," a woman said. She was huddled around a small trashcan with a fire in it.

"Don't worry about me, ma'am. I'm looking for trouble tonight," I said. *I think the smile on my face is disconcerting to them.* "What do you know about the 'dark underpass', as you all call it?" I asked.

"It's a place you shouldn't go. Bad things happen to those who go there. Some of us who are sadly new to the street, man or woman, set up down there and they die. The police and ambulances always say it's an overdose or a street fight got out of hand over food or drugs or something. But we aren't all like that and they know it. We don't know what's happening, and we don't want to," the woman said.

"I can understand that. Well, thanks for talking to me tonight, and stay warm," I said.

As I turned, I could hear some of them cursing about my hearing or sanity. None of them knew I already had a hunch about what I was walking into. If my theory turned out true, then it would be a long night. And if it was some crazy killer just hunting for vulnerable people? He'd be human, but he's still going to see what I can do.

Where I parked my car had been pretty much empty at this time of night, but the highway was busier and dangerous. After a few close calls, I was across and able to finally see my destination as I crested a small hill. The underpass at the bottom was old but was still in use. I'm not a city planner, but my guess was that it was part of the first interstate system in the fifties. From my view on the hill, I could see the busier sections of the newer highway. I watched for a minute and only saw a few cars travelling by, and the road underneath was murky and dark. My phone rang, startling me – it was Allison.

"Are you calling to tell me it's dangerous and I should leave this to other, better magic users?" I asked. The silky, but low tambor voice answered back.

"I always say you can stop chasing evil and dark shit in cold and sad places, and stay inside with me," Allison said.

"I know and I want to, but this is a bad one and I must handle it. Don't worry. Plus, I have an idea. How about brunch tomorrow at our favorite taco place?" I asked.

"You know a way to a woman's heart. You stay frosty out there, okay?" Allison said.

I made a smart remark about walking the back streets of highways late at night and what could go wrong. We made some more sweet talk and said goodbye.

She only calls on the scary ones, I heard one of my anxiety monkeys shouting in the back of my head. That's what I call those impulses - your gut, sixth sense, etc. Mine can go crazy and tip into panic mode, and tonight it was. But over the years I had learned to put that feeling in its place.

As I walked closer, a little light filtered down through the night and I could see abandoned tents and belongings. I could feel it watching as I got closer and knew nothing else was alive. I stopped walking right in front of the tents and trash. Some would think this was just a dump for druggies, or criminals, or the homeless, but I knew. This was the remnants of what it had taken.

I wasn't looking for more than five seconds when I heard a low growl, deep and vibrating through the earth. I was going to speak, but it beat me to the punch.

"If you've come to do anything other than die and become my dinner, please don't waste my time, let me get to it and eat," it said.

I could see the large beast in the upper pylons of the underpass. During the day it would be easier to see, but tonight, I could only see a huge and disproportioned black shape in the limited light.

"I don't know how you got here and where you came from. I'm sorry, but the killing, the disappearing homeless, kids, law enforcement, all the rest. The missing dogs, cats, horses - it's going to stop. Tonight. It's my turn. I'm not an ordinary joe walking around at night. I can use magic. That's why I'm not running," I said. It just growled.

"You think you can stop me. Have you ever even seen anything like me?" it said. I smiled.

"Yes, I can read and use a computer. Others have. There are stories and I've read them all. But I would like to hear the story of how a hell troll got here," I asked. I pulled out my vape pen and took a drag while I looked at the moon and sky. Even in this tense situation, I can't help it - I really think it's pretty.

"I do like your stupidity and death wish, mortal. You want to hear the story. One whatever you call a "day" in hell, I was left unchained, and I found a hole in the fabric of where I was. I looked around and I was here, in this city. Killed a few mortals I found to feed my appetite from my journey, and I worked around the city until I found this little spot. Not too many people, just enough to feed. And I will continue to feed," the hell troll said.

"I see," I said. I fiddled inside my jacket and grabbed a small bag. I palmed it subtly like a magician and went back to listening.

"You see nothing. You are mortal. If I hadn't just eaten, I would suck the marrow from your bones," the hell troll said. At the end of his sentence, I heard something thump onto the concrete of the underpass. In the darkness, a small object the size of a basketball rolled down and came to a rest in the sand by the road. The dim lighting showed teeth and what was left of the flesh. I looked back to the shape of the hell troll.

"You're done. I'm giving you one last chance. Go back to where you came from. If you continue to mess with me and this plane of existence, I will do something you will regret," I said. The only reply was laughter.

"I am not scared of you at all, little man. What tricks do you think you have? The loud banging thing – sure, it hurts, and I usually rip off an arm. What else?" the hell troll asked. I grabbed my phone and started a text to Allison.

"Sorry, I'm telling my girl I won't be home until morning for sure, the way you are acting," I said nonchalantly.

"I grow bored. I will kill you. While I hate leaving you meat sacks to rot in the little hole I made in this dark, you shall be my breakfast at the start of your tomorrow night."

I heard what sounded like a herd of buffalo running towards me. The sand, the dirt, pebbles from the road were all vibrating and the darkness brought a cloud of debris with it. I threw the sack I had palmed towards the opening of the underpass. As the sack unfurled, it hit the troll mid-charge. I felt a split moment of flight or fight response, and then when the bag hit, only relief and pride.

As the white powder contacted the air, the concrete, the hell troll...it bound it. The special spell I'd included made the underpass into a sealed unit. A barrier shot up instantly in front of me, blocking the troll's rampage, and like a line of napalm, flashes sealed off the other sections in unison. Nothing would happen to mortals or the cars that passed through, but now, the hell troll was...

"Trapped! How can this be? You are not powerful enough. I would have sensed it," the hell troll said.

"You don't think I would have left the house to come and meet you without a protection spell, do you? Why do you think I let you think you were in control?"

"What have you done? I can't break through this!"

"And you never will. Ever. Unless I command it. There is only one shot here. Go back to where you came from. You can still use your powers down there and leave all of us up here alone. If not. I will leave you here to rot," I offered, trying not to show the anxiety below the surface.

"You cannot do that. I will break every bone in this body trying to break free, and if I do..."

"I'm sure you will. I was taught this spell is pretty much infallible for your kind," I said.

"True, but you also know the one ability all demons have to make you feel your shames, your regrets," the hell troll said.

Before I could reply, I was hit with a deep sense of being inadequate. My mind raced to Allison. *Why does she love me after this dark stuff I've put her through? I'm just a charlatan, not a true wizard like her father.* My muscles tensed and tears threatened. I knew I was risking going hand-to-hand with the monster, but something in my subconscious kept shoving me forward.

"Nice try. I've been fighting against your kind since I was small. I've beaten myself up more than you could even imagine. You guys can always creep to the surface and attack the vulnerable spots, but a human will spend days, months, years, their entire life flogging themselves. I know, and I go there and still fight it to this day. But it's between myself and a higher power. That fight isn't worth some troll in a dirty underpass," I said. I could hear that low growl again and the rocks falling as the troll made its move. It bounced off the spell and I felt a brief thump on my chest, like getting hit by a football or basketball. It was probably preferable to the other option of no protection at all.

"I told you, last time. Time to leave. You can open one of your portals and go back. If you don't, well..." I said.

The troll replied with another bounce off the edge of the spell. He growled and grabbed some of the trash, flinging it wildly in a rage.

"All right. I am setting this spell into a complete box. You cannot escape from any angle. You're right. I can't get in and you can't get out. That's the idea. Your box will slowly get smaller, and smaller, and smaller. I know you live longer than mortals, so I put it on your schedule. For the next twenty years, if I did my math right, you won't be able to put your hands on anyone or anything. People like me can still see you, but regular humans will just feel a chill down their backs. You will starve for twenty years, and you will have to stay and watch this world, living with things I know will send a chill down your spine - boredom and starvation," I said.

"You. You take this off now. If *you* want that woman and others you care about to remain safe," the hell troll said.

"I came prepared. I hoped you would know that," I said. I reached into my jacket and took out a beaker of holy water from my order. One night I asked for it through the old school channel of mail, and almost one week later to the minute the letter was written, the holy water had appeared at my desk at home, in all its spooky glory. I opened the bottle and threw its content. The water flew past the spell line, creating what looked like little static electricity sparks, and sparking again on impact with the hell troll. The troll began screaming in pain.

"I cast you out. From skin to bones and thorn to toe. You do not belong," I said. The hell troll raged and bounced off the concrete. The aged and rusty material started to crack under the force of the troll's body.

"You did that to me! How dare you do that to me?" the troll screamed.

"One last time, are you ready to go back?" I asked.

"Never!"

I could now see its face, furious and burnt by the holy water, and its reflection of the moonlight. *This one's mean.*

The hell troll was screaming again, trying once more to run and attack. My anxiety was still there, but easing a bit as its efforts were proving useless. If I hadn't had protection up, being torn to shreds would be an understatement. I could see the troll's dark black and brown nail-hoofs slashing and thankfully becoming translucent in the walls of the spell.

"Now for some bookkeeping. I am going to send your location and what I did to the higher ups. They might send some people, or they might just let me deal with you," I said. I knew the creature didn't care, but going through the procedure was comforting. The laughter from the creature was unexpected, with a hint of calm.

"You think you are the only one with help?" the troll said.

The light purple glow of the sky began to change. The blanket of clouds parted. The wind died down and the soft buzz of the outside world went still. The troll's laughter carried on the wind. I felt a new energy - someone was watching.

"You are new. I haven't met you before," I said. I sensed a presence and looked up to the top of the underpass. Someone was standing clad in a hood, cutting a dark silhouette against the stars. The only thing I could make out was a single strand of dark, long hair peeking from the hood.

"She's in my corner. She's got a lot more power than some special water, or you," the troll said.

"I will let it go back to where it's from, and you and I can have a conversation," I offered to the figure. No reply. She just stood. The next sound was the sound of my spells and protection dropping. The snarl of delight from the troll was palpable.

"Oh no," I said. It was all I could say as I began to run towards the side of the underpass. The panic set in. Thoughts started rushing into my head. *Allison. Death. Home.* Many things. I reached into the secret pocket inside my jacket towards the back and sealed with Velcro. It had been so long since I had opened it, it took a few tugs, but I yanked hard and pulled out a special black case. A normal human might have thought it was a plain jewelry box. I looked back. The hell troll was bounding towards me. I opened the case and inside, a glimmer of moonlight shone off nine stones of different colors. I grabbed the smallest one my discombobulated brain could find.

"I can't believe I'm going to use one of these," I said to no one in particular. I stopped and threw the stone.

The stone hit the hell troll, embedding into its skin. But it didn't stop there. Once inside, the stone melted and began to turn the skin around it black and boiling. The hell troll screamed in pain and fear, its screams echoing throughout the underpass. I saw movement in my peripheral vision and looked up. The hooded figure was looking down at the scene, but from the body language, I felt whoever it was wasn't expecting that.

The figure spoke. Of course, the voice was skillfully masked, and I couldn't tell who it was.

"You're going to be someone...fun," the figure said.

With that the figure rocked back and was gone (with magic or just on foot, I couldn't tell). I looked back at the body of the hell troll. It had slowly crumpled in on itself as the burnt blackness spread, and now the void had taken most of its skull. In a few more minutes the troll's entire being would be gone, not just back to where it came from, but deleted permanently from all of space, time and energy. *These are rare, and I used it on one little troll.* I was starting to beat myself up, so I did what I always did when my head was bad. I called Allison.

"Hi love, I've got a crazy story to tell you. I did something tonight and used one of those 'please don't use' items. I think the others like me are going to want an explanation."

"Really, you think it's that bad?" Allison asked. I looked back up into the sky, and as if by magic, the clouds were back, enveloping the world in a soft purple glow.

"I used one of the Casilli Stones," I said.

"Oh, I see," Allison said after a moment. "Well, get back and we can start getting safety rituals and weapons ready."

"I'll be home in a few," I said. I checked and most of the troll's body was gone now, aside from its legs. It wouldn't be long now. I decided to make the trek up the sharp embankment, my legs burning with the effort. Once up at the top, I could see the lights of the city and its people. He stopped for a moment, feeling their life and energy.

I won, even though I don't feel like it, I thought to myself. *That's the job.*

Such a Time as This

Christa Planko

Esther first saw the apparition on the brink of a hill—on the brink of her death.

It was the summer of her 13th birthday. She had officially been a teenager for a month, but she was already certain her teen years would be unbearable. Her first year of middle school practically wrecked her. The former Catholic school girl couldn't find acceptance among the streetwise youth at Chaddsford Middle School. Instead, she found herself used for sport, taunted and pranked by the other kids.

This accounted for half the reason why Esther ended up on the cliff.

The other half came from her home life. An only child, Esther often felt she had no one. Her father, Tom, was an architect, always working. He was hardly around. And while her mother, June, was around, she was emotionally distant. She walked about in a daze, never really present. Esther couldn't talk to her or get any kind of invested attention. In fact, her mother's dissociation had gotten so bad that her father suggested a remote family getaway. It was intended to rebuild connections.

The family had driven three hours to the cabin in the hills. Her parents had been there before Esther was born. It was owned by one of her father's work colleagues and had gorgeous surroundings. There was a nearby lake and plenty of trees, wildflowers, and hiking trails. It was removed from society, which made things perfect. There was nobody around.

Nestled in the hills, the cabin stood about a mile from a cliff's edge. Esther discovered the cliff on a solitary morning walk while her parents slept. The trail was isolated in these remote parts. As she walked, she noticed the cliff several feet away. She moved toward it, inching her way to the edge. Unintentionally, her foot dislodged a stone. Her breath caught as she craned her neck forward to watch it plummet. It made a small splash as it plopped into the stream thirty feet below. Then nothing but silence and peace.

Esther closed her eyes. Silence and peace. How she longed to silence the echoes of the taunts and names that resounded in her mind. How she yearned to experience peace—the peace she felt in the darkness when she closed her eyes, shutting out the world.

She inched closer to the cliff's edge. A mere leap separated her from the silence and peace she so desired. She drew in a breath and paused, about to take the plunge.

"Help me."

The voice caused her to stumble backward. She tripped over a large rock and landed on her rear end. Startled, Esther looked around. She was certain she had been alone. She didn't hear anyone approach and nobody appeared in view. Maybe she imagined it. Could it have been her own internal voice, coming from somewhere deep within?

"Help me," the voice sounded again. A child's voice. Esther turned toward the wooded area to her right from where the voice emerged. In the shadows of the trees, she could see the figure of a young girl. Although translucent, she could make out the clear outline of two outstretched arms and two legs beneath a sundress. Esther's eyes panned up the dress where there was a definite face. The mouth was an open O, perhaps awaiting a response. The eyes fixed on her were hollows in the dark.

Esther tried to scream, but no sound escaped her throat. She crawled backward on the ground as the apparition began to approach. Struggling to find her footing, she finally lifted herself up. She ran back, heart pounding all the way. She never looked back.

Once she reached the cabin, Esther flung open the door. She slammed it shut, plastering her back against it. Her breath escaped in short, frequent gasps.

"Esther, is that you?" Her father, Tom, entered the room, still in his robe. Esther stepped away from the door. "You're shaking!" he noted as she came over to him. He put his arms around her to comfort her. "What are you doing up so early? What happened?"

"I went for a morning walk, and I saw...something," she said, unsure how to describe it.

"Something or someone?" Tom asked.

Esther wondered—is a ghost some-*thing*? Or some-*one*?

"I'm not sh-sure," she said, continuing to tremble.

"You're going to have to tell me more if you want my help."

Now her mother, June, was in the room, eyebrows furrowed with concern. "What's going on, Tom?" she asked, seeing Esther burrowed in her father's arms.

"That's what I'm trying to find out," Tom said.

"I saw a ghost, ok?"

The reply was muffled as Esther kept her face pressed against her father's shoulder. The words felt awkward coming out, but she knew what she saw.

"A ghost?" Tom laughed. "You know there's no such thing!"

Frustrated, Esther pulled away.

"I know it sounds crazy, but I went off the hiking trail and saw a ghost in the woods. There was nobody else around. Then this girl appeared out of nowhere. Only I could see *through* her!"

Her mother clucked her tongue. "It was probably the sun through the trees. You thought you saw something. The mind plays tricks sometimes. What were you doing in the woods by yourself anyway?"

Esther shrugged. "I wanted to get some fresh air."

Tom sighed. "Your mother's right. It was probably a trick of the eye," he said, then added more sternly: "And you shouldn't be wandering through the woods by yourself."

Here comes the lecture. Now they won't let me out of their sight.

"How about I make us some breakfast?" her mother asked.

"That sounds wonderful, June," Tom said, then chuckled. "As I understand it, a full belly keeps the ghosts away."

But Esther didn't laugh. She did see a ghost. Period. Not only did she see a ghost, she heard it speak. Esther rolled her eyes. *Try telling my parents that.* They would probably have her evaluated for mental illness. So, she decided she wouldn't speak again about what she saw.

Later that night, after dinner, Tom and June decided to soak in the backyard hot tub.

"Want to join us, pumpkin?" Tom asked. "The warm water calms the nerves."

"No, thanks," Esther replied. "I'll probably go sit on the swing out front and read for a bit."

"All right, then," Tom said. "Reading also settles the mind. Just don't wander away from the cabin."

Esther pulled a book out of her backpack and held it up for her parents to see. "I won't. Have fun, you two."

As her parents slid open the glass doors leading to the back deck, Esther watched. They each stepped down into the bubbling spa. Once she saw them settle into their spots, glasses of wine in hand, she slipped out the front door.

She set the book on the porch swing. But she didn't sit down. That ghost she saw wanted desperately to communicate. It wanted something. *She* wanted something, if what she saw was, in fact, the ghost of a young girl. It sounded like she wanted Esther's help.

As an only child who often felt alone in her problems, Esther felt that she should muster up some courage to do something. She imagined that little girl alone in the woods. How frightened she must feel. How cold and lonely.

She went back to the trail, to the wooded area near the cliff. Maybe the ghost girl would show up again. This time, Esther would be brave and ask the girl what she wanted.

As she walked, Esther clutched her cell phone in case she needed its flashlight feature. Although still daylight, dusk was fast approaching. She followed the trail until she spotted the area in the woods which jutted out to a cliff. Slowly, she stepped off the trail into the wooded area. The lowering sun made the woods seem ablaze. An orange glow permeated the trees. Long shadows stretched along the ground. Esther swallowed as she glanced about.

"H-hello?" she called out to no one in particular. She found the large rock she had tripped over when she first heard the voice.

"Hello, do you need help?" Esther squinted into the woods where she had seen the apparition to the right.

"Will you help me?"

The voice came unexpectedly from the left. Esther gasped as she whipped her head toward the voice. With the sun behind, Esther could see the full apparition in the shadowy woods, just several feet away from her. The figure was transparent, but clearly a girl of about eight years old. She had long, poker straight hair like Esther. It may also have been blonde, although color was difficult to detect in the shadows. Her eyes were large and pleading. She fidgeted with a bow on the front of her sundress. Earlier that day, the apparition had seemed to glide, but Esther noticed now that she did have feet. In fact, they were in sneakers. One turned nervously inward toward the other as the girl stood, awaiting a response.

It's just a little girl.

Esther's heart began to pound. She could feel the hair on her arms begin to rise, but she determined to speak to the child. "Yes, I will help you," Esther said.

Then the girl smiled. She released the bow and clasped her hands together in excitement.

See, just a little girl.

She smiled back. "What do you want?" she asked.

"Find the lamb," the girl said.

Esther's mind went to images from nursery rhymes about little lambs and lost sheep. "I didn't see any lambs or other animals around," Esther said. Then she put herself in the mindset of a child at that age. "Did you lose a stuffed animal?"

The girl shook her head side to side. "No, the lamb with eyes of love."

Esther was baffled. What did this girl mean?

"I'm sorry, I don't understand what you're looking for," Esther said.

She heard her name being called in the distance. It was her parents. They were looking for her.

The girl's eyes widened. "I have to go!" she said. "Meet me tomorrow morning at the boat house. We'll find it together then."

"O-OK," Esther stammered. "Wait! Do you have a name?"

But it was too late. The ghost glided backward into the shadows and Esther found herself alone. She turned and ran back to the trail to get home to her parents.

The next morning, Esther sat at the breakfast table with her parents. She thought about how she would convince them to let her explore the boat house alone. They were initially upset when she again wandered the night before. But after noting that Esther was calmer and (according to her) learned her lesson about going off trail, they let it slide. They seemed much too absorbed in their own conversations to worry about Esther being unsupervised. And so, they continued their private discussions well into the night.

"I noticed a boat house down by the lake," Esther finally managed to say.

"There is an old boat house," Tom replied. "I believe there are some kayaks and canoes in there, too, that we are free to use."

Esther feigned intense interest. "Really?" she asked, eyes widened. "Can I take a kayak out on the lake?"

"Well, sure," Tom said, searching June's eyes for approval. "It would be nice for us all to paddle around the lake a bit this afternoon."

"This afternoon?" Esther asked.

"Yes, your mother and I would like to continue a talk we were having last night. Besides, it should be much sunnier this afternoon."

Esther could see through the kitchen window that the sky was overcast. There was also a slight fog. "Well, while you two chat, will it be alright if I check out the boat house?" she asked. "You know, to make sure there are enough kayaks and paddles."

Tom looked at June as if to get a read from her face, but she appeared emotionless. "That sounds like a good idea," he smiled. "Why don't you go do that?"

Immediately, Esther pushed away from the table. He didn't have to tell her twice. "Great!" she said. "I'll check it out and bring back the full report!"

"You do that, pumpkin," he smiled at her, then turned back to June.

June stared blankly at the wall, which was not uncommon. Esther saw her respond when Tom took her hand in his.

Let them have their conversation. That will keep them occupied while I find out what the ghost is looking for. Some kind of lamb—maybe a toy or drawing? Hopefully, the girl will meet me at the boat house as promised. Maybe the fate of the ghost depends on me to help her move on to the other side. How many other people would understand and be able to act without fear? Maybe I was made for such a time as this.

The boathouse was situated near the lake, at the bottom of the hill. Esther walked around to the back of the cabin and began the descent. It wasn't a steep walk, and Esther could see the top of the boat house poking out through the fog. It completely blanketed the lake, drifting in smoky swirls.

When Esther reached bottom, she found herself about knee-deep in fog. She stepped slowly and carefully. Her eyes stayed lowered to ensure she wouldn't trip over anything like a half-hidden tree stump.

As she approached the boat house, the door creaked open on its own. Esther stopped in her tracks. Her heart began to pound. "Hello?"

But there was no one. She crept toward the door of the boat house. It was dark inside and cobwebs draped the corners of the doorway. She entered carefully, the fog rolling in with her. Suddenly, an arm burst upward, reaching straight out of the swirling smoke. Esther screamed and staggered backward into the door. Startled, she grabbed the doorframe, preparing to run out.

"Please don't go!" The little girl's voice sounded so sad. The figure stood up out of the fog, rising to full height.

Esther paused. "Wh-what were you doing down there?"

The girl cocked her head and blinked. "Seeking the lamb."

"The lamb," Esther repeated. "How big is it? Is it a figurine? A drawing?"

The ghost girl held her hands out about six inches apart. She tried her eight-year-old best to describe it.

"This big," she said. "The lamb's heart shines through his eyes. So, whoever looks at him knows that they're loved."

The description sounded very touching, but didn't help Esther much. She still wasn't sure what it was she was looking for. She pulled out her cell phone and turned on its flashlight feature. She shone it down into the fog where the girl had been kneeling. There were a bunch of boxes stacked against a shelving unit.

The girl pointed toward a gap that formed behind two of the stacks.

Esther approached the boxes and aimed the light downward. Something dark and rectangular wedged between the stacks. It looked like a tackle box.

"Is that box what you're looking for?" Esther asked.

The girl nodded her head.

Esther unstacked the boxes and moved them out of the way. She tossed them aside, nearly choking on the dust cloud billowing from them. The tackle box was also covered in dust. Esther tried to blow the dust off the top when she lifted it, but to no avail. She set it on top of one of the stacks and shone the light on it to see.

"Open it," the girl said, eagerly.

Esther set her phone down and tried to pry it open in the dark.

"Do you have a name?" she asked the ghost as she fumbled with the latch.

"It's Cora," the girl said.

Corazon popped into Esther's head. She detested her first year of middle school, but it was the first time she ever had to take a language, which she enjoyed. She chose to learn Spanish. *Corazon was the Spanish word for "heart".* This made Esther smile.

"I'm Esther," she said. "Nice to meet you, Cora."

A large smile warmed Cora's pale face.

Frustrated that the box wouldn't open, Esther lifted her phone and shone the light on it again. She noticed a lock.

"The box is locked," she told Cora. "That's why I can't open it."

"Oh, nooo!" Cora whined.

"This lamb is really important to you, huh?" Esther asked.

Cora nodded.

"Why is that?"

"I need to give it to them," she said. "They need to see it."

"Who needs to see it?"

"Tom and June," she said. "My Mom and Dad."

Esther's eyes widened. Now she had goosebumps.

"Tom and June are *my* parents," she spoke her words with slow, punctuated speech.

Cora looked confused.

"Didn't you know?" she asked. "You're my little sister."

Esther shook her head back and forth. *No. How could this possibly be?* She stepped backward until she stood in the sunlight offered by the open door. Then she turned and ran all the way back to the cottage.

Once inside, she closed the door behind her. She bent forward, both hands on her knees, sucking the air into her lungs. The run uphill left her winded. Yet, she knew the dizzy feeling reeling through her brain was the revelation from Cora. Was it true? Did she have a sister? Would her parents not have told her?

She stumbled into her room and dropped onto the bed. Thoughts raced through her mind. Her mother's cool distance. Her father's absence. The invisible wall she sometimes sensed between her parents when they were together.

Did it all somehow point back to Cora? What happened? How did she die? Did her parents really love her, or could she never replace the hole left from a deceased child? The questions flooded her thoughts. They left her overwhelmed and frightened, even.

Then came the tears. They welled in her eyes until they burned. When they began to stream down her cheeks, leaving warm, salty tracks, her hands flew up to her face. She sobbed aloud into her palms. The emotion was too much to contain.

"Pumpkin?" Tom now stood in the doorway. He appeared flushed, as though he had come back from a walk.

Esther couldn't manage any words. She just looked at her father as she continued to sob.

Tom entered the room and sat on the bed beside Esther. He put his arm across her shoulders. "What's wrong?" he asked, wiping a tear from her cheek.

Sniffling, Esther rubbed her palms across her cheeks. A new emotion overtook her now. She glared at her father.

"You never told me!" she choked. "You and Mom. Neither of you ever said a thing!"

"What's this about?" Tom asked. "You'll need to be more specific, Esther. This is crazy talk unless you tell me what's the matter."

Crazy talk. She would need to keep her words in check so her father wouldn't think she was off the rails. If she brought up Cora and he wondered where she got her information, she couldn't very well tell him a ghost told her. And what if Cora's words weren't true? How would she explain herself then?

"Never mind," Esther collected herself. It took all her strength as her emotions swept through her in tumultuous waves. Anger, worry, fear. Loneliness, in spite of having two parents who possibly loved her? She wasn't sure they truly did.

"Well, something upset you," Tom said. "You can't deny that. Now what was it?"

Esther hesitated. Maybe she couldn't say anything to him, but she might be able to show him. There was something in that tackle box that Cora wanted desperately for Tom and June to see. Esther looked him in the eyes. "I saw something," she said.

Tom dropped his head. His mouth twisted into a smirk. "Not this again," he sniffed. He glanced at Esther. "Was it a ghost?"

"No," she lied. "Something else. Down in the boat house."

Tom looked concerned. "Was somebody in there?" he asked. "Because we should be alone here from what I was told."

"Not somebody," she said. "Something."

Tom cocked an eyebrow.

"I have to show you."

Esther hopped off the bed.

"Come on!" she grabbed her father's hand and led him out of the room.

June was wandering aimlessly about.

"Is everything ok?" she asked when she saw them. Her tone was flat and robotic. Her eyes glazed over. She was having one of her off days.

"It's fine, June," Tom answered. "Esther and I were just going to take care of some things in the boat house."

"Okay," June said. But she already had her back to them as she turned her pace in the opposite direction.

Tom and Esther marched downhill towards the boat house in silence. When they reached the door, Esther paused, looking at her father. Pulling out his cell phone, he tapped on the flashlight, then opened the door. Esther stayed close on his heel.

Tom stood inside and flashed the light around the perimeter. There was nothing but shelving, boating gear, boxes, and cobwebs.

Esther tugged at Tom's shirt and pointed down toward the corner of a shelving unit.

He shined the light in that direction. There lay the tackle box, turned over on its side as Esther left it.

"It's some sort of toolbox," Tom said. He drew nearer, squatting beside it. He lifted it upright.

"What do you know?" he chuckled. "It's my old tackle box. I haven't fished in years and never really thought twice about what could have happened to it."

"I think you need to open it," Esther said.

Tom looked up at Esther. She simply nodded. He reached for the latch.

"Locked," he said.

"Why would you lock a tackle box, Dad?"

"You were a little girl," he said. "I didn't want you getting into the hooks and hurting yourself."

"I never came here with you guys," Esther affirmed. "I wasn't born yet the last time you were here."

Tom flushed a little, not knowing what to say. "Uh, that's right," he mumbled. "I must've forgotten. That's true."

"But don't you want to know what's in it?" she asked. "For nostalgia's sake?"

Tom shone the flashlight around. He spotted a hammer on a nearby shelf. He grabbed it and struck it against the locking mechanism. It cracked. He opened the lid of the tackle box. Laying on top was something wrapped in paper. Tom stared, unsure what it could be.

"That's it," Esther said. "See what it is."

As Tom lifted the object out of the tackle box and began to unwrap it, Esther noticed a translucent glow toward the back. It was Cora.

"You found it?" she whispered, looking directly at Esther. Esther looked toward her father. He didn't seem to hear the child's voice.

"It's a lamb!" Esther exclaimed triumphantly as her father revealed a flat, ceramic ornament in the shape of a lamb. It had clear marbles for eyes.

"It's him!" Cora exclaimed. She clapped as she bounced up and down. "See the love in his eyes?" She clasped her hands beneath her chin and awaited Tom's response as he shined the light over the lamb's face.

"Look, Dad," Esther said. "There are hearts etched beneath the marbles."

He turned the lamb over, shining the light on it. There was writing.

"What does it say?" she asked.

Tom gulped as he fought back tears. "'Love, Cora,'" he choked. He lifted the lamb to his lips and kissed it as the tears began to flow.

Cora's face fell. "Why is he crying?" she whispered. "He should be happy."

"They're tears of joy, I think," Esther whispered back.

Tom slowly raised his head.

"Who are you talking to, Esther?" he asked.

Esther stepped away from her father's view. "Hi, Daddy..."

"Who...? What...?"

Tom's eyes widened with fright when he saw the apparition.

"Cora?"

Esther placed her hand on his shoulder. "It's okay, Dad," she said. "I think she has something she wants to tell you."

Cora looked at Esther who smiled and nodded. Cora smiled back. She turned to Tom.

"Daddy," she said. "I'm sorry. I wasn't very nice when I found out Mommy was going to have a baby."

"Oh, Cora," Tom whispered between tears. "Your mother and I loved you so much. We brought you here to share the news that our family was growing—so we could all spend time together and celebrate. I'm so sorry we punished you by sending you to your room. You were so angry when we told you. We thought you were acting out..."

"I know, Daddy," Cora sniffled. "I was worried at first that you would love the new baby more than me. But then I was happy and excited to become a big sister. So, I made the lamb for you and Mommy—to let you know how much I loved our family. The day I wandered off was so I could hide this for you. It was a surprise."

"We should have checked in on you...paid more attention," Tom sobbed.

"I snuck out through the window," Cora said. "To hide the lamb in your tackle box because I knew you were planning to take us fishing. But it was raining when I left the boat house. I slipped on the mud and slid into the lake."

"You couldn't swim," Tom choked. "And it was dark. Oh, Cora. We have never been the same since the day we...lost you."

Cora looked at Esther and smiled.

"But you have Esther," she said. She reached for her hair. "Her hair is like mine. So are her eyes. You could always look at her and see me."

Cora beamed with pride. She turned to Esther. "You're very pretty," she said, coyly. "I'm proud to be your sister. You are part of my family and I love you, too."

Esther smiled as her eyes welled with tears. "I didn't know you existed before now, but I love you, too, Cora."

"If it wasn't for you, I would never have the chance to tell anyone that," Cora said. She clasped her hands again. "You found the lamb! I hope it reminds you all how much you're loved."

"I know a great place where we can hang this and see it every day," Tom smiled.

"Then you like it?" Cora asked.

"I love it," Tom replied. "And I love you."

Cora's smile broadened. She tugged shyly at the bow on her dress. "I'm so happy," she said. "But I have to go now. Don't worry—you'll all be fine. Love will hold you together. And I know I am so loved." Cora touched her heart. "I feel it right in here."

She stepped back until she slowly faded away. A twist of sparkling light ascended through the roof and vanished.

Tom and Esther stood in place for several seconds before falling into each other's arms.

"I'm so sorry I never told you," Tom said. "It has been a sensitive topic for your mother and me. We thought we'd get past it once you were born. But keeping it quiet, like it never happened, only made things worse—for ourselves, for us, for you. It hasn't been fair."

"I understand," Esther said.

"I'm sure you have a lot of questions," Tom said.

Esther nodded.

"Come on. Let's go back and have a talk," he said, holding up the lamb. "We'll share this with your mother."

Back at the cabin, Esther and her parents had a long talk. Emotions abounded from tears of grief, to tears of guilt, to tears of joy. But underlying it all was love. It drew them all together— just as Cora said it would.

The accident at the boat house was so tragic that Tom and June could never bring themselves to discuss it. They had decided they would never let Esther know that she had an older sister. But silencing it had only created a rift. Tom had worked to forget. And June had emotionally distanced herself. Now that it was out in the open, the family vowed they would spend more time focused on their living daughter.

The day they returned home, June found a spot to hang the lamb above the pantry door in the kitchen. This way, it would be as though Cora was present with the family during meals. Tom got out a step ladder and hung it.

June stepped back, staring lovingly at the ornament hanging above the pantry. The curtains in the kitchen window began to billow. June closed her eyes against a gentle breeze that lifted her hair for a second. Then her eyelids shot wide open, shiny with tears.

"Did you hear that, Tom?" she gasped. Her fingertips grazed over her face as though checking whether she was really there, in this moment.

"Hear what?" Tom asked, curious.

"For a brief second, I thought I heard a little girl's voice whisper, 'I love you, Mommy.' And the image of Cora's face with a warm, beaming smile filled my mind and I knew that, wherever Cora was, she was happy and full of love."

Now both Tom and Esther wiped at their tears. June embraced Esther, drawing her in for a hug.

"Thank you for bringing us all back together again," June said to her daughter. "And by 'us,' I mean Cora, too. You brought her back to us, metaphorically speaking."

Then, the words Esther would never forget. The same words she once thought to herself: "Perhaps you were made for such a time."

And perhaps she was. But she knew she didn't act alone. There was a greater force behind it all. It brought Cora to her and her to her family. It united them all and made them complete. It was the power of love. As long as love existed, so would her family, including Cora who lived on through them.

In that moment, Esther's heart filled to overflowing. She smiled and reached for both her parents' hands and squeezed.

The Boy Who Loved Horses

Joseph Carrabis

I was born in a town like this. Mine's on the eastern ridge and closer to Raleigh. My town had the same dirt roads, the same one-room wooden church, the same old store where you asked for things instead of getting them yourself, the same people but with different faces, the same old men carrying coon rifles, girls getting married when they're thirteen and younger, having kids before they're through being kids themselves, the same sense of what's ours and what's not. I left my town and got educated. Made it into the extension service. Decided to come back and help others in towns like mine. My education didn't take all the hill out of me, though. Knew enough to carry a gun in case I got too close to a still. But it did take some of the hill away. I forgot about towns like this.

I came here about a year ago; my big, state-issue Buick all shiny as it passed suspicious eyes. The state needed a count of school age children to qualify for funding and I came to count the children in this town.

Hill're wary of anything new. They saw my car and suit and whispered "city" as I passed. It was true. When I come to this town, I acted like I was an educated man, and everybody was suspicious of me. I went into the general store and bought a pop, sat down and tried to talk with some of the folk. Took me a while, but I got a nod, then a wink, then a smile. Turns out some of us had kin.

Eventually, had to tell them why I came. They got quiet after that. I asked if there was some place I could spend the night. Nobody said. I should've left. I know hill. I know the signs. One of the men, Burt, left. The rest of us talked some more and, when there was no more to say, I thanked them all and left.

I saw Burt as I drove out of town. He was walking, two steps forward and one step back, and I could tell he was tasting squeeze since he left the store. Should've kept on driving. Should've known. Hill's got mysteries they need to keep. "Hey, Burt, you need a ride?" I opened the door for him, and he winked and handed me his bottle, getting in.

Burt lived in a cabin up a short, rutty, old road about a mile out of town. We drove there talking hill, talking kin. By the time we got to Burt's cabin, he was smelling like a coon's been rolling in 'shine. There was another jug on his table. He offered me more but drank most of it himself. "They won't tell you about the boy," he said.

"What boy's that?"

"Lem's son, the boy who loves horses."

He was quiet for a bit, so I said, "You going to tell me, Burt?"

Burt rolled up the sleeve on his left arm. It was covered with deep scars, like something didn't take a liking to it. "I used to keep hawks. The boy turned my birds against me. You stay the night if you want. Then you best leave."

"What do you mean, the boy turned your birds against you? Did he poison them? Is he twisted?"

Burt rolled down his sleeve. He was about to pick up his glass when he slammed his hand down on the table.

"What's wrong?"

He pulled his hand back and wiped it on his shirt. There was a black pus puddle and eight twitchy legs where he hit the table. "Boy's not twisted. But he twists." He looked at me then. I could tell because he shook my arm. "Calm down, son. Just a spider, is all."

Now, I've been shook by spiders ever since I was four. I was walking with my pa. He heard something and told me to stay put, but I didn't listen. I tried to follow, got lost, and fell into a pit of spiders. Lord Almighty, how I shrieked. Big, fat, fuzzy things, crawling all over me, in my hair, on my face, up my legs, down my arms. I started screaming and my pa came and got me. He slapped them off. Some squashed right on me, so big you could see their eyes bulging as they popped against me. Never got over it. Not then, not ever.

Burt pushed the jug at me, and I finished it off, at least what didn't slide down my chin.

About eleven, eleven-thirty, Burt's snoring woke me up. I went outside and walked around. It was a clear, full mooned night, a night where the hills smother you in smells of wet hay and laurels. There was a field down the road from Burt's cabin. I walked down there.

I get closer and I hear horses. In the center of the field, in the light of the moon, there stands a boy, twelve or thirteen, no more, in the middle of twenty head. He was waving his arms like he's conducting an orchestra, but it's dead silent save those horses. They's following his motions and jumping and snorting and playing like he was one of their own.

Then, he saw me and his arms came down, and the horses got between me and him.

"Boy," I called, but nothing.

The next day I went into town and asked if anybody knew about the boy. They told me no such boy existed. Too much squeeze, they said. I wasn't sure. Some others brought their children to me, and I took down names and guessed at ages.

Should've known. I was hill. Too much education. Should've known. I drove back that night and went to Burt's cabin. No one was there. I started walking, flashlight in my hand, to the field where I saw the boy. Only marks there was a day old.

I drove to town and there's the boy. The same boy, in the middle of the street this time, with more horses around him. Stallions and mares, paints and quarters, Morgans, Arabians, Belgians, Percherons; there were so many I couldn't tell what all was there. But there they were, prancing in the moonlight, the boy like some ringleader in a circus and his horses on display. I got out of the car and started towards him. He saw me then. His arms shot out and the horses ran off. I dodged a Belgian and saw the boy head into the church.

Cornered him there. Just me and the boy. The windows didn't have shades or blinds and the night shone through. The place's filled with moonlight and shadows. His eyes wide on me and he's backing up, each step driving him further up the nave, and I followed, pew by pew. I got close enough to get a good look at him. There's nothing different about him; he's just a boy is all. Black hair and eyes, clean clothes, patched, but as clean as hill clean gets. No shoes.

"What's your name, son?"

He didn't answer. He just kept looking at me.

"Boy, what's your name?"

He stops, his back up against the pulpit, his head just beneath the Cross.

All of a sudden, the doors of the church burst open. I turned around to see. The horses are coming into the church. Two big Percherons, probably twenty hands each, broke the doors off the hinges and bowed the frame getting in. They came down the sides of the sanctuary, all the time snorting and stamping like they scent a lynx or a bob, and there's a foal in the field. Then came the others. I could see them in the moonlight, four stallions, throwing their heads up and down, their eyes opened wide and right on me, looking at me like it's the Apocalypse and I'm unworthy to ride. The chairs and pews are going everywhere. Wood is splintering, hymnals is flying, Bibles getting trampled into dust.

The horses are close, and I grabbed the boy, one hand on his arm and the other in his hair. "You stop them, boy. You hear me? You stop them now or you'll be dead before tomorrow, boy."

His eyes darted from me to the horses. I squeezed his arm so tight I could feel his pulse in my hand. "I mean it, boy. You send those horses away."

The horses started going out. The stallions first, then the two big drafts. It's just the boy and me. And as I'm looking at him, something moved right above his head. Right there at eye level, eight legs arcing and its web glistening, I see a spider, its web attached to one arm of the Cross, the spider swinging to the other.

The boy moved away. He saw me, and I could tell I was pale even by moonlight, but I ain't letting that boy go until I get back to my car.

That's when I heard footsteps outside, in the street, and I made for the door. We stopped in the doorframe. Must've been all the townsfolk there. They're looking at me and looking at the boy.

"You let him go, mister. We got no truck with you. The boy's not your concern. You let him go and we'll let you be."

That much hill, no education takes away. I let the boy go and I wouldn't take a step before Gabriel's horn come calling me. "I'm going to my car and this boy's coming with me." I took one more step and heard some hammers cock. The moonlight glinted off some stocks and barrels.

I took my gun out of my pocket then. "Anybody wants a go, I say I can shoot this boy dead before I see my maker. Anybody wants a peace; I'm going to start walking. And if my car don't start and move when I step on the gas, this boy's dead. And just so that no one thinks I'm too city to shoot this boy, remember some of us got kin. I'm from the other side of this ridge." I gave them time to think about that. "I'll let this boy go soon as I'm clear of this town. You don't know me, but some of you know my kin. You got my word; I'll let this boy go; you just let me out of this town."

If I wasn't city, they'd listen and let me go. But not now. Now I was city, I wasn't hill. And they knew the same as I did; soon as I could, I'd be back with people to get this boy. Boy had a gift and city'd want to know.

The look in their eyes. Knew they didn't believe. I pulled the boy to put him between me and the crowd. Then I saw one man looking straight at the boy. "This your boy?" I asked him.

The man nods and I guessed the boy saw him because he nods, too. The man says "Yeah, that's Luke. He's mine. And I'm his pa. I got nothing else but that boy in my life, mister. That boy and the horses I trade when the breeders come looking for hot or cold blood. That boy loves his pa, mister. Just like you must love yours. You love your pa, don't you, mister?"

I tugged on the boy's arm, not wanting to answer. All of a sudden, I heard a scuttling above me. I looked up and saw all these legs and eyes staring down. The boy's heart was pounding, I could feel it, but I didn't care. The spiders started dropping down, not even coming down on threads. Some were so big you could hear them splat when they hit the ground. I let go the boy's arm and started shooting at the roof. But it was no good by then.

I was in Burt's cabin when I woke up. There was food on the table, but I couldn't eat it. I found a broom and went all through the house looking. Couldn't find one. That's when Luke's pa come by to tell me. Luke doesn't like to hurt anybody. Doesn't want to, either. Just wants to train horses. Boy's got a natural way with them, loves them and they love him. But Luke's pa also tells me I can't leave. Says if I ever try to go away, Luke'll send more spiders.

Can't go away, never. Hear that? Scuttling on the roof? Listen. Real soft? That's more of you, isn't it.

Isn't it?

Inside Out

C.R. Johansson

He looked up, squinting. The sun was directly above him. *It must be close to noon.* The temperature would continue to rise for another two to four hours before it started its slow decline. *If I'm lucky, I'll be dead before it reaches its lowest point near dawn.*

He twisted at the waist, his movements didn't disturb their feeding at all, and he reached behind his back and pulled his phone out of his back pocket. Cellphone coverage was nonexistent in this part of the woods, but he wasn't planning on calling for help. He wiped the sticky blood, his blood, off the phone onto his T-shirt.

"Huh," he made a small noise of overconfident indifference when he looked at the phone. *I was right. It's twelve-ten in the afternoon. I must look like hell,* he thought. *But this needs to be done.* He started to record a video and began to narrate.

"This is," he stopped and cleared his throat which was dry and scratchy. His water bottle was in his truck, and he hadn't had any in hours. *Why would I want to prolong this, anyway.* "This is Dr. Alan Riker Forensic Entomologist, reporting from the Olympic National Forest in Washington State. Scarabaeidae 981 live-bait feeding patterns and behavior study experiment number one. This is the first and last experiment of this type. Bait consists of large warm- blooded mammal of the Hominidae family." He paused briefly. "Well, it's me." He chuckled and rolled his eyes in embarrassment at admitting to his clumsiness. While his laugh was a sign that his hysteria still lingered in the shadows of his mind, behind the antiseptic scientific front he was trying to portray on his recording.

His girlfriend warned him not to do this experiment, but he couldn't stop himself. *And I would have been successful if that damn bird hadn't scared me.* He met his girlfriend at his friend's Halloween party last year. She was dressed as a pink and purple alien. They moved in together three months later, when her roommate moved out. Even though she wasn't a scientist, she fascinated him. Her unique ideas, thoughts and opinions on science bordered on an awakening that hadn't existed in the field for centuries. Last night before they fell asleep, she confessed to him that she didn't want him to perform the experiment because she had a feeling that he would succeed, and that scared her for some reason. *That was the motivation I needed to forge ahead.* The experiment wasn't innovative, other scientists had tried it before, but her premonition told him all he needed to know. He would succeed where they failed. So, at four in the morning, he kissed her cheek as she slept, crept quietly out of the apartment and drove to what he thought was the perfect spot.

Scarabaeidae 981 existed all around the world: in the jungles, the forests, and the deserts. They were even found on the ocean beaches. They were first discovered in the 1920's devouring a corpse from the inside out in the Amazon jungle. They were logged and classified, and weren't seen again until the 1940's when there was a sudden increase in sightings. Surprisingly, none were found in the cities. Though small remote villages and towns were subjected to their terror regularly. None of the parasites survived in captivity or the labs, and their life cycle was unknown. Scientists around the world believed they were scavengers, perhaps a distant relative of the skin beetle. *But what if they aren't scavengers eating something that's already dead? What if they caused the death? What if they kill by consuming their victim from the inside out?* He needed to know the answer.

Scientists couldn't figure out where they came from. Scandal magazines and the internet claimed they were from outer space. Others believed that they escaped from a scientific lab. Some sort of terror weapon. *Close to eighteen thousand new organisms are discovered each year*, he thought. *These things might have been hibernating for all this time. Maybe they were living deep underground, deeper than any of our mines have gone, and finally reached the surface.* He wiped the sweat on his forehead and again gazed up at the sun.

"The original experiment consisted of a canine as live bait," he continued. "A coyote which may or may not have starved to death by now, depending on when my bones are discovered, is housed in a kennel in the back of the van. For full exposure, elements of this experiment changed when I fell while setting up the last camera and suffered a compound fracture of the tibia resulting in bone protrusion. Cameras are positioned in an isosceles triangle shape around the experiment site and are recording. The video will support my claim. The first scarab appeared ten minutes after I fell. Confirming my theory that they are attracted to fresh blood and live bait, not just corpses."

I didn't even see where it came from, he remembered with a nervous laugh. It reminded him of the year carpenter ants overran his apartment. *It was like they were magical or something.* One second the bathroom wall behind him was void of ants, and in a blink of his eye, one was scurrying up the wall. When the first beetle-sized parasite appeared standing on his foot, it felt like he was in a surreal nightmare. He waved his hand to shoo it away, but the predator wasn't even phased by his action. Its antenna twitched, twisting and turning, assessing the situation. *And calling other parasites.* In seconds, close to fifty of them surrounded him. Then without warning, at least one dozen raced up his pant legs while two others sped to the rip in his jeans at his injury site where his bone protruded. Panic stricken he screamed, waved his arms, squirmed on the ground rolling his hips back and forth. He even wiggled his legs despite the searing hot pain from his injury, trying to scare them off, but they didn't flee. When the first parasite bit into his leg, he shrieked in horror. He spent the next hour hysterical, as one parasite after another feasted on his body, until fear led to shock and shock led to resignation. That's when it dawned on him to make the video.

"I don't know how many responded to the initial signal from the dominant scarab, but one fact worth noting is they do not swarm or behave in a frenzied feeding pattern like other insects, reptiles or mammals. The alpha scarab continues to reside on the top of my shoe. Perhaps controlling the feeding? I don't know. I believe they have some sort of anesthetic and paralyzing element in their salvia, like mosquitoes or the rattle snake." *Or that demon from the horror movies.* "Perhaps its more akin to a venom," he said for the recording, "as I discovered my legs are now numb as more of them feed."

He felt his mind wander, space staring at nothing for a second before his gaze settled on a nearby tree trunk where little ants scurried up and down the trunk. *Why aren't the ants afraid of them?* He had to admit Scarab 981's design was simple and its purpose even simpler; to live, to eat and to reproduce. *Maybe they're like ant nest beetles. Not much is known about them either and they're rarely seen. All we suspect is that they live with ants when they're in their early stages.*

"Bark! Bark! Bark!"

Alan's eyes popped open. It was twilight outside. For a second he didn't know where he was. Then his mind cleared. He didn't even know when or how he fell asleep. *Perhaps passed out is more like it. I'm sure I've lost a lot of blood.* He looked at his bloodied jeans. In the distance he heard another coyote's response.

"Bark! Bark! Bark!" This time the coyote's bark blended into a deep howl, intended to intimidate a foe.

What was that? A dog? Struck by fear, Alan moved his head side to side and saw nothing. *The coyote in the van.* His thought gave him a little relief. Other coyotes and scavengers would come to investigate eventually. The alpha scarab's antenna twitched and twisted. *Does it know the coyote is trapped and vulnerable too? He looked at his phone.* Five hours had passed. *I hate daylight savings time.* In the distance the primitive reply from another coyote echoed and his fear returned.

He gazed at the stars just beginning to appear above. *Please let me die before the wild coyotes get here.* He'd been bitten by a dog when he was a kid, and fear of it plagued him even now as he lay here being eaten alive by something no bigger than his fingertip. When people think about being eaten alive, they fear the large predators like sharks, bears and mountain lions. They don't think about the small predators in the world. *And if they do, they think of bees, spiders and snakes.* Survivors, on documentaries, share how in a split second, as the grizzly bear bit down on their leg, they made the decision to live and survive their attack. *There are no documentaries on those who die. I know I'm being eaten alive, but there's nothing I can do about it. Like people who are dying of cancers, bacterias, or viruses. But, unlike people dying of cancer who have time to distance themselves from the joy of life and their loved ones over the course of months as they prepare to die, I'm stuck with a hasty, quiet acceptance that feels like it's dragging on forever.*

He picked up his phone which he had dropped in his lap to resume documenting his experiment. It was the only weapon he had against his fate. He'd gotten used to the gentle tugging as the scarabs pulled pieces of his body away. The tugging reminded him of having stitches removed. Beneath his clothes, he watched their round shapes moving about. Very soon they would invade his torso. He couldn't understand why he hadn't bled out yet.

"A feeding pattern has emerged," he said. "The scarabs feed for about ten to fifteen minutes, like a variety of young mammals who suckle for ten to fifteen minutes and then sleep. Then, the scarabs who have fed, retreat and are replaced by ones who haven't fed yet. The alpha scarab remains at its position on my foot. Perhaps it's more than an alpha, perhaps the feeding scarabs are its offspring."

"Yelp! Yelp!" The coyote in the van thrashed about for a second or two. Then it whined and went silent.

I didn't see any of the scarabs leave the clearing. Maybe there's another colony of them nearby. I wish I had a camera set up near the van so it could verify my suspicion.

"I don't know why I haven't bled out yet." He questioned out loud for the recording and looked at how the legs of his jeans flattened, as if there was nothing inside them. "Though I can't visualize what's beneath my jeans, my legs must be close to bones now. The scarabs will start consuming my torso next. They must secrete ecarin or some sort of coagulant which is keeping me alive."

"You're a smart man, Alan." The tiny, but not quite twangy voice had a strange, foreign accent which he'd never heard before, but that didn't matter.

I'm saved! His heart leapt with joy.

"Oh, thank god you're here," he said and moved his head side to side again, trying to find the person who spoke. "I'm hurt, and I need medical help right away."

"I'm not here to help you, Alan."

The cold hand of death gripped his heart like a vice, and he stared in horror at the alpha scarab on his foot. His breathing increased, tears filling his eyes.

No, it can't be.

"It can't be," he whimpered. "I'm having predeath hallucinations now," he recorded. "I'm imagining that the alpha scarab is talking to me."

"I am talking with you, Alan."

He stared at the beetle for a second of two, a little unsure of what to do. "Ok," he conceded. "Let's say you are really talking to me and not a hallucination. Why are you talking to me? Why are you eating me?"

"Every organism needs to feed."

The scarab's logical response pissed him off, and for a second, he thought about throwing his phone at it, even as the scarabs beneath his clothes vacated, but he suppressed the urge. "Ok." There was no way he could mask the sarcasm in his voice, and if he could've moved, he would have given the insect more attitude. "If you are a talking scarab who just needs to feed, why are you taking time to talk to me?"

"I want you to know everything you think about us is correct."

"Right," he said with a sarcastic sigh, realizing his suspicion was right. "You're just a predeath hallucination intended to comfort me as I die by telling me that my life meant something in this world and that I made a difference."

"I'm not a hallucination," the scarab insisted as it started crawling across the empty legs of his bloody jeans and up his t-shirt.

"Ok, if you're not a hallucination, I might as well get some answers. Are you of this world?"

"We are one of the oldest organisms of this planet. We live in the deep earth."

"Why didn't you stay down there?"

"We were hungry. We can kill just as easy as we can clean up something that's already dead."

"I knew it!" He couldn't help but smile at his success. *All my time and research has paid off. I was right and because of my experiment everyone will know it.* He sighed, relief washing over him. *It wasn't a waste of time.*

The alpha climbed up onto his chest, where it stared at him with its beady black eyes. Its antennae twitched and twisted. All the other scarabs gathered, encircling him the way they did when they first appeared. This time, instead of being afraid, he had the funny thought of the children's story about the little people.

"Are you happy with your discovery?" the beetle asked.

"Oh yes," Alan sighed. At this moment, nothing else mattered. *I was right. And it wasn't a waste of time.*

"Goodbye, Alan." The beetle lunged forward and sunk its mandibles into his eye.

"Ahhh!" He screamed as the entire colony attacked.

Sangoma, Zombie Elephants, and Tokoloshe, Oh My!

Kaye Lynne Booth

Nelwazi and Nhlanhla lazed in the warmth of the jungle floor as they reclined against the jackalberry trees, popping the fruits into their mouths.

"What should we do today?" Nelwazi asked, plucking a piece of buffalo grass and putting it to his lips to blow. A long squeaky sound like a duck came out. "I'm bored."

"I know of a sangoma *(shaman)*, Ngobizitha, who lives not far from here, who has been sending tokoloshe to cause havoc in the village. Maybe we should pay him a visit and ask him to stop."

"Tokoloshe!" Nelwazi said, scoffing. The tokoloshe were mythical creatures which liked to torment children. According to the legends, an evil sangoma would capture them and make them do their bidding. "They are not real. The elders just tell those stories to make children behave. Even you must know that."

"You'd better watch what you say," Nhlanlha replied. "Ngobizitha is a powerful sangoma. Very old. It is rumored that his training involved a test of such difficulty that, although he triumphed, it left him bitter and angry.

"Oh, you're right," he said with wide eyes, teasing his friend. They had grown up together in the Zulu village and Nelwazi couldn't help but make sport of Nhlanhla whenever the opportunity arose. "Perhaps if we look here, by the river, we can capture a tokoloshe and make it do our bidding. Then, we'll send it after that old sangoma, eh?"

Nelwazi jumped up, running to the river's bank. "Come out, Tokoloshe!" he cried. "Come out wherever you are."

"Nelwazi, you are a fool," Nhlanhla said, rushing to grab his friend by the shoulders. "You must be a sangoma to control a tokoloshe. You should not mess with such creatures."

"There is no such thing," Nelwazi said, sticking out his tongue at the other boy. "But if we did come across one not under a sangoma's control, I bet I could make friends with him. He'd do what I asked because I'd be kind to him, not because of some magic spell. Not even a tokoloshe can resist love. My Gogo *(grandmother)* says love is the most powerful magic. It can cure anything."

A splash came from the river above them and they turned their heads in that direction, startled. "What was that?" Nhlanhla said, sounding a little frightened. "Did you hear it, too?"

Nelwazi couldn't resist this additional opportunity to tease his friend. "Yes, I heard it," he said, crouching at the river's edge and scooping up some water in his hands.

"What do you think it was?" the other boy asked, eyes darting up and down the riverbank as if he expected something to jump out at them.

"Look out! It's tokoloshe!" Nelwazi cried, tossing the water at his friend as he ran back up the bank toward the sheltering trees, laughing.

"Very funny," Nhlanhla said, giving chase. "I'll get you for that!"

Nelwazi stopped at the jackalberry tree, looking over his shoulder to see his friend charging up the slope after him. But Nhlanhla wasn't laughing. His eyes were bulging, and the cocoa skin of his cheeks was tinged pink. He looked angry, and he was headed straight for him like a charging rhino. Nelwazi turned and ran through the trees, not wanting to find out how angry his friend really was.

Every time he looked back, Nhlanhla was a little closer than he was before, so Nelwazi just kept running, crashing through the surrounding bush. They had been friends for as long as he could remember, and Nelwazi had never seen his friend this angry before. He ran, and ran, not daring to stop. He was faster than his friend, so he hoped the other boy would soon run out of steam and give up. Maybe then, he could discover why his friend had gotten so upset at his playfulness. In all of his fourteen years, he had never seen his friend so angry.

Nelwazi's toe caught on the edge of a stone, projecting him forward, where he landed face first in the dirt.

Before he could get back to his feet, Nhlanhla was upon him. The other boy grabbed him and lifted him off the ground, plopping him down on his behind. "You stupid jerk!" he cried, slugging him in the shoulder. "You can't be joking around about sangoma magic. You'll bring down bad juju on both of us. Do you want to bring down evil upon us?"

"You're serious?" Nelwazi said, gazing at his friend in disbelief. "I was only joking around. Take it easy, will you?"

But when Nelwazi looked up at his friend, towering over him, Nhlanhla was gazing past him, over his shoulder and all the color had drained from his face. He turned to see what had so disturbed the other boy and saw a Zulu hut behind him, tucked so deep in the bush that it was almost completely hidden.

"What is the matter with you?" Nelwazi said, not seeing anything remarkable. "It's just a dumb old hut."

"Bad juju. I told you," Nhlanhla said, slowly backing away. "You've brought us right to Ngobizitha's door. This can't be good."

"Are you kidding?" Nelwazi said. "What makes you think this hut belongs to the sangoma?"

"Who else would live up here on Ghost Mountain?" his friend asked. It does not take a genius. I told you shouldn't joke around like that."

"Don't be ridiculous," he said, rising from the ground. "Even if this is his hut, which it probably isn't, the place looks deserted. Look at how the trees and brush have grown up around it. Let's go have a look. I'll prove it."

He took a single step toward the hut, but Nhlanhla grabbed his shoulder, holding him back from going any further. "Wait!" his friend cried. "You can't seriously want to venture inside. You are messing where you have no business messing."

Just then, the winds picked up, thunder cracked above them, and the sky grew dark. "The ancestors are angry," Nhlanhla cried.

"It will be alright," Nelwazi said, laughing as he pushed his friend's hand away. "No one will know. Don't you want to know if it really belongs to your sangoma? We'll just take a quick peek."

"You can go look if you want," Nhlanhla said, crossing him arms over his chest, and planting his feet firmly in the dirt. "I don't care to get any closer than I am right here."

"Fine. Suit yourself," Nelwazi said with a shrug of his shoulders. He acted as if he didn't care, but now he had something to prove. "I'll be right back." He swallowed the lump that was forming in his throat and headed through the thick brush surrounding the hut without looking back to see if his friend was following.

The closer he got to the hut, the more the anticipation to see what was inside increased within him, but he forced himself to tread slowly and quietly, like he'd been taught by the Zulu hunters. He would be a hunter soon, and this was good practice.

He crept toward the hut, taking care not to snap a stick, or crack a twig in the thick growth which surrounded the hut. He kept his eyes focused on the structure, watching for any sign of movement which might indicate that someone was inside.

When all remained still, he moved forward a few feet and then stopped, watching for movement once more. He repeated this process until he had reached the heavy door of the round, thatched hut. The mud walls were thick, and there was no way to know if there was someone inside. He had reached the point of no return. If it really was a sangoma's hut, once he entered the dwelling, there would be no going back. He looked back, over his shoulder once more, to see if his friend had followed, but there was only sprawling jungle behind him.

Taking a deep breath, he placed a hand on the heavy, wooden door, pushing it open and stepping into the dark room. He left the door open for the daylight that it provided, illuminating most of the open space before him. He gasped at what he saw.

The skeletal framework of the wall directly in front of him was covered with bones and skulls. Perhaps Nhlanhla had been right. This could truly be the sangoma's hut. Another lump formed in his throat, but he swallowed it down with a gulp.

Stepping the rest of the way inside the beehive structure, the ceiling rose, accommodating his tall, thin frame. He had told his friend he was not afraid, but he really wished Nhlanhla were here with him. However, Zulu warriors were brave and Nelwazi was determined to demonstrate his courage. If he could find something to prove he'd been inside a sangoma's hut, he could do that.

He quickly glanced around the room. There was a straw mattress on top of a reed mat to the left of the skull wall. Below the skulls was a counter, which he hadn't seen before. On it were several jars and piles of powders. He stepped up to it, taking in each item. Any of the powders might prove that he'd been here, and that it was a sangoma's hut, but some might be simple herbs. There was no way of knowing what they were, so he didn't know which one to take a sample of.

Then he noticed that some of the jars were labeled. He read a few, but the names didn't mean anything to him. He was not a sangoma, or an inyanga, and he did not have the proper training to decipher them. He wished again that Nhlanhla had accompanied him. He had a small amount of training in the healing arts and would perhaps make a good inyanga one day. He might know what some of these substances were.

A voice from outside, which could only be Nhlanhla, called out. "Nelwazi! Help!"

His friend was in trouble. Nelwazi glanced around the room once more, then snatched up an empty jar and scooped a pile of powder into it, before dashing out to go to his friend's aide.

Outside, a crack of thunder rocked the ground and the sky opened up, letting loose a torrent of rain, soaking him instantly. He slashed his way back through the thick, wet branches of the brush, trampling bushes in his path in answer to his friend's cries.

When he broke through into the clearing, he saw Nhlanhla running to and fro, jumping and ducking, as if he were being attacked, but Nelwazi could not see his adversary.

"Help!" Nhlanhla cried. "Help me!"

"Nhlanhla, what are you doing?" he said, scratching his tight, curly black locks in confusion. "What is going on?"

"It's tokoloshe," his friend cried. "You've angered the sangoma, and they are poking and prodding me. Ouch! Ouch!" Nhlanhla jumped up, and then back, then spun around quickly as if something had attacked from the opposite direction. "Do something! Help me!"

Thunder rumbled and lightning flashed in the distance. The rain came down in torrents. Wiping the rain from his eyes, Nelwazi pushed against the wind to go to his friend's aid.

Lightning flashed and thunder clapped, and a jolt of lightning shot through him, knocking him to the ground. Nelwazi regained his feet, shaking off a million pin pricks which raced through his body, as his friend cried out once more.

"Nelwazi, help me!"

He wiped the rain from his eyes, but he still couldn't see what it was that was attacking his friend. Nhlanhla grabbed a large stick, swatting at the air with it. One swipe came to an abrupt halt and produced a loud grunt. Apparently, his friend had hit something, even though Nelwazi could not see it.

"What can I do?" he said. "How do we fight something we can't see?"

"I don't know! But do something!" Nhlanhla cried, swinging the stick around in a wide arc. Then, he jumped straight up in the air, as if he had been goosed. "Ouch!" He looked at Nelwazi, pleading with his eyes. "Please help. I can't get away."

Nelwazi wasn't sure what to do. His friend was obviously being tormented by an invisible foe. It could only be tokoloshe. If they were controlled by the powers of the sangoma, then surely the man himself would be here soon. He knew he needed to act quickly.

All he could think was to fight magic with magic. So, he reached his hand into the jar he was carrying, pulling out a handful of the powder. He didn't know what the powder was, but it was what he had to work with.

"Can you find it with your stick, so I know where it is?" he called to the tormented boy.

Nhlanhla swung the stick madly, making swishing noises through the air until at last he met something with a loud 'thwack!', and a loud yelp sounded. Nelwazi ran forward and blew the powder from his palm in the direction the yelp had come from.

The white powder filled the air, and as it settled, the form of a tokoloshe took shape, revealing a squat, hairy beast with its long penis thrown over its shoulder.

"There it is," Nelwazi said, pointing to the creature. "Now you can hit it."

Nhlanhla smacked the creature in the head with the stick. It cried out once more and then, it vanished.

Nelwazi ran to his friend's side. "Are you all right?" he asked, placing a hand on his shoulder in concern.

But Nhlanhla pushed his hand away. "This is all your fault!" he yelled, glaring at him with eyes as sharp as daggers, taking a step back. "You just had to enter the sangoma's hut! You didn't believe in the tokoloshe!" He paced back and forth in front of Nelwazi. "Well, let me tell you something. That was a tokoloshe we just battled! Do you believe in them now? I ought to smack you with this stick for all the trouble you've caused."

Nelwazi was taken aback. He had not expected such outrage from his friend after saving his life. But he realized Nhlanhla was right. All of this was his fault.

"Hold on. Hold on," he said, holding his hands up in front of him to ward off any blows, should they come, and taking a step toward his friend. "You are right. It is my fault, and I'm sorry. It's not that I didn't believe in the tokoloshe. It's just that I didn't want you to think I was scared."

Nhlanhla dropped his stick and stared slack-jaws at his friend. "You were really scared?" he asked. "But, you acted so brave. You were braver than I was."

"Nelwazi shrugged his shoulders. "No. I was foolish. How will I ever become a brave warrior when I do such dumb stuff? I could have gotten us both killed."

"It wasn't going to kill me," Nhlanhla said, shaking his head. "It just tormented me, but I couldn't fight what I couldn't see. Thank you for your help." He held out his hand, and Nelwazi took it. Things were good between them once more. "What was that powder? That was smart thinking."

"I don't know," Nelwazi said with a shrug of his shoulders. "I took it from the sangoma's hut as proof of my courage."

"What?" Nhlanhla said, his mouth agape once more. "Are you mad? Already, Ngobizitha knows what you've done. That is probably why he sent the tokoloshe. We must leave this place now. That may be the powder he uses to create zombies and control tokoloshe. It made the creature visible and then it disappeared. What else could do that? You had better leave that jar here, and perhaps Ngobizitha will not be angered."

"Or it could have been a healing powder used to cure the common cold. That doesn't prove anything," Nelwazi said, pulling the jar in close to his body. "Even though it was foolish, it represents a lesson learned on my quest to be a warrior. I can't leave it behind."

"What about me?" Nhlanhla said. "Did I not battle bravely against the tokoloshe? I too, should take a trophy to represent my lessons and prove my courage."

"What lesson did you learn?" Nelwazi asked, cocking his head and raising his brow.

"But before Nhlanhla could answer, a voice thundered through the air. "Thieves! Who has been in my hut?"

Nelwazi glanced toward his friend, who looked as if he might be ill. "Grab your stick and let's get out of here!" he said. Then, he broke into a sprint, running into the forest as fast as he could, cradling the jar filled with mystery powder in his arms.

He looked over his shoulder, spotting Nhlanhla crashing through the brush after him, stick in hand. They had their trophies. Nelwazi slowed his pace to let his friend catch up. Breathing heavily, he came to a halt near a large sausage tree, dropping to the ground. "I think we lost him. It looks like we are safe for now."

"That was close," Nhlanhla said, sinking to the ground next to him. "Ngobizitha the Conqueror is one to be feared. I don't think he will give up so easily. We had better keep going and get far away from Ghost Mountain."

"Wait," Nelwazi said, shaking his head. "My mouth is too dry for me to continue running. I must slake this thirst, before going on."

Nhlanhla wrinkled his brow in thought as he scanned the area. "The river is not far from here," he said as his face lit up with dawning recognition. "Follow me. It should be over in this direction." With that, he rose, offering Nelwazi his hand.

A loud, hollow voice reverberated through the forest. Nelwazi could have sworn the trees swayed with its vibration. "THEIF! I WILL FIND YOU!"

Ignoring his friend's pro-offered hand, Nelwazi scrambled to his feet. "I guess we'd better keep running, thirsty or not."

But Nhlanhla was already headed off toward the river. Nelwazi took off after his friend.

They ran a long way, until Nelwazi's mouth was so dry that it felt like he'd consumed a mouthful of desert sand. He needed water, and he needed rest. "How much farther to the river?" he called out to Nhlanhla. They had run a long way, even for young, healthy boys. He didn't know how much longer he could keep up this pace.

The sharp crack of rifle fire rang through the air. Nelwazi dropped to the ground, and Nhlanhla followed suit.

"What was that?" his friend said. "Is that the sangoma after us again?"

"No, I don't think the sangoma would use a firestick when he has magic at his disposal," Nelwazi replied. "The sangoma would just send more tokoloshe. More likely, in this part of the bush, it is poachers."

"Maybe we should go back," Nhlanhla said. "We can find another route to the river."

"Would you rather face the sangoma, then?" Nelwazi asked, shaking his head. "Besides, I'm too thirsty to go back and take a longer route. Let's crawl through the bush to that clearing up ahead, keeping our heads down. We can just peek to see what's happening and then decide."

Nhlanhla nodded in agreement, and they began to crawl through the bush as if they were warriors sneaking up on an enemy.

When they reached the edge of the clearing, Nelwazi peeked through the thick brush. He couldn't believe what he was seeing. There was a killing field before them. He dropped down behind some bushes to keep out of sight, and Nhlanhla followed suit. Elephant carcasses were scattered about the clearing, near a watering hole. The coppery smell of blood filled the air.

A group of poachers were gathered around a large female elephant, sawing off her tusks for the ivory. The elephant emitted sounds of distress, too weak to put up any more fight. The poachers had done great damage with their big elephant guns. It broke Nelwazi's heart to the cries of the beast, but he dared not reveal himself, so he remained hidden. When the men finished, they carried away the tusks, loading them onto a big truck, and drove away.

Once he was sure the poachers were gone, Nelwazi emerged from the bush, and ran across the clearing to the wounded animal. The elephant was still breathing in hard, labored breaths. There were tears in the corner of her honey-orbed eye. "Hey, girl," he said, dropping to the ground near her head and rubbing the rough skin of her trunk softly. "Don't be afraid. I won't hurt you anymore. I'd like to help you, if I can."

"What are you doing?" Nhlanhla said, coming up behind him.

"She's dying," Nelwazi said, with tears slipping from his own eyes. "I must help her, if I can."

"But, what can you do?" his friend asked. "The poachers left her for dead. I fear it is too late to do her any good."

Nelwazi opened the jar in his arms, scooping out another handful of powder.

"Are you mad?" Nhlanhla said, placing a hand on his wrist with a look of horror. "That is a wild elephant you are sitting next to. If you spook her, you might be killed. Besides, you don't know what that powder will do."

Nelwazi pushed his friend's hand away and held the hand with the powder above the elephant's enormous mouth, letting the powder pour into it. The elephant curled her lower lip, pulling the powder into her mouth with her gigantic tongue. He didn't move, waiting to see if perhaps he had helped her in some small way.

"Nelwazi, get out of there!" Nhlanhla said, backing away to the edge of the clearing once more. "What do you think you can do? You can't heal the damage the hunters have done."

"I gave her some of the sangoma's powder," he said, looking back over his shoulder, but still not moving. "It was all I could think of to do."

"But you don't know what that powder does besides getting rid of tokoloshe," Nhlanhla said. "It might be zombie powder. I don't know what else would do such a thing."

"Maybe it's a healing powder, and it will take away some of her pain. They took her tusks and left her here to bleed to death," he said, holding back sobs at the thought of the cruelness of it. "I know she is dying, but I had to try."

He turned his attention back to the elephant, but her eyes were now closed, and no more huffing breaths emitted from her mouth. She had slipped away into death while he had been distracted. It didn't seem the powder had done much good.

"It doesn't matter now," he said, gathering up his jar of powder and rising to his feet. "The poor thing has gone on to be with her ancestors."

He walked back to the edge of the clearing to stand with his friend, but before he got there, a mewling sound came from the bushes on the other side of the clearing, drawing their attention. As they watched, an elephant calf emerged from the bushes, swishing its trunk from side to side, and emitting the sounds they had heard. The calf headed straight for the mammoth form of the dead female.

"Nelwazi, get out of there," Nhlanhla cried in warning. "Elephants are unpredictable. You don't know what that calf might do."

The elephant calf was large, but it was still a baby. It was cute. It didn't appear to be aggressive, but he knew his friend was right. The female must have been its mother. There was no telling how the young one might react when it realized she was dead. Nelwazi began backing away slowly, so as not to alarm the calf, but keeping his eyes on it, just in case.

Once he'd reached the edge of the clearing, he hunkered down in the brush next to Nhlanhla to keep out of sight. They continued to watch the calf to see what would happen.

The calf went up to its dead mother, touching her trunk with its own, still emitting those soft mewling sounds.

It was sad what the poachers had done, and it made him angry. Nelwazi hated that this little one had lost its mother, and he hated the cruelty of the poachers, who would leave such a majestic animal to die in pain.

"Those poachers should be made to pay for what they've done," he said to his friend. "I wish the elephant had stomped them into the ground."

The calf gave out a cry of distress and went running back into the bush as if it smelled a lion nearby.

"I wonder what that was about," Nhlanhla said, scratching his curly, dark head.

Nelwazi just pointed at the carcass of the mother elephant. The animal's eyes were now open, and its tail flicked back and forth in the dust. It raised its head, and its trunk began to sway in the savannah winds. Then, the elephant rose to its feet, trumpeting loudly, its eyes glowing red.

"It can't be," said Nelwazi, backing further into the bush.

"I thought you said it was dead," Nhlanhla said, looking to him for answers.

"I know it was dead," he said. "Even her calf knew it. She was dead."

"Then, how is she up and walking around now?" his friend asked as the elephant headed off in the other direction. It was the same direction in which the poachers had headed. Her movements were jerky, and the ground thundered with her every step.

"I don't know how," Nelwazi said, puzzled by this strange development. "She was dead. I'm sure of it."

"I'll tell you how," Nhlanhla said. "It was that powder. It really is zombie powder, and you created an elephant zombie! Now what are we going to do?"

"How could I do that?" Nelwazi replied. "I'm no sangoma."

"I don't know, but somehow you did," Nhlanhla said. "Now only you can control it. You can't leave it walking around unchecked. An elephant zombie could be very dangerous. We must go and stop it."

"And do what?" Nelwazi asked, questioning everything now. Was his friend right? Had he created an elephant zombie with his powder? He knew that sangoma used a powder ground from tokoloshe bones to create zombies and control them. That was how they controlled the tokoloshe, too. What other explanation could there be? To Nhlanhla, he said, "I am not a sangoma. I've had no training. I don't know how to undo whatever spell has been cast. What do you want me to do?"

"I don't know, but you'd better do something," Nhlanhla said. "That monster could destroy villages. You must try."

Nelwazi considered his friend's words. Of course, he was right, as usual. Nhlanhla had always had a good head for reasoning things out. Somehow, he had made the elephant live again, and he would be responsible for any damage that it caused. He must figure out how to control the creature.

"Then, we'd better get going before we lose track of it," he said, rising from the bush and heading across the clearing at a trot. He paused to look back at Nhlanhla, who remained at the edge of clearing, seeming hesitant. "This is my doing. You don't have to come. It could be dangerous. I have no idea what I'm doing. It will most likely end in disaster."

"Are you kidding?" Nhlanhla said with a grin. "You are my friend, and we are in this together. Let's go."

"I think I may know where she is going," Nelwazi said, tucking his jar of powder under his arm and setting off once more in the direction the zombie elephant he had inadvertently created had gone with a lighter heart. "If she's doing my bidding, she must be after the poachers. I wished for her to stomp them. Now I just need to find her and stop her."

If he was right, he now knew how to control her.

He was halfway across the clearing when he heard Nhlanhla cry out. "Ouch! Ouch! Ouch!"

Nelwazi stopped, turning to gaze at his friend, who was hopping around as if he were being attacked once again. Before an answer came, he felt a pinch on his upper thigh. "Ouch!" he cried. Then, he felt a poke in his abdomen and cried out again. "Ouch! Tokoloshe!"

He quickly opened the jar and scooped out another handful of powder, throwing it up into the air. Just as before, the tokoloshe appeared before him, and vanished just as quickly. He scooped another handful and ran to his friend.

"Ouch!" Nhlanhla cried.

"Where is it?" Nelwazi asked.

"Ouch! Ouch!" his friend cried again. "I don't know. It comes at me from all directions." Nhlanhla jerked his foot off the ground as if he had been bitten. "Ouch!"

Nelwazi held up his hand, opening his fist to let the greyish powder rest in his palm. He stepped up next to the other boy. "Stay behind me," he said as he turned in a circle, blowing the dust into the air, exposing not only one, but three tokoloshe before they vanished an instant later.

"Thanks," Nhlanhla said. "I guess the sangoma has not forgotten about us."

"No, I guess not," Nelwazi replied setting off on his trek once more. "Hurry. Catch up with the elephant zombie before it can do harm to anyone."

"All right, but how do we know where it is going?" Nhlanhla said, catching up to him. "Where are we headed?"

"I believe the creature is on the trail of the poachers who killed her," Nelwazi said, sharing the theory he'd been working out in his head. "I think I ordered it to stomp them into the ground."

"So, you believe that speaking your thoughts aloud about the poachers, you ordered the elephant zombie to go after them?"

"Why not?" Nelwazi said, shrugging his shoulders. "If a sangoma creates a tokoloshe, he controls it. I created that monstrous creature out there the same way, so I should be able to control it the same way. It makes sense, and besides, the creature is leaving a clear trail through the bush in all its clumsiness, knocking over trees and smashing down the flora."

When they finally caught up to the zombie elephant, Nelwazi could see that he was too late. Dead poachers were lying around the overturned truck, like the beaded dolls his little sister played with, discarded and tossed aside.

The elephant zombie held one of the poachers above her head, wrapped in its trunk. The man was screaming in fear as he dangled high in the air. As the creature raised its trunk even higher, Nelwazi cried, "No! Let him go!"

The elephant zombie stopped at the sound of his voice, staring at him with blood red eyes. Then, the creature tossed the man away with its trunk, much as Nelwazi might toss away the burnt husks of the boer-bean once the cooked seeds have been removed. The man let out one final scream before the impact shattered his skull against the frame of the overturned truck.

"Wow! It worked," Nhlanhla said. "It really does your bidding."

"I did not bid it to do that!" Nelwazi cried. "I meant to save that man, if I could."

"Then, you had better watch how you give your commands in the future," his friend said, placing a hand on his shoulder. "That creature follows your commands to the letter. You did not say let him live. You said let him go. The creature did as you bid it."

"I never asked for this," Nelwazi said, sinking to the ground and placing his hands on top of his head. "I wanted to control her, so she couldn't harm anyone else, but I don't want to be responsible for what this beast might do. I must find a way to reverse the powder's magic."

"Reverse it? Why?" Nhlanhla said with a puzzled expression as he sat down on the ground next to him. "You control an elephant zombie. Imagine what you could do. You could use it to plow the fields. It would be quite helpful in farming the crops of the village. It could help build walls and move large logs which otherwise couldn't be moved. All you need to do is command it to do these things. The people of our village will love you."

"No. That wouldn't be right," Nelwazi said, shaking his head. "Look at her eyes. They are blood-red, instead of the color of glowing honey, and they are dull and blank. There is no life in them. She is no longer the mighty elephant she once was. I may be able to control her, but this is not living, it's existing. It is to be among the undead." He ran his fingers through his tight curls of hair. "And to do as you suggest and turn the creature into a slave..., it would be evil and wrong. It would make me no better than a sangoma who creates and commands tokoloshe to torment people."

"You're right. The creature is evil," Nhlanhla said. "So, what will you do?"

"No. The creature is not evil. She did not ask for what has happened to her," Nelwazi said. He needed to make his friend understand. "It's the wielder of the magic which created her that is evil."

"You are not evil," Nhlanhla said. "You didn't know what would happen."

"But I am responsible for the outcome, no matter my intent," he replied, admitting what he had secretly feared all along. "I am not a sangoma. I have no secret knowledge or power. I am still trying to figure out how all of this happened in the first place. You are the smart one. What do you think I should do?"

"I certainly don't know how to reverse what has been done," said Nhlanhla, placing a fist beneath his chin and leaning his elbow on his knee while he thought the problem through. Then, his eyes grew wide and his face lit up as he stared at Nelwazi. "But, I may know someone who does." He stood, grabbing Nelwazi by the hand. "Come on, Let's go."

"Please don't suggest we go back and ask the madman we've been running from," Nelwazi said with a groan as he rose to his feet. "Only a sangoma would have such knowledge."

"Or an inyanga (herbalist)," Nhlanhla replied, raising his brow. "I know of an herbalist who lives somewhere along the river, near here. All we need to do is go back to the river and find her."

Nelwazi felt the beginnings of hope spread through him at his friend's words. Perhaps they could find a way to undo his foolishness. He spoke in his head to the ancestors as they walked, promising to stay away from dark magic forever, if he could only undo the evil that he had inadvertently unleashed.

"Lead the way," he said, picking up his step to keep up. "At least we have a plan now. That's more than we had only a few minutes ago. What would I do without a friend like you?"

"You would be in trouble," Nhlanhla said with a sigh as he led Nelwazi through the brush toward the river, shaking his head. "I don't know why I let you drag me into your troubles. I'm always fixing your shenanigans. One day, you are going to get us into something that we can't get out of."

"You love all of our adventures, and you know it," Nelwazi said with a big grin. "We always come out all right."

"Yeah, well, I just hope we can find a way out of this one okay," his friend said, nodding his head back toward the creature, which was standing in the clearing, swishing its trunk from side to side with a dull look in its red eyes. "Zombies don't eat, so it is not grazing. I don't think it knows what to do. But we can't leave it there. You'd better bring it along."

Nelwazi looked back at the zombie elephant and said, "Come on. Follow me." A flash of red sparked in the creature's eyes, and it set out toward the two boys.

"If we find the inyanga, everything will work out. I know it will," Nelwazi said to his friend, forcing a smile and hoping that he looked more confident than he felt.

Nhlanhla was right. They had never been in this kind of trouble before. He had messed with dark magic to appear brave. But he was not brave. He was foolish and now, they had to find a way to undo his mistake. He was reassuring himself as much as he was his friend. "I am certain of it."

The boys searched up and down both banks of the river for the inyanga's hut, but found nothing except trees, bushes, and tall grass. They came to a stone bridge which was used to travel from one side of the river to the other. Nelwazi spotted something strange in the grass beneath the bridge. He climbed down under the bridge to check it out. There, he found the sleeping form of a tokoloshe curled up in the grasses, his large penis thrown over his shoulder and tucked under his head, as a pillow.

"Look at this, Nhlanhla," he said, pointing to the sleeping creature. "I bet that is how the sangoma catches them. He waits until they are sleeping and then snatches them up."

"Tell me you are not going to capture it," Nhlanhla said. "Or perhaps you should. You have the powder to make it do your bidding. You could send it after Ngobizitha and give the old sangoma some of his own medicine."

"No! I don't wish to control this creature," Nelwazi said. "That powder has gotten us into enough trouble already. Besides, I don't know what it would do if used on a living creature, and I am certainly not going to kill that creature or any other." He crept closer to the sleeping tokoloshe.

"Don't disturb it," Nhlanhla said, placing a hand on his shoulder and pulling him back. "You can't just walk up and start a conversation with such an evil creature."

"But, he might know where the inyanga lives," Nelwazi replied. Tokoloshe are only evil when under a sangoma's control. They do not ask to be captured, killed and turned into zombie slaves, any more than that elephant over there asked for her fate."

He shrugged his friend's hand off and continued toward the sleeping creature, the tall grasses crimping under his feet. Soft snores issued from the creature's mouth, accompanied by tiny vibrations, making his large, thick lips wiggle with each exhale and setting the hair on its upper lip aquiver. If not for the long, stringy hair covering his body, he would look akin to a hunched old grandfather taking an afternoon nap.

Nelwazi's toe caught on a small stone, turning it over and sending it rolling down the bank and into the river with a loud splash. It must have startled the tokoloshe, for he sprang up in alarm and let out a squeak, his small, narrow eyes growing wide in alarm. He snatched up a stone from the bank in his small, child-like hand, taking a defensive stance with his long arm pulled back as he scanned the area for danger.

"Wait," Nelwazi said, stepping forward toward the tokoloshe with his palms held open to show he posed no threat. "I mean you no harm."

"Get out of there, Nelwazi!" Nhlanhla cried from above him on the bank.

The creature squinted his beady little eyes as Nelwazi approached, as if he were still suspicious of him. Then, it let out a short grunt. "Ungh."

"Don't be afraid," Nelwazi said, moving toward him slowly, open palms in clear view. "I won't hurt you. I'm looking for an inyanga. Do you know where she lives?"

As the creature watched Nelwazi approach, he let the stone drop from his small hand.

"Hello," he said to the tokoloshe, extending his hand to softly rub the creature's hand. Then he pointed to himself. "I am Nelwazi." Then, he pointed at the creature, raising his brow in question.

The tokoloshe looked him up and down with his beady eyes. Then, he leaned in and sniffed Nelwazi's hand with its large, bulbous nose and grunted once more. "Ungh."

"Ungha," Nelwazi said. "I will call you Ungha.

"Are you mad?" Nhlanhla called from above him. "You don't know what that thing will do."

"Look at him," he said to his friend. "He won't hurt me." He reached out and gently stroked the creature's long, stringy hair, which hung down over his pronounced brow, nearly hiding those beady little eyes. "I told you. They aren't evil unless they are under a sangoma's control."

The elephant trumpeted behind them, reminding Nelwazi of the problem at hand. But the sound startled the tokoloshe, and it vanished in an instant.

"Come on, Nelwazi," Nhlanhla said. "We must find the inyanga's hut. Your new friend up here isn't exactly patient, and I don't want to find out what happens if we keep her waiting too long."

He ran back up the bank to join Nhlanhla as the zombie elephant trumpeted again. Then, he saw why. Halfway up the hill, he turned to see if the tokoloshe had returned to being visible, only to find Ungha standing directly behind him, his long penis tucked between his legs so that he appeared to have a tail.

"Ungh," the creature said, poking Nelwazi in the back with a stubby pointer finger.

Nelwazi turned to face his new-found friend. "No. You must go back," he said, shaking his head, then pointing to the bridge.

Ungha poked Nelwazi's stomach and said, "Ungh."

The elephant trumpeted once more. This time, it was accompanied by a thunderous boom, and the earth shook beneath their feet. To Nelwazi, it sounded more like a thunderous groan.

"Nelwazi, come on," Nhlanhla cried. "The tokoloshe are attacking your elephant."

"I've got to go," he said to Ungha. "You must go back. Go do... whatever tokoloshes do. Just disappear."

With that Ungha vanished right before his eyes. Nelwazi turned and ran back up the hill to join his friend, who was gazing with his mouth agape at the scene in the clearing. The elephant zombie thrashed the brush with her trunk, stomping the flora with her thick, heavy feet, as if she were being attacked from all sides by an unseen foe. And he knew who those foes were.

The ground rumbled with every stomp of her enormous feet, her trumpeting cries ringing through the air. Although hollow and lifeless, Nelwazi detected a ring of distress beneath the surface.

"We have to help her," Nelwazi said, taking yet another handful of powder from the jar.

"If you go over there, you may be stomped to a pulp," Nhlanhla said, grabbing Nelwazi's arm. "They are driving the elephant mad. She's out of control."

"But I have the power to rid her of her foes," Nelwazi said, pulling his arm from Nhlanhla's grip. "You know they are looking for us. I cannot let her suffer even more for my errors."

He ran into the clearing where the elephant trumpeted loudly, stomping the ground in a rage. Her red eyes seemed to glow even more fiercely than they had before, but the grey sheen of her hide had faded to a dull alabaster.

Nelwazi opened his hand and loosed the grey powder into the air. Instantly, several forms of tokoloshe appeared, and the elephant's trunk smashed into two of them before the rest disappeared. The two that had been hit were knocked to the ground, where they vanished with a large poof of air, sending loose remnants of the powder floating to the ground.

Nhlanhla came running up behind him. "That was amazing," he said, smacking his friend on the back. "You got rid of all of them with a single handful of powder. Maybe we don't need the inyanga after all."

"No. We still need an inyanga to help reverse the spell," he said as the elephant gazed down at him with dull red eyes. "I don't think the powder kills them. They only disappear temporarily, then they come back in force. And my supply of the powder is dwindling." He held up the jar for his friend to see. There was less than half a jar of powder left.

In an instant, the jar was snatched from Nelwazi's hands, and it vanished into thin air, just as the tokoloshe had. A twitter of laughter filled the air.

"No!" Nhlanhla cried. "Now you have none! Now what will we do?"

"Don't panic," Nelwazi replied. He suspected this most recent mischief was not of a vile nature, but only that of an invisible prankster. "Ungha, please show yourself."

Instantly, the little tokoloshe appeared before them, jar in hand. "Ungh."

"Give it back, Ungha," Nelwazi said with a stern look.

Nhlanhla stared gape-jawed at the hairy creature, as it handed the jar back to Nelwazi with a gape-toothed smile. "How did you do that?" he said. "Did you use the powder on him? Why does he follow your commands?"

"He was only playing," Nelwazi said. "What commands this one may be more powerful than dark magic. It is called friendship." He turned to the tokoloshe. "Thank you, Ungha."

The creature reached out with a long bony arm, rubbing his stubby fingers lightly over Nelwazi's hand. "Ungh."

"Great!" Nhlanhla cried. "Now we have a zombie elephant and a tokoloshe following us. I don't see how this improves our situation."

"You're right. It doesn't," Nelwazi said. He turned to Ungha. "Thank you, friend. But now, you must return to your home by the river, and I must be on my way."

Ungha cocked his hairy head to one side, raised his protruding brow in a puzzled expression, and said, "Ungh?"

"It's all right. You go," he said, pointing toward the bridge. "I must go with the elephant and my friend. I will come back for you."

Ungha grunted, looking over his shoulder at the bridge, then back at the two boys and the elephant. He looked away, averting his small, narrow eyes toward the ground and headed back toward the bridge with another grunt. "Ungh."

Nelwazi wanted to tell the creature that he was not rejecting him, that they were still friends. He could feel the creature's pain like it was his own. But Nhlanhla took ahold of his hand and said, "Come on. We must still find the inyanga. My friend from the village visits her regularly. I think this is the path which she takes. We must be close."

Nelwazi gave a look back over his shoulder, but the tokoloshe had vanished once more. The zombie elephant followed sluggishly as the two boys followed the path. Her movements were jerky, as if she couldn't control her limbs. Her dull red eyes looked sad to him. He had seen tears escape her eyes on several occasions, and there was one rolling down her big grey cheek now. "I must find a way to give her peace," he said, as strode up the path. "Just look what I have done to her. I've turned her into something which her own calf runs away from."

"It's not your fault what the poachers did," Nhlanhla replied. "You were trying to help. The calf would be motherless either way."

"Still, this is no life for an elephant," he said. "All she does is follow me around all day."

"Because she is not alive," Nhlanhla said. "It is undead; a zombie elephant; a dangerous monster."

Before Nelwazi could reply, the elephant reared up, trumpeting loudly. He urged her to continue forward, but she swung her trunk wildly, red eyes blazing, refusing to move. It had to be the tokoloshe once again. What else could stop his unstoppable friend?

"What is this at my dooryard?" said a female voice, coming from a group of trees just ahead of him.

He looked up at the sound, to see a small elderly woman emerge with a big walking stick which was taller than she was. She stopped, leaning on the stick as if her hunched form needed it for support.

"Who are you?" she said. Then she pointed her stick toward the elephant. "And what is that unnatural creature with you? What business do you have with Gugu?"

Nelwazi stepped forward. "Sawubona, Gogo, *(Good day, Granny)*. We meant no offense," he said, "We are searching for the herbalist who we heard lives somewhere nearby. Would you know of her?"

"Why are you looking for her?" she asked, eying them suspiciously. "Why do you travel with that unnatural creature?"

"That is why we seek the inyanga," he said. "I am Nelwazi, and this is my friend Nhlanhla. We need her help. Do you know where we might find her?"

The woman's gaze shifted between the two boys and the elephant, then back again. "And what about this one?" she said, pointing to Nhlanhla. "Does he speak, or does he just follow you blindly?"

"Sawubona, Gogo," Nhlanhla said, stepping forward.

"Which one of you is responsible for that vile beast in my field, stomping my crops?" she asked.

"I am," Nelwazi said. "I seek the inyanga's assistance to put the poor beast to rest. This condition occurred quite by accident."

The old woman was silent for several moments. Her stare made Nelwazi feel as if she could see right through him. Then, she nodded, as if she had come to a decision. "I am Guelethru, but most just call me Gugu," she said, turning to walk back up the path the way she had come. "I am the inyanga that you seek, but I have no cure for that abomination."

"Ouch!" cried Nhlanhla, jumping up, twisting and turning in the air. "Stop! Help!"

Gugu raised her brow, gazing at Nelwazi. "Tokoloshe, too?" She shook her head, turning to continue on her path.

"Please, wait, Gugu," he said, holding up his forefinger. He opened the jar, taking out a pinch of powder as the inyanga watched. The supply in the jar was getting low, so he used it sparingly. He placed the pinch of powder in his open palm. Running toward Nhlanhla, he blew the powder into the air, dispersing it.

A tokoloshe appeared briefly before vanishing from sight.

Gugu stood, staring at the place where the tokoloshe had been. "You have tokoloshe after you. You boys have angered a sangoma."

"Ngobizitha," Nhlanhla said, offering up more information than requested. Nelwazi scowled at him.

"It is even worse than I imagined," Gugu said. "Perhaps you should tell me how all this came about."

"It is my fault, Gugu," Nelwazi said, standing before her. He knew it was the truth, but it was painful to admit that he had caused this whole mess. The time had come for him to face up to his mistakes, and he would now have to explain to the inyanga all that he had done. He could only hope that she would know how to undo all the madness he had created. "I wished to prove my courage, so I stole this powder from the sangoma's hut, but I did not know what the powder was..."

When he had finished his tale, Gugu shook her head and clucked her tongue. "My, my," she said, rolling her eyes up to the sky. "Only the sangoma whose zombie powder you have taken can reverse its power, and you have angered him. It is not likely that he will help. I may be able to help you rid yourselves of the tokoloshe, but the price of an inyanga's powers are quite high. What do you have to offer in way of payment?"

The two boys looked at one another. They both knew they had nothing to offer the inyanga.

Nelwazi turned his gaze back to Gugu. "All I have is the zombie powder," he said, holding the jar out to her. "If you help us get rid of the tokoloshe the sangoma sent, I won't need it anymore. I know now that it doesn't prove anything, except that I am a fool. I will give it all to you."

"It is not yours to give, child. I imagine Ngobizitha will be wanting his powder back," the inyanga replied. "I cannot accept it. I do not deal in the dark magic."

"But, I have nothing else to give you," Nelwazi said, feeling the small hope he'd been holding onto slipping away from him. "What else can I do? How will I ever make any of this right?"

"I will give you this stick," Nhlanhla said, stepping forward with his stick in his hand. "It is a sign of my courage. I fought off the tokoloshe with it. It is a mighty weapon."

"Ah, a valuable item, yes," said Gugu with a toothless grin. "But you are not the one who needs my assistance. You would offer this for your friend?"

"I would, Gugu," Nhlanhla said with a nod. "Nelwazi is like a brother to me. He has a kind heart and a great need to make right what is wrong. I will do whatever I can to help."

"You are a good boy, Nhlanhla, but it is Nelwazi's debt. He must be the one to pay."

"But...," Nelwazi said, intending to beg if he had to, but Gugu silenced him with an opened palm held out in front of him.

"You, Nelwazi, will owe this debt to me, which I will collect on at a future time," she said. "If you agree to this, I will do what I can."

"I agree!" Nelwazi said, nodding. He answered without considering it twice. He resisted the urge to throw himself down at her feet and kiss the ground she walked on. "I am so grateful."

"Then, let us be on our way. There is much work to do," Gugu said, turning and heading back through the trees without looking back. "There's a kraal behind my hut which we can use to set a trap for the tokoloshe."

Assuming they were expected to follow, Nelwazi turned to Nhlanhla and said, "Come on." Then, he turned and headed off after the inyanga.

The earth shook behind them as the zombie elephant stumbled after them. Nelwazi looked back at her. She was not looking good. Her stride was more staggered now, and her skin seemed to be sloughing off her body, leaving patches of raw flesh. She drug her trunk along the ground, as if she didn't have the strength to hold up the great weight of her head.

Nelwazi watched her over his shoulder as he walked, convinced more than ever that he must help the creature, until he walked right into Gugu. She stopped, with her hands on her hips, blocking the path in front of him.

"No. No. No," she said, shaking her head as Nelwazi regained his balance. "That creature stays. It is unnatural and of the dark magic. It's too close to my home already. It shall go no further."

"But, she must come with us," Nelwazi said. "Alone out here, she would be unprotected from the tokoloshe. I can't let them torment her. Even if she could see them, she's much too slow."

The inyanga looked at him with a raised brow, remaining silent.

"Please. I promise she will be no trouble," Nelwazi said, seeing an opportunity to convince her. "She doesn't eat or drink. It's my fault she is what she is. Am I not responsible for her?"

"Yes, it is true," Gugu said with a sigh. "You are responsible for your handiwork." She paused before continuing. "The creature must stay here, but I will make her an elephant-sized amakhubalo amulet for protection. "Come." Again, she was off up the path without waiting to see if the boys would follow.

Back at the hut, Gugu cooked up a large pot of the medicine they would need to lure the tokoloshe on her hearth. A foul odor filled the room as it simmered over the fire while they smeared lion fat all over their bodies to protect them, and drank Amasi, or fermented milk, to give them strength. She made an amakhubalo from a large piece of bark and instructed Nelwazi to place it in the zombie elephant's mouth to suck on.

When he returned to the hut, something poked Nelwazi in the side as he opened the door to enter. As he reached into the jar for a pinch of zombie powder, a tokoloshe appeared before him. "Ungh."

"Ungha, what are you doing here?" he said in surprise, letting the zombie powder fall through his fingers, back into the jar. "Why aren't you back at your bridge? You were supposed to wait for me there."

"Ungh," the tokoloshe said, poking him in the arm.

Just then, the hut door opened behind him, as Gugu backed through the door, speaking to the boy inside. "Bring the bowl out to the Kraal. The night approaches and there is still much work to do before the moon rises. As she turned to exit, Ungha disappeared, but not before the inyanga caught sight of him.

"What is this? Another one?" she exclaimed "So soon? Come inside, quickly."

"No. Wait, Gugu," Nelwazi said. "This is Ungha. He is not enchanted. He is my friend, and I think he is lonely." He looked at the spot where the creature had disappeared. "It's all right, Ungha. You can show yourself."

Ungha reappeared next to Nelwazi, his long penis thrown over his shoulder. "Ungh."

The inyanga stared at boy and beast in amazement. "How can this be?" she said. "You must be a chosen one."

"I don't know about any of this," Nelwazi said, shrugging his shoulders. "I found him sleeping by the river when we were looking for your hut. Now, he doesn't seem to want me to leave him."

"You must send this one away," Gugu said with tight lips.

"But he is not enchanted. I swear," Nelwazi cried, startling the creature and causing him to vanish once more.

"If he stays, he could get caught in the trap we are setting," she said. "Enchanted or not, he is still a tokoloshe, and my magic would affect him, too."

"Here is the enchanted powder which you made," Nhlanhla said, appearing in the doorway of the hut with a large bowl in his hands.

"Fine. You come with me to the Kraal," Gugu said to Nhlanhla. Then she turned back to Nelwazi. "If that creature is your friend, you will send him back where he came from and make him stay there." Then, she moved past Nelwazi, following Nhlanhla to the kraal.

As soon as they were out of sight, Ungha appeared once more. "You must go back to the river and wait by the bridge," Nelwazi said, pointing toward the river. "It isn't safe for you here, but I will come find you soon."

The tokoloshe peered at him through the long, stringy hair which hung down over his brow, concealing his beady, black eyes. "Ungh," the tokoloshe said, reaching out and poking Nelwazi's arm.

"No. You must go," he said, waving his hands in the air, shooing the creature away.

The beast stared at Nelwazi. A single tear slipped from the corner of his eye and ran down his cheek. Then, he disappeared, faster than Nelwazi could blink.

Nelwazi stared at the spot where his new friend had been just a moment before. He knew the creature did not understand why Nelwazi had sent him away. But it was for his friend's own good, so he turned and headed to join his human friends at the kraal.

They were both inside the kraal when he got there, with Nhlanhla following Gugu around the diameter, carrying the powdered mixture she had cooked up, while the inyanga sprinkled it on the ground, forming a large circle of white.

"We must lure the creatures into this circle with the cow's milk," she said, looking up at him. "But the cow is old like me, and I do not want her tormented, so Nhlanhla will lock her away inside, where she will be safe. You are what they are after. It will be up to you to lure them into the trap and keep them there."

When she had completed her circle of enchanted powder, she sent Nhlanhla to lock the cow in with the chickens to keep them safe and turned to Nelwazi, handing him an amakhubalo of bark, similar to that she had made for the zombie elephant, but smaller. "Suck on this for protection," she instructed. "You will stand inside the circle and will draw them in with a bowl of cow's milk. Once they are inside the circle, they will lose their power of invisibility. You must disperse them with your zombie powder, but not until you are sure they are all inside the circle and cannot get away."

"But, I only have a small amount of powder left," Nelwazi said, examining the jar with the powder inside. "What if there are too many tokoloshe and I run out?"'

"It only takes a few grains of the powder to disperse them, so make it count," Gugu said. "Without the power of willful invisibility, my magic will strengthen your magic, and they will not be able to return to earthly form ever again, so they won't bother you anymore."

"So, I must allow them to torment me until I'm sure they are all there?" Nelwazi asked, a lump forming in the back of his throat. He had a bad feeling about this.

"No one said this would be easy," Gugu replied. "All magic comes with a price. In the dark arts, the price is often as high as the giving of a life. Your price is to withstand the torments of the tokoloshe for a short time. Your body will be covered in lion's fat, which will protect you from evil, but also make your body slippery. You must suck on the bark of the amakhubalo I gave you to protect yourself from madness."

"That doesn't offer much comfort," Nelwazi said, sulking. He did not feel much better about Gugu's plan, despite her assurances.

"It is what you must do," she said with a shrug of her shoulders. "Once you disperse the tokoloshe, you and I will pay a visit to Ngobizitha. He's been dabbling in the dark arts. The ancestors will not be pleased."

At her words, Nelwazi felt a glimmer of hope stir inside him. He had not known how he would convince the sangoma to help him, but with Gugu by his side, perhaps there was a chance.

But first, he needed to deal with the tokoloshe. As the moon appeared on the horizon, he took a deep breath and step inside the white circle. He stood in the center, gazing at the surrounding landscape, as the moon rose higher in the night sky. He began to wonder if the tokoloshe were going to come at all.

"Perhaps I've already disposed of them all?" he said to Gugu and Nhlanhla. He didn't see how that was possible, but it was the best reason he could think of. "Maybe there are no more."

"Be patient, boy," Gugu yelled out. "They will only come when the moon is at its zenith."

As he continued to wait, he hoped that he was right, and Gugu was mistaken. He knew that he must face this trial to right his mistakes, but it was difficult to be brave, especially when he knew the danger was there, but not when it was coming. Soon he would become a warrior and there would be no room for such thoughts.

But, right now, he was still a boy, and he could admit, at least to himself, that he was scared.

It was a clear night, but just as the moon reached its apex, dark clouds blew across the sky, hiding the big white globe and blocking most of its light. That is when Nelwazi felt the first pinprick, causing him to jump back, where a sharp stick poked him the back. "Ouch! Ouch!" he cried.

He spun around to find himself face to face with a large, bearded tokoloshe that pinched Nelwazi's belly. "Ouch!"

Gugu's enchanted powder was working, and his attackers became visible as soon as they crossed into the circle, but it was filling up fast. There were too many of them. He couldn't poke and pinch fast enough. They had him jumping and spinning, trying to avoid their painful prods, but it was useless. He finally dropped to the ground, rolling himself into a ball, covering as much of his body as possible, and tucking the jar in close as they continued to assault him.

"Get up!" Gugu yelled. "You must disperse the powder!"

"I can't," he yelled back. "There are too many of them."

Small fingers pinched him everywhere. Sticks prodded him no matter which way he rolled. He sucked the amakhubalo amulet Gugu had made for him, dampening the volume of the screeching and chittering which must be only in his head. These were the voices of madness which Gugu had warned him about. The amulet dampened them, but they were still there, prodding at the edges of his mind, just like the tokoloshe prodded at his body.

He heard a skirmish within the circle as the tokoloshe's torment eased up a bit. He rolled over to see a pair of human feet among all the hairy-toed tokoloshe feet.

Thwack! Thwack!

Nelwazi looked up to see Nhlanhla fighting back the tokoloshe with his stick.

Thwack! Thwack!

"Get the powder!" Nhlanhla said, swinging his stick, and dodging the creatures with the skill of a seasoned warrior. "I don't know how long I can hold them off. The noise in my head is unearthly. Make it stop!"

Nelwazi rose to his knees and removed the lid from the jar. As he regained his feet, he resisted the urge to jump when he felt a pinch on his buttock. As he dipped his fingers into the jar, a tokoloshe poked him in the shoulder. He pulled his hand from the jar and tossed the powder in his face, and the creature's form dissipated immediately.

Another moved in behind Nhlanhla, preparing for a pinch with his little fingers, and he tossed another pinch of powder in that direction, dissipating the tokoloshe before he could do more harm.

His friend had come to his aid with no thought for himself. Nhlanhla had no protection from the madness. It was up to Nelwazi to be his protection, just as Nhlanhla had protected him. He sprang to his feet, breaking his amulet in half and giving one half to his friend.

"Suck on it," Nelwazi said, instructing him as Gugu had. He blew powder on a tokoloshe which was prodding Nhlanhla with a stick.

Nhlanhla stuck the bark in his mouth and swung his stick as two more approached from the left. Nelwazi blew the rest of the powder in his hand onto two tokoloshe approaching from his right, and dipped his hand back into the jar, which was nearly empty.

"Where are they all coming from?" he cried. "They are everywhere!"

There were too many left for him to count, but he only had a small amount of powder left. Nelwazi didn't know what to do.

"Get off me!" Nhlanhla cried.

Nelwazi spun around to see a rather plump tokoloshe sitting atop his friend's back, pinning him to the ground and pinching him mercilessly. He leapt to his friend's side, blowing the powder from his palm into the creature's face. Instantly, it was gone from atop Nhlanhla, but two others took its place before he could rise to his knees.

Still another jumped upon Nelwazi's back and he spun around to face the creature, but it had a grip on his shoulder and refused to let go. Its long penis drug the ground behind them both, sweeping the feet from under another tokoloshe and knocking him to the ground. Nelwazi saw this and began spinning around, faster and faster, using the long penis of the tokoloshe on his back like a weapon, smacking the other tokoloshe with it and knocking them off their large, hairy feet. He spun so fast, the tokoloshe on his back lost his grip and went flying into the invisible barrier created by the circle of white powder as if he had hit a stone wall. "Ungh," the creature said, hitting the ground with a thud.

Nelwazi took the lid off the jar and emptied the remaining contents over the fallen tokoloshe, dissipating them one after the other. When they were all gone and the jar was empty, he sank to his knees in exhaustion. "They're gone Nhlanhla," he said, gasping for breath. "We did it!"

But there was no response from Nhlanhla. Nelwazi looked up to see his friend still face down on the ground. "Nhlanhla!" he cried.

He crawled over to where his friend lay and rolled him over. His body cried out in pain from the tokoloshe's pokes and prods and pinches.

Then, Gugu was there. "Quick, bring him inside."

Nelwazi got to his feet, ignoring all the aches and pains caused by the tokoloshe, and scooped his friend up in his arms, carrying him back to the hut, where Gugu took his friend and laid him down on her bedding.

"I think he's either dead or dying," Nelwazi said. "Please help him."

"Go out and gather firewood for our breakfast and give me room to work here," Gugu said without looking back. She was focused on her patient. "Check on that elephant while you are out there."

Tired and sore from his battle with the tokoloshe, Nelwazi did as the inyanga had instructed. He headed into the trees with the elephant zombie staggering after him with dull eyes, often dragging her feet on the ground, not having the strength to pick them up properly. She stumbled in the thick grass and went down on her front knees with a thundering thud.

Nelwazi gathered the wood as quickly as possible, anxious to return to the hut. He was worried about Nhlanhla. His friend had jumped into the circle to fight at his side, unprotected from the dark magic of the tokoloshe. If his friend did not recover, he would be responsible for Nhlanhla's death.

With his arms filled with wood for the fire, he turned to head back to the hut, but before he took no more than three steps, he heard the wailing call of a black-backed jackal, stopping him in his tracks. And answering call wailed back. Then, there was another, and another, until the combined cacophony of calls built to a maddening crescendo.

Nelwazi was familiar with these predatory beasts which frequented the bush surrounding his village. They are both cunning and daring, and they hunt in packs. The amukhabalo which hung around his neck offered no protection from beasts such as these. The black-backed jackal are the oldest dog species in South Africa, and he took their calls as reason to hurry back to the safety of the hut.

He stopped when he came to the edge of the bush, where it opened into the veldt. He would have to cross it to return to the hut. The jackal calls seemed to be getting nearer, spreading out around him.

On the veldt, he would be exposed, but he knew if he ran, it would be a signal to the canines to give chase. Even on a good day, it was unlikely that he could outrun the quick-moving predators, and as tired and sore as he was from the tokoloshe, he didn't feel that he had a chance. But he couldn't remain here on the edge of the veldt, with nothing to fight them off but a bundle of sticks.

He broke out in a sweat as the calls turned into the rapid yapping signaling that they were onto the scent of potential prey. He decided to take his chances on the veldt. Dropping his bundle of wood, he broke into a run, sprinting off across the veldt at the fastest pace he could muster.

Yip. Yip. Yip. Yap.

He glanced over his shoulder without slowing his speed to see the pack of jackals closing in on him, as he had feared. They were fast and the distance to the hut was too great. He could not outrun them, but he couldn't give up. He found an additional burst of speed from within when he felt one of the jackals nipping at his heels. "Stay away from me!" he yelled.

The ground began to shake and tremble. Nelwazi ran as fast as his legs would carry him, not pausing to assess the situation, until he heard the loud trumpeting of the elephant from behind him. Then, he chanced glancing back to see the zombie elephant crashing through the trees and emerging onto the veldt, shaking the earth with every shambling step.

She trumpeted once more, and the jackals halted their chase, watching the zombie elephant approach. The elephant's unnatural red eyes blazed as she raised her trunk again, and the jackals scattered back into the brush, yelping in fear.

The ground continued to shake and rumble until the zombie elephant came to a halt in front of him.

"Thank you, my friend," Nelwazi said, staring up at the behemoth. As he stared up at her, he noticed a ring of golden honey outlining the scarlet-red iris of her eye. It saddened him that this was all that remained of the creature she once was. "I shall call you Umngane."

The elephant stared down at him with that single gold-ringed eye, and he saw a single tear slip from the corner and run down her wrinkled, grey cheek. "Don't worry, Umngane," he said, reaching up to wipe away the tear from her face. "I will find a way to end the evil I have created and allow you to rest in peace. I swear."

He reached out to rub Umngane's trunk to reassure her. Her skin was rough and flakey, and small pieces came away on his fingers, making him even more determined. "I'm sorry," he said. "I did not mean to make you into a zombie. I just wanted to ease your pain."

He turned to head back to the hut, but realized he no longer had the firewood he had collected for Gugu. He had dropped it on the other side of the veldt, in his fear of the jackals. "Oh no," he cried aloud. "I need that wood I dropped. Now I must go back."

Umngane shambled around, heading for the trees, and Nelwazi headed after her. Before he had made it half-way across the expanse, the elephant was headed back toward him carrying a bundle of sticks in her trunk much bigger than the one he had dropped.

"Thank you, Umngane," he said, taking the sticks from her. She had more than he could get his arms around, so she carried the rest in her trunk. Nelwazi was so exhausted that he could have laid down there on the veldt, in the tall grasses and gone to sleep. But he had to get back to check on Nhlanhla. With Umngane's help, at least he didn't have so far to walk now.

Nelwazi was thrilled to see Nhlanhla sitting up, sipping from a cup when he entered the hut. "How are you feeling, my friend," he said with a smile.

"I feel like I had a run-in with a rhinoceros, and it ran right over the top of me," Nhlanhla said with a weak smile. "The herbs Gugu gave me are working to make me feel better, but they work slowly."

"Nhlanhla will get better, but it will take time, and much rest," Gugu said, handing a cup to Nelwazi. "You sip this, and you will feel better, too. You must regain your strength. We have only taken care of part of your troubles. Drink up."

Nelwazi took the cup from her and drank down the bitter brew as fast as he could. The tokoloshe were gone, but he still had to help Umngane, and he didn't have time to waste. He could not rest until he found a way to release her from her torment.

"Yuck! It tastes awful," he said, wiping a drip of the liquid from his chin. "Are you sure it won't kill me?"

"That is why I told you to sip," Gugu said with a frown, placing her hands on her hips. "I also say, you both need time and rest. You will get some sleep, and then we will pay a visit to Ngobizitha and see what we can do about the unnatural abomination outside."

"Umngane is not an abomination," Nelwazi said. "She is a most innocent victim of dark magic, and she is suffering. She cannot wait. Her carcass is deteriorating rapidly. While I rest, she will suffer longer."

Gugu's frown deepened increasing the lines in her wrinkled face. "I see in you the potential for a great sangoma, but you are no match for Ngobizitha. You must be as strong as possible when you face him. Without proper healing you will not be."

"I am no sangoma, but I must help Umngane. I will face him as a warrior. That is what I know," he said, crossing his arms in front of him stubbornly. This was one issue he was not willing to bend on, even for Gugu. "If we wait, she might be unable to make the journey. Her carcass is falling apart, and she is stumbling all over. Already, she will leave pieces of herself along the way. If she falls on the journey, she won't die. I have cursed her for eternity. Don't you see? We must leave immediately."

Gugu was silent as she considered his words. He couldn't tell what she might be thinking. He had been disrespectful in his desperation to help Umngane. Now, she might refuse to help such a disrespectful boy. Then, he would have to deal with Ngobizitha by himself.

"Please forgive me, Gugu," Nelwazi said, already sorry for his rash outburst. "I am so worried about Umngane. I did not mean to speak disrespectfully. I just wanted you to understand why I cannot do what you have asked."

"I understand only too well, Nelwazi," she said, giving him a weak smile while her eyes still looked sad. "It is good that you take your responsibility in all this seriously. But, still, you must wait until you've regained at least some of your strength. You will sleep tonight, and I will send you off at daybreak tomorrow."

Nelwazi wanted to argue, suddenly he was having trouble thinking straight. His eyelids grew heavy, and it became difficult to hold his head up.

"I was just waiting for that potion to take effect," she said, smiling at him from across the table, which now seemed very long. "I was afraid you might not want to rest, so I put a little something in it to help you sleep. See you in the morning, Nelwazi."

In the morning, Gugu greased him up with lion's fat once more, and bid him to drink another cup of the bitter concoction.

"I'd rather not, if it's all the same to you," he said, pushing the cup away. After the way she had tricked him last night, he wasn't taking any chances. He wasted the whole night sleeping when he should have been traveling with Umngane. Although, he had to admit that he did feel much better this morning, stronger than he'd been the previous evening. He felt ready to face the sangoma. "I'd like us to get going as soon as possible."

Gugu shook her head. "Nhlanhla is not strong enough to make the journey. We cannot go today."

"But you promised we'd set out at daybreak," Nelwazi said, feeling betrayed by the inyanga.

"I said I would let you go now, and I will, if that is what you want," Gugu said. "I will tell you how to find Ngobizitha, but I must remain here to care for Nhlanhla."

"I am much better now," Nhlanhla said from his sickbed, pushing himself up onto his elbows. "I think I am strong enough to make the journey. We should all go."

"No, my friend. Gugu is right," Nelwazi said. "All of this is my doing. You have followed me, even when you knew I was wrong, and come to my aid, risking your own peril. I cannot endanger those I care for any further. I will face the sangoma on my own."

Gugu gave a knowing nod. "The tokoloshe are gone for now, but the one who created them is powerful, and he can create more," she said, placing her hands on his shoulders and staring directly into his eyes. "His magic is very dark. You will need all the protection you can get."

Then she placed a swatch of beaded cloth into his hand. "You give this to Ngobizitha when you see him, and tell him it is from me," she said. "He will understand their meaning."

Nelwazi closed his hand over the cloth. "Thank you, Gugu," he said nodding to her. "You take care of Nhlanhla. He is a good friend, and very brave. He will be a courageous warrior and fight by my side someday. Now, tell me how to find Ngobizitha."

Nelwazi set out to find the sangoma and somehow convince him to help him undo the evil which he had done, with Umngane shambling along behind him. He didn't need to check to be sure she was there, because he could tell by the ruckus which she made as she crashed through the forest. He didn't see a single living animal along the path, and even the birds scattered as the zombie elephant approached.

When he looked back, he saw large chunks of flesh hanging from her carcass, with more falling off with each step she took, but she was still upright and moving forward, if slowly and clumsily.

He followed the river until he came to an enormous Sausage Tree at the base of Ghost Mountain, where the ancestors reside and the sangoma lives. There, he veered, taking a game trail that Gugu said would take him up the mountain through the trees.

Twice he stopped, waiting for Umngane to catch up, but as soon as he felt the ground rumble beneath his feet, he set out again, even in the hills when he couldn't see her. He didn't have any time to waste, but the creature could not go any faster.

When he reached the clearing around the sangoma's hut, Nelwazi stayed low in the tall grasses, crawling on his belly like he'd been taught. He stopped between two Euphorbia trees, being careful not to touch their poisonous fruits, staring out at the thatched beehive hut of Ngobizitha. This time, the sangoma sat, cross-legged in the dooryard, tossing the bones in a white circle of powder on the ground in front of him. He wore a black and white, beaded headdress, with ostrich feathers adorning his head.

"The hyena bone tells me that a thief is approaching," he said, in a voice which was both deep and loud. "Come forward, thief. Show yourself. Have you come to return what was stolen?"

Nelwazi swallowed hard, forcing the large lump which had formed in the back of his throat to go down with much difficulty. The sangoma knew that he was here, and it was time to face him. If he didn't do this now, he would fail Umngane. And he would fail his friend who always had faith in him, even when Nelwazi didn't believe in himself. If he did not succeed, Umngane might be destined to spend eternity as a zombie. Already, she had places where the flesh had fallen off and the bones beneath were showing. Soon, she would be a walking skeleton, instead of a walking corpse.

Nelwazi resisted the strong urge to flee, and instead, rose to his feet and faced the sangoma, steeling himself for whatever came next. He didn't know what to expect, but he had formed ideas of several possibilities on the trek here that made his knees quake at the thought.

"I am here," he said, stepping forward. "But I cannot return your powder. I used it up. There is none left. I have come to ask your help in undoing the dark magic I have created."

"You are a thief," Ngobizitha said, pointing a finger at him. "You stole from me. Why should I help you?"

He held out the beads Gugu had sent. "The inyanga, Gugu. She sent these to you," Nelwazi said. "She said you would understand their message. I used your powder and now, I must undo what I have done. Gugu says you are the only one who can help me."

The sangoma looked at the beaded cloth Nelwazi handed him, and his large, fat lips formed a smile. "Gugu believes that you have been chosen by the ancestors to train as a sangoma. Why would she believe this of a thief?"

"I don't know anything about being a sangoma," he said, shrugging his shoulders. "I will become a warrior soon. Perhaps she thinks that because I dispersed the tokoloshe you sent after me. All I want to do is reverse the magic and help the poor elephant I have cursed with your powder. I should not have taken it, I know. I did not know what it was or what it would do."

"Gugu must be mistaken," the sangoma said, laughing heartily. "The ancestors would not choose one so foolish. How did you disperse my tokoloshe?"

"I... I sprinkled them with the powder, inside Gugu's circle of magic," he replied, hesitantly.

"And you created a zombie elephant with that same powder?" the sangoma asked.

Nelwazi nodded.

"All you need do is sprinkle some of the powder on the zombie creature to disperse it, as you did with the tokoloshe," Ngobizitha said with a belly laugh. "You had the answer all along."

Nelwazi felt very foolish, indeed. "The powder is gone. Can I trade you something for more?" Nelwazi asked. "I used all I had to disperse the tokoloshe.

"Foolish boy," the sangoma replied, anger flaring in his eyes. "I cannot give the powder to you. You are not a sangoma. You are a thief! You must repay me for that which you took."

The elephant trumpeted outside. To Nelwazi, it was a cry of distress. "Listen to her," he said, pleading with the sangoma. "You are a sangoma healer. Gugu says the ancestors are displeased with your use of the dark arts. They will be even more displeased if you let that innocent creature suffer."

"The creature would not exist if you had not broken into MY hut, and stolen MY powder, thief!" Ngobizitha said, raising his voice and glaring at Nelwazi. He planted his feet firmly and placed his hands on his hips. "I will use the powder to create more tokoloshe. You have no more powder to disperse them now. They will torment you forever!"

"I must have your help!" Nelwazi said. "I am not a sangoma. I cannot reverse the dark magic. But I know about being a warrior. I will fight you for your help."

"Foolish boy," Ngobizitha said, shaking his head. "You are no match for this powerful sangoma. Even a real warrior would be no threat to me. Take your zombie elephant and go home while I'm still willing to allow you to walk away from here."

Nelwazi was desperate. He lunged at the sangoma, intending to knock him down, but the moment they came into contact, a jolt of electrical energy surged through his body. It felt as if he'd been hit by lightning. The sangoma's body stiffening as the current shot through him, as well, creating a connection between man and boy. Nelwazi tried to release his grip, but he was unable to severe the connection, as the current flowed through both of them. When the surge of energy had run its course, he was able to let go, slumping to the ground.

He rose from the ground on shaky legs. The old sangoma remained slumped next to him, unconscious. Nelwazi left him there, staggering to the hut. Several piles of powders lay on the table as before. He felt drawn to the pile of grey powder lying on the far corner. Before he could think twice about it, he scooped some up and ran back outside to where Umngane waited in the trees.

Nelwazi held out his hands to the zombie elephant, offering her the powder. "Take it, my friend," he said in his most soothing voice. "This will set you free."

The creature moved her trunk over Nelwazi's hands, sucking some up. There was a loud pop as the zombie elephant dispersed, just as the tokoloshe had done.

"Good-bye, my friend," Nelwazi said, wiping a tear from his cheek.

"Thief!" Ngobizitha cried, coming up behind him. "You have dared to cross Ngobizitha, not once, but twice! I will rip you apart with my bare hands."

Nelwazi turned to see the sturdy bulk of the sangoma, twice his size charging at him. He snatched a stick from the ground to defend himself, but before he could take a stance, Ngobizitha slammed into him, knocking Nelwazi to the ground. The sangoma's huge fist pummeled his head as he struggled to catch his breath. He looked up to see a tokoloshe with a long stick in his hand and his penis thrown over his shoulder.

Before Nelwazi knew what was happening, the creature smacked Ngobizitha on the back with the stick. The sangoma jumped to his feet, swinging his fist at the tokoloshe. Before he could make contact, the tokoloshe disappeared.

Nelwazi sat up, rubbing his head as he watched the sangoma swinging at the air. When the tokoloshe reappeared, he recognized his friend, Ungha, as he poked the sangoma with his stick once more, and then disappeared again. He had to laugh at the old sangoma as he tried to fight an invisible foe.

Ngobizitha twisted and turned, trying to avoid the pokes and jabs of Ungha's stick, which seemed to come out of nowhere. The old sangoma cried out, running into the bush, trying to escape his unseen assailant.

"It looks like this hut needs a new sangoma," Gugu said, emerging from the trees with Nhlanhla by her side.

"Did we miss all the excitement?" Nhlanhla said.

"But I am not a sangoma," Nelwazi said, puzzled by her strange declaration.

"The ancestors have chosen you," Gugu said. "Ngobizitha won't bother you anymore. The hut belongs to you now. You have earned it."

"I made foolish choices and caused great pain and grief to my friends," Nelwazi said. "How have I earned anything? Besides, I am a warrior."

"It is not up to you to decide," Gugu said with a smile. "You have been chosen, and it seems that your training has already begun. Your first lesson was learning to take responsibility for your mistakes and recognizing when you are wrong. You have befriended creatures which most shun, and shown empathy and kindness. You will be a great sangoma one day."

"How did you beat Ngobizitha?" Nhlanhla said. "Only a sangoma could do that. Wait until the other boys hear this."

Nelwazi considered the words of his friends. He had beaten the sangoma, but he couldn't explain how it had happened. The jolt that went through them could only have come from the ancestors. Was he really chosen, as Gugu believed? Could it be his fate to be, not a warrior, but a sangoma?

He considered these things. Ngobizitha used his knowledge and power for evil purposes and that evil was his undoing. But what had happened with Umngane, and his new friend, Ungha, proved that kindness is a far greater strength. It was true, he had the spirit of a warrior, but he also had great compassion; something Ngobizitha seemed to have lacked. Perhaps he could become a good sangoma with support of good friends. After all, who was he to argue with the ancestors.

Them Doore Girls

Joseph Carrabis

You hear that? Kind of like a ship's horn, waiting to get piloted into land. Starts low and keening, then suddenly high. Won't do much good looking. You can look everywhere you want in these parts, and you'll never find it. Ain't none of us could ever find it, and we looked some. Pilot Farley, he took his skiff out far into the fishing waters and found nothing. He'd be able to find it if any could, that Pilot Farley.

You wait right here, though. Few minutes is all. You'll see them Doore girls come out that shop across the way and start walking to home.

See, I know what makes that noise, and it ain't no ship fetch up on the rocks. It's what's calling them Doore girls, and it ain't nothing human, at all.

I found out long time ago when I was just about your age – you're being what, twenty? Twenty-five? You just rest a while, sip that soda pop slow, and give that fancy car of yours a rest while I mind the store, and maybe I'll tell you. I'll tell you because there ain't nobody around here going to listen. You can ask, they won't say nothing. Women want their husbands and sons home at night.

Ya. That's them Doore girls. They ain't hard to look at, are they? That's Ruth and Livy, front door and back door, if you get my meaning.

Now Ruth, she's right comely, ain't she? Ruth, she's my age – don't roll your eyes, son. There's more to this town than you could know. Livy, she's being a year and a half younger. But that Ruth, she's always the kind of woman, somebody'd see her walking, and we'd all get up from the card game just to have a look. Some of the others of us, some like Johnny Walker – his parents weren't too proud when they named him, were they? – come outside and sit like we're doing now, right on the porch, and he'd keep right on looking as she'd go past. Ain't known much pleasure, that boy.

Always had a warmth for Ruth, I did. When I was a young man, I had my own boat and a home right up on the bluff. I protected my home good against both summer and winter. Nowadays they call that "solar design". Don't matter. Just knowing where you live, is all. Sold my boat so long ago I don't hardly think of it. Don't go out on the water now. Them others, they don't mind. They'll go out 'cause they know their children's safe. They got them Doore girls to thank, but none of them will.

I was shy back when I was young. Wouldn't talk to no one. But I'd known them Doore girls since we was born.

The Doore girls live by themselves. They lost their parents to the water when the sisters were entering their teens. That ain't odd, people dying on account of the sea. But ain't nobody died on the sea since then, neither.

Come when I was thirteen, their tragedy struck. Ruth and Livy and their Ma and Pa went out to the island to do some clamming. It was a big church supper and we was all bringing something.

They won't tell all, that I know for sure. But as they'd start coming back, here comes that sound like something looking for something it can't find. The Doores were caught out in it, no more than a mile from shore either way, something every newborn pup knows how to swim, and their Ma and Pa is gone. Next day we found Ruth and Livy fetch up, looking terrified and sick, and both of them, their eyes got a fear couldn't be described. Old Evie Halpren took them in, but they wouldn't hear none of it. "We got our own home to look after, Mrs. Halpren," they said. We all thought they still had the sun in them. Pilot Farley said letting them live alone was about as sharp as a sack of wet mice. But they wouldn't hear none of it, and being they's Doores, just like their parents, – Tommy Doore, God bless him, many's a day we'd see him standing in his field, arguing with a stump – we nodded and let them be.

Well, they grew up, was all. But they grew like I told you, front and back door alike. That Ruth Doore, the way she moved, stay with a man like the taste of strong licorice on the back of your tongue, or maybe that first taste of coffee after pulling up the morning's nets in a too heavy fog. And that Livy – and this ain't showing no disrespect for the wonders God's done – you just know she'd keep a man warm and awake at night. Ruth, she knew how I'd feel. Never told her, but let her know the best I could with a look and a nod when the church socials was over. She'd always smile back, but kind of sad, and I kept my words to myself cause of that.

But whenever they'd walk past, we'd all go see, then shake our heads and smile. We'd all come back in and sit down to the game again. I guess my feelings must have showed strong one day, cause Old Farley – You'll know him when he comes. Got a stump like Ahab. Warn't no whale, though, just caught his leg in the ropes pulling up the nets. That's when they started using Diesels. Didn't know about no clutches back then – he'd whoop his stump under the table; whack, whack, whack, then look at me and smile. The others joined in and I could feel my face getting hot then cold.

"Wouldn't be the first man or boy asked to sit beside a Doore in church, or maybe brought them the pride of his catch," he said.

Clem sighed, "Would be the first they invited in, though," and they all laughed again.

I was about to throw my cards down when Pilot Farley puts his hand on my arm. "Don't mean no harm, Noah. Don't want to shame you none. But you can't sell what you don't advertise, son. You got a feeling for one of them girls, you go tell them. Ain't no shame in hearing a 'no'. Only shame is in not hearing anything at all."

Clem and the others nodded, not looking at me, but watching me over their cards. I put my cards down and left.

I walked the shore then, from the docks down to Indian Point and up east to River's Spring. Thought maybe they'd be clamming, but they weren't. Went to their home then, but they weren't there neither.

Now about this time, it's getting dark and a heavy fog's coming in with the night. And from low beyond the island, there comes that sound. I could hear the lobster boats churning and making back water, pulling for the dock rather than sit out in the bay waiting for Farley to lead them home.

Easiest way home for me from their house was on the shore, so I headed down the path until I was walking on gull tracks and sand when I heard their voices.

It was full dark now, and the fog was hanging on you like a sweater soaked in snow. But I saw them Doore girls down by the water. I looked, thinking to call to them, but stopped and watched. They weren't clamming, and they weren't swimming. They was waiting, was all.

I lay down in the grass just to watch, thinking maybe they had somebody coming from one of the towns east or south, and maybe that's why no one got close to the Doores.

Then that sound come again, deeper and nearer, like it was carried on the mists of the fog itself. Them Doores, they start moving like cattle expecting a storm. There was one more blast from whatever it was coming across the water, then I saw it.

Something big and dark, looking like a man and rising like the crest of a wave, coming close to where the Doore girls watched. Bigger than night and darker than the pitch we poured on Old Farley's stump when he got his leg twisted in the Diesel.

A wave like a man's hand washed up against them and Livy shook, shook hard and her legs opened so the water could go high. Ruth's blouse was pushed against her, flattening her breasts against her chest. The next wave took Livy down to the ground and the wave after tore open Ruth's blouse and pulled off her dress.

I jumped up then and shouted, "Ruth, Livy, what is it?" and like a fool wanting to shake hands with Devil, I ran down thinking I was to save them.

"No, Noah. Don't. Go back," yells Ruth, and they both started crying and covering themselves, their voices sounding so sick like whatever's happening to them is the worst curse out of God's own mouth.

They started backing away, though I couldn't tell if they was backing away from me or the sea which was surrounding them.

"What's happening?" I hollered.

"Go back, Noah! Go away before it finds you!"

Something dark come up out of the water then. Something like I'd never seen, and don't want to see again. Something looking like a man, but no man could move like it did. I backed away and slipped, falling into sand wet with the tide. Whatever it was, it didn't have no face that I could see, but you could tell it was looking at them Doore girls as they moved up into the grasses, and out of the reach of the water.

Next thing I know I'm deep into the water, and it's feeling like a stone-cold vise pushing the life out of my chest. I hear that noise, too, deep inside me, and I'm thinking for sure Jonah's whale's got me in its jaws.

I come up out of the water once, something holding me in its hand above the waves, and again that sound bellows through me. Ruth, I heard her call my name. Heard both Doore girls, crying and shrieking, and this thing bellowing and shaking me, until finally them Doore girls started back down to the water.

Whatever it was moved up against the Doore girls. First one, then the other. Until they were washed in the waves and this thing was rolling with them, moving onto them and finally into them. And they was screaming, screaming as if making love to the tides.

Next thing happens, I'm thrown far up onto the rocks. When I woke up it was morning and them Doore girls was gone.

That's it, that's the story. Ain't no one else around here going to tell you why them Doore girls lost their parents and them two survived, or why ain't no others died on the sea since them Doore girls washed up. Something was looking and found what it wanted. Something took a liking to them. Something that's keeping them all for itself.

They ain't changed much since then. Ain't got a gray hair between them, least not one as you'll ever see. And that ain't showing no disrespect. It's the truth.

I'm telling you this because, boy at your age, you should know there's some things made just for looking, ain't never meant to be touched, ain't never.

No.

Cattails

Robert White

J.J.'s life went downhill like a greased toboggan after his parents' divorce. He went from a two-story brick Tudor and a private academy to a trailer park and a rural public school at the other end of the state overnight—or so he complained to his mother after she told the news they were leaving comfortable, middle-class Livonia "for a new life, just you and me, in the Upper Peninsula."

J.J. didn't like the Legran Trailer Park the moment he saw it from the passenger seat of the U-Haul truck. Worse, he hated his new school. Three boys from the Legran "Toilet Paper" attended the same school. Dale, the biggest and toughest, was the alpha male, although he didn't talk as much as the brothers, Frank and Richard. Richard shared some of J.J.'s classes.

The teachers were indifferent, most downright lazy, and even the principal was intimidated by coaches, no matter how many rules their boys violated. Half the faculty were new every year, shunted from better schools where they failed to pass muster.

J.J. didn't fight back when his homeroom classmates made "Kick Me" signs and slapped them on his back. He never reported anyone for dumping his gym bag into the urinals. He failed to make friends with a boy wearing glasses who sat in front of him in math. Dale saw them talking one morning. J.J. noted the look of fear in his classmate's eyes. The boy instinctively knew J.J. was marked by Dale's hostile stare the way a lion spots a limp. He wanted no part of it, or the new kid.

Three weeks into the fall semester, J.J. was desperate. He found solace wandering by the St. Mary's River, exploring the woods, talking to himself about his problems at school and home. Behind his school was an overgrown field and a path that led to a cyclone fence. Generations of boys from school had dug a hole beneath the fence to go to the river to fish or smoke weed. A big metal sign on the fence proclaimed the area a "NO TRESPASSING ZONE UNDER THE AUTHORITY OF CHIPPEWA COUNTY" as part of the Soo Locks.

Returning home late, he found his mother's boyfriend in the La-Z-Boy chair and his poster of *Shane* in his bedroom ripped into tiny pieces, spread out over his bedspread. The image of Alan Ladd leaning down from his horse to say goodbye to Brandon deWilde was like a talisman to J.J., engraved into his neocortex. His only reminder of times when his parents were together and life was normal. The longer Randy remained a fixture in the trailer, the more he resembled Jack Palance, the black-clad gunslinger Shane had to kill to save the sodbusters.

"Hey, punk, want a sip of whiskey, a man's drink instead of that circus water you guzzle?"

"No, Randy, you drink it. You will anyway." J.J. hoped he would pass out—his last chance to get the extortion money his three bullies demanded.

"You keep calling me 'Randy,' 'stead of 'sir,' you're gonna pull back a bloody stump, you hear?"

Randy made a half-hearted effort to rise from the chair, laughing when J.J. scooted down the hall to his bedroom.

School on Monday was as bad as J.J. expected. Cornered at his locker by Frank and Richard, he had to face Dale at lunchtime. They told him what was going to happen after school.

All afternoon, he failed to concentrate on his classes and was scolded for fidgeting at his desk and for daydreaming by Mrs. Corchoran. When Mr. Casey gave him a detention in math, he could have wept with gratitude. His relief was short-lived, however, as he was barely off school grounds before the trio swept behind him from hiding spots to run him down like attack dogs. The bruises they inflicted were hidden by clothing. The worst was Dale's short, snapping punch to the solar plexus, which left him gagging on the ground. Richard added a kick to the liver for good measure that took away what little air he could suck into his lungs.

"Look at him puking," Richard gloated, the tag-along bully.

J.J. lay on the ground a long time after he thought they'd run off. Instead, his head was jerked up by the hair. Dale's face was inches from his.

"Twice the money tomorrow, or what you got today was nothing," he hissed.

He shoved J.J.'s face hard into the grass. Despite the time of day and the fact this was a residential neighborhood, no one looked out a window or came to help. He sobbed on the walk home.

Other than commenting on how "late the bus was," J.J.'s mother had little interest in his arrival as he walked to his room.

By Thursday, J.J. was an emotional wreck. He didn't know when the next demand would be made, or from where the next attack would come. He didn't know how to make it stop.

Richard approached him at recess, all smiles, as though his kick to J.J. had happened in an alternate universe. J.J. was startled and confused. He failed to grasp what Richard was saying—something weird about "killing muck rabbits down by the river and selling them."

It finally dawned on J.J. that Richard was inviting him to come along.

"Me?"

"Yeah, what you think I been sayin'? Me, you, them other two guys."

"I'll think about it."

"Here comes Dale. He don't like no for an answer."

Dale occupied most of the space in front of J.J. "Hey, what's up?"

"Nothing."

"Rich here asked you to come along with us tomorrow after school, right? It'll be a blast."

J.J. needed his refuge by St. Mary's more than ever. Everything told him this was wrong from Richard's phony invitation, glancing around him in a 180-degree scan as he spoke to see if anyone noticed him talking to Dale's appearance. He approached his clearing in the cattails in high agitation, nervously gesturing with his hands, talking aloud to himself like that crazy man outside the paperback store where he bought his Zane Grey novels.

His mind was in such torment that he took several steps into the clearing before he noticed the boy standing inside.

J.J. stutter-stepped backwards, then froze. He was on the verge of fleeing when the boy smiled and said, "Don't run off."

Like a command, J.J. stood still.

"Who—who are you?"

"Nathan."

He was taller than J.J., bigger without altogether losing the physique of early adolescence, and fair-haired. But sported an old-fashioned hair style unlike the shags, buzzcuts, faux hawks, and fades popular at school.

"How did you find my . . . this place?"

"I come down here a lot."

J.J. puzzled through that response. He'd never seen the kid before that moment.

As if reading J.J.'s mind, Nathan said, "I collect cattails. Lots of things they're good for."

He opened his hand to reveal three of the brown, cigar-shaped tips.

The only use J.J. had for cattails was to pluck the tips and throw them at targets for something to do.

Nathan's fingernail plucked at one of the tips. It looked like stuffing that popped out of old furniture. "My mom adds this to flour for making stews and soup," he said. "Thickens it right up. You can boil the green shoots. They taste a little bit like cucumber. Dip them in oil, you got yourself a homemade torch."

J.J. wasn't sure what this strange boy was saying was true. He tensed his body to flee in case this was a trick.

"Most people, they don't know shit from Shinola about nature. I'm part-Indian. My mom's First Nation."

His father used that expression. J.J. relaxed slightly, but he still wasn't sure whether the boy was lying. For one thing, he was fair-haired, blue-eyed. Every Indian J.J. saw on television was dark, swarthy. The Native Americans living at the trailer park and the Ojibwe around town had glossy black hair, sometimes worn long, in braids.

A dozen red-winged blackbirds burst out of the cattails. J.J. flinched, but Nathan didn't bother to look at the gurgling ruckus over his shoulder where a dozen males fluffed their bright shoulder patches or lit on the swaying cobs.

"Swamp birds, J.J. Nothing to fear."

Did I tell him my name? I must have . . .

What Nathan said next took the breath out of his body. Red spots dazzled his vision; his knees almost buckled.

"Those three, you know they're going to kill you tomorrow."

J.J.'s eyes welled with tears that overflowed and spilled down his cheeks. Instead of exclaiming, or denying, or refusing to believe the cruel words, he pleaded aloud: "Why?"

"They don't need no reason, kid," Nathan said. "Dale's a sociopath. Them other two do what he says."

"How do you know that . . . that—"

J.J. couldn't finish the sentence. The thought was too monstrous.

"I live at the T.P. You know, what everyone calls the Legran Park. Frank's mother has a trailer there. She's a prostitute. Richard is a trick baby. I overheard the three of them talking right under my bedroom window. They plan to bash your head in with the bats they're bringing to kill the muck rabbits."

J.J. knew it was true, knew he was the "rabbit." Something in the way Richard sidled up to him with that phony story of selling dead rabbits.

"If you live at the trailer park, how come I never saw you around?"

"Because I'm home-schooled," Nathan replied. "My mother doesn't believe in the white man's ways." He laughed.

J.J.'s mind tried to focus. "I'll phone the cops."

"They won't believe you no more'n your mother or her deadbeat boyfriend."

"I'll make them believe me!"

"Stop playing at make-believe," Nathan said. "Time to grow up, J.J. I'm talking about the next . . ." checking his wristwatch—"twenty-one hours and forty-two minutes."

That was the time he was supposed to meet Richard at the track after school.

"What do I do!"

"Stop whimpering, for one thing. You got everything you need except the bat under your bed, which you need to fetch and get down here before nightfall. Don't look surprised. I checked your stash when I found this place. I saw the shovel, the *puukko*—"

The hair on J.J.'s neck stiffened.

"How do you know that knife's a *puukko*?" His father had given him the Finnish knife for his twelfth birthday.

"It's got a tang," Nathan said.

"I know what a tang is," J.J. replied.

"The blade goes all the way up the haft in case the handle breaks off—"

"I know what a goddamn tang is!"

"Too bad you didn't bring it here when school started up."

J.J.'s cheeks burned at the humiliating memory. Barely two weeks into school starting, when Frank and Richard jumped him near the river. Frank jammed a bagworm into his face and asked him how the worms tasted.

"Tell me what to do."

Nathan laughed. "Hey, you already know what to do."

The terror that wracked him all day ceased, a feeling of serenity replaced it. J.J. couldn't explain the abrupt change, especially after that weird day's agitation and nervous fretting. His calmness didn't penetrate Richard's charade of chumminess, even though totally unreciprocated. To J.J., it all seemed surreal, as though Nathan were waiting down there for him, stiffening his spine.

A greasy film of perspiration on Richard's forehead. An unattractive kid with bulging eyes and a small head, he reminded J.J. of a photo of a hyena from the ancient issues of *National Geographic* in the library.

"The air's cold," J.J. said. "Why are you sweating?"

"I ain't sweating, man."

Richard's reaction told J.J. everything he needed to know about his classmate's state of mind. *He doesn't know how he'll react*, J.J. thought.

J.J. ran headlong toward his fort; the sandy ground slowed him down and sank him in its grip. As the cattails loomed closer, their green stalks and brown tips waved in gusts of wind off the river.

"*Cattail corn-on-the-cob makes for good eating, you know. . . .*"

Nathan must have snapped off a dozen more stalks to help him find his entrance hole more easily, maybe knowing he would be in a panic. J.J. bent low and moved through the narrow path he'd stomped to get to the clearing, stalks lashing his arms and face. He ignored everything to get to the far corner where he'd hidden the *puukko* and its sheath. He tucked them behind his belt. He picked up the bat he'd stashed there.

The crackling of cattails behind him told him that Richard must have raced to catch up.

"What the hell you doin', man? You're—we're supposed to go—I almost lost you in all this bamboo shit!"

"Cattails, Richard. They're called cattails."

Richard composed himself, thinking hard, resumed his frenetic eye-darting glances. His expression was a mix of malevolence and fear, a Judas goat irked by the sheep he led to the kill chute. His face was scratched. He'd missed the entrance by a couple feet and blundered headlong into the mass of cattails. He turned around and raised his arms to head back through the cattails the way he'd come in.

J.J. stood there staring back, unable to move his feet.

"*Don't let him get back outside once he's in or you're dead meat . . .*"

J.J.'s scream was a *kiai* that welled unexpectedly out of his esophagus. He flew toward Richard whose back was about to disappear behind a curtain of green stalks.

Part of the blow from the bat was deflected by the cattails but enough of it struck the top of Richard's shaggy head to stop him in his tracks. Richard stumbled backwards. His body shook like a small fir tree about to collapse. He half-turned toward J.J., who had the bat raised behind his head for another blow. Richard's spastic arms weren't able to follow the brain's command to protect his head. The second blow made a crunching sound. Richard's eyes rolled to the back of his head, and he dropped into the cattails and lay there. One of his tennis shoes extended into the clearing; it twitched and stopped.

J.J. fought back the nausea climbing up his stomach, breathing in and out for several seconds. He tossed the bat behind him.

"*Richie, God damn it, where the fuck you at?*"

Frank. He had no time to shove Richard's leg deeper into the cattails.

"Come out, come out, wherever you *aaarrre*," Frank crooned to the spot where J.J. stood riveted. In his normal voice, he shouted: "Dale's waitin' on us, man! He's got some rabbits for you two."

"Come in here for a second, Frank," J.J. said in a quavering voice. "Rich has something for you." J.J.'s voice rose too high at the end.

Silence. Then a crashing through the cattails. Frank found the path.

J.J. rushed to the point where the path debouched into the clearing. His heart hammered like a bongo, his mind jumping like a droplet of grease on a hot skillet.

Frank is big . . . Frank is too big . . . Nathan's voice superimposed his warning: "*He'll be on you so be ready for him.*"

"Where you at, God damn it?"

J.J. didn't trust himself to reply. He assumed a position like a weightlifter in a squat.

Frank's face appeared feet from him. J.J. had practiced the move in the bedroom mirror until he had to stop before he pulled a muscle or ruptured a ligament.

"*. . . right under the jaw . . . Don't think about it . . . Do it!*"

J.J.'s bent legs straightened like springs. The *puukko's* flat blade back allowed the user's thumb or hand along it to concentrate the force for the blow. When J.J. sprang up, Frank's eyes hadn't yet focused in the semi-dim light. He never noticed J.J. hunkering near his feet. He certainly never expected J.J. to be armed. J.J.'s hands, wrapped tight on the handle, flew upward as the blade plunged deep beneath Frank's jaw before Frank was aware of what was about to happen. J.J. was barely in time with the thrust. Frank's head snapped backwards when the glint of recognition appeared in his eyes, and he understood. *The muck rabbit had turned on him.*

Frank dropped backward onto the path, hands clawing at the thing biting him below the neck. A red geyser spouted from the hole. Frank slapped and pulled the knife free. He scrambled crab-like within the confined space, but his feet were unable to get purchase in the sticky, black mud. When he turned to regard J.J., surprise, horror, pain, and rage comingled in the look.

"Don't stand there admiring your work, neither!"

Nathan's warning snapped J.J., back into action. Had it not been for the cattails hindering Frank, J.J. could not have picked up the bat and raised it in time. J.J. whirled around, stepped between Frank's splayed legs for maximum impact, and as Nathan had commanded, brought the meat end of the bat down on Frank.

But he missed the top of Frank's head in the slick footing. The bat caromed off Frank's head and slammed down on his face, shattering the nose, blinding Frank. The bat end finished its torque over Frank's upper lip breaking teeth and nailing his upper lip to the jagged row of his bottom teeth. Frank went down on his rump in the black muck, too stunned to move. Blood and spittle mixed with fragments of tooth dribbled down Frank's chest.

J.J. swung again, his aim truer. "*Put him* hors de combat *once he's down* . . . Nathan borrowed a Zane Grey phrase J.J. recalled from one of the prairie novels.

J.J. flew out of his clearing, hit the back exit with bat and knife in hand just as a loud, crashing behind him announced Dale charging, bull-like, into the clearing.

The jolt of adrenalin in J.J.'s belly fought a seesaw battle with nausea as he ran, the thick mud acting like a boat anchor to his speed. He ran blind through the snapping fronds and stinging cobs, but he knew where to turn and head for the cyclone fence as though he had a GPS in his head. The whipping stalks that assisted made his progress a zigzag instead of the straight line he'd mentally prepared for.

Dale's bellowing in a maddened rage spurred on. Exhausted, he ran on, panting, knowing he was no match for Dale's long-legged stride. A gun added to his bat and knife might not have been weaponry enough. He kept running through the dark green maze until he detected a lighter swatch of lime ahead where the thickest of the cattails ended in wind-whipped hillocks of sand adjacent to the river's edge.

J.J. knew he still had a half mile to go yet before the fence. It wasn't much of a lead if the bigger boy left the clearing and spotted him.

"Pace your run, don't suck in air like a fish out of water, hands tight to the body..."

J.J.'s inner gyroscope zeroed on the fence. He had little time even if Dale stopped looking for him among the cattails. One thing in his favor was that Dale had to leave the same way he entered—through that hole beneath the fence.

He saw light glinting off the razor-tipped fence ahead and redoubled his effort. By this point, he was gasping for air, his arms and legs were lead. But, thank God, no terrifying Dale on his tracks.

J.J. had his spot picked out last night before dark fell when he went to fetch the bat under his bed—a last gift from his father before the divorce. A clump of thorn bushes lying thirty feet from the ditch where the hole was. A stunted forsythia bush with branches that swept the ground was better suited, but J.J. deemed it too thin to disguise him except in pitch-black dark. And he did not want to wait that long.

When Dale emerged into view, he was a fast-moving silhouette against the treeline. It wasn't yet full dark. His form trotted low to the ground and reminded J.J. of the childhood book that he refused to let his mother read to him again about goblins and their dark shapes, like the humped backs of red-eyed raccoons, which terrified his imagination. That was Dale—big, fast, moving in the darkness as though he'd wrapped it around him like an old-time villain in a cloak.

Dale zigzagged, hunting J.J.'s spoor. Something he scented on in the cold wind, like a wolf sniffing the air for prey. He moved in and out of J.J.'s vision across the rough terrain.

J.J. crouched, straining his eyes, but held his body to its long stillness. Before his mother's alcoholism ruined her marriage, she practiced power yoga. J.J. used some of her moves to keep his limbs from stiffening while he waited. Another molasses-slow tick-tock of time wedged past before J.J. picked him out again. Dale stepped in front of the forsythia bush.

Mere yards away, close—

Without hesitation, J.J. stood up and charged the form in the sandy trough of ground at the center of the cut in the fence. Dale twisted around at the sound of the attack, tried to yank his sweatshirt free of the snag.

A body blow wasn't as effective as the head shot J.J. needed to make. He put everything into the swing and brought the blunt end of the bat end down on Dale's spine. Dale's howl could be heard across the blackened landscape.

"Don't stand there admiring . . ."

J.J. brought the bat down again and again, harder each time, on the lower back of the bigger boy. He knew it wasn't going to be as easy as Richard or Frank, no matter how many times he hit him.

Dale reacted with instinct: he tucked his legs into his chest and rolled away in the dirt, his hoodie a rag left on the barbs of the fence. Knowing Dale would not flee, would charge him and try to kill him as soon as he recovered strength for the charge, J.J. sidestepped from his swinging position to get closer, not farther from his enemy, a tactical move suggested by Nathan. Now the full darkness was to J.J.'s advantage, not Dale's. Dale's guttural scream guided J.J.'s aim. He stepped into the swing like a batter in the box. The bat met Dale's temple in a satisfying shock that rippled from J.J.'s hands up his forearms.

Dale's legs buckled, he went down in a heap. J.J. stood over the body and hit him savagely, mercilessly, over and over. The bat struck muscle, bone, pulped flesh. J.J. prodded Dale's head and swung again until slushy sounds replaced thuds or cracking bone. Dale's last sound was a throaty, liquid gurgle like the red-winged blackbirds that made J.J. shiver.

He dropped the bat and fell down beside Dale's body, panting, just inches from Dale's destroyed head and face.

The night sky was spangled with stars. He breathed in and out, unable to move. He felt encased in a concrete crucifix. His mind left and came back several times before he felt the urge to rise. Night calls of animals flowed over him like those water molecules Mr. Dupree spoke of in science class. Once or twice, a larger animal approached and made snorting or sniffing noises—raccoon, skunk, or possum—he wasn't able to tell which. No light to magnify the phosphorescence of their eyes.

J.J. picked himself up in slow stages. Each one, a laborious exertion of muscles that screamed for relief. He trudged back to his cattail fort over the course of the long night fetching the rope for

Dale and the shovel to bury all three in one grave. He knew the place. Richard and Frank would keep while Dale had to be dragged back before dawn. Although it was illegal to let dogs run loose, hunters from the trailer park did it to sharpen their dogs' prowess. J.J. did not want to meet up with a pair of Labs or Rottweilers in his weakened condition, much less with a dead body he was dragging.

He tied a bowline around Dale's ankles and began hauling his cargo back. He had to stop and rest so many times that he was unsure he'd make it by first light.

The grave he dug was behind his fort and was, mercifully, less difficult than he anticipated. The soft muck yielded to his shovel easily. The trick was to keep the backflow from undoing his work. By the time he could make out the difference between the maple and the oak leaves from the nearby canopy of trees, he'd dug deep enough for all three. He didn't know if it was deep enough for coyotes, but it had to do. Time was fast running out.

Dale went in first. He rolled Frank on top of him and then little brother. Richard's eyes were half-lidded; black flies had already discovered the scent of decay and were trooping in and out of his nostrils and mouth, half-opened in that derisive sneer J.J. recalled.

He covered the grave and stomped it flat. Gathering his equipment into a pile, he covered everything with cattails until he could get all of it back home and wash it off. Most of Saturday was spent hauling items from the fort and avoiding people and cars, ducking behind trees, or crossing the street ahead of pedestrians to avoid being seen.

His sleeping bag held a rank odor of swamp that wouldn't come out, so he cut it up, stuffed it into a couple garbage bags. One went into the dumpster at school; the other went into the dumpster in the alleyway between the paperback store and the diner. No CCTVs to record him doing it in either place.

His *puukko* and shovel were disassembled, sawed into pieces like the bat and dumped into several sewer grates a dozen blocks from the trailer park. By the end of Wednesday, J.J. had destroyed or thrown away all evidence. In weeks, as the weather turned harsh and the icy winds blew down from Canada, his fort would be flattened and demolished.

One week after killing and burying three boys, J.J. heard the rumors of the missing youths at the trailer park and in school. Two detectives went to school to interview students who knew the boys. Because J.J. lived in the same park and shared classes with Richard, his interview lasted longer than most. He answered every question, didn't offer information, and when they asked him if he knew where he thought the boys were, he said he had no idea.

"You were one of the kids picked on most," said the male cop.

"Yes."

The interview took place in the back of the cafeteria. Food smells lingered after lunch hour and were exaggerated by the boiling steam of dishes being cleaned. The hissing sound of the hoses was audible to where he and the big cop shifted uncomfortably in the fold-up, bingo chairs.

"That Richard," the male cop said; "he had classes with you, right? Did you two ever talk, get together, do anything?"

"No."

The lady cop, with her blonde ponytail was pretty, so J.J. avoided staring at her. She spoke for the first time: "When Richard and his brother shoved that bagworm—is that what it's called? — over your head—"

"Not over my head," J.J. corrected. "Into my face."

"Yes, well, didn't that make you mad?"

"Yes."

"Didn't it make you want to do something—get revenge?"

"I was happy when they decided to leave me alone after that."

He thought of the boy in math class who had shunned him for fear of drawing the rabid dogs to him.

"Uh-huh."

The male cop stretched his legs out and groaned. "Man, I forgot how awful these chairs are on my poor fat ass."

He winked at J.J., hoping the profanity might warm him up a little.

"Did Dale ever hit you?"

"He gave me rabbit punches in school."

"Rabbit punches. Well, if you think of anything else, you can call us at this number."

He handed J.J. a business card. "If you think of anyone who might have wanted to get even with them, let us know. I hear they were all bad apples."

J.J. said nothing. Neither cop seemed in a hurry to get up. Finally, the lady cop stood up, brushed her skirt of invisible crumbs, and said to her colleague, "Let's go."

J.J. knew from the start she had the power. Her eyes reminded him of a tercel's from the cattails. She had the same tea-colored eyes. He watched it sit on a small blackbird while blackbirds set up a din and fluttered all around it to get it away. It barely moved other than to shift its talons deeper into its pinned victim.

A week later, the Michigan state police announced a nationwide search for the missing boys. The chamber of commerce offered a $5,000 reward for information. Dale's father appeared on the local station appealing to the public for help. He looked like Dale, only gone to seed. The homeless man downtown who slept rough had the same beaten look in his eyes. He didn't look like the killer biker J.J. was told about.

J.J. avoided going down to the river. Cops had searched the area, but the papers didn't say what they found, if anything.

J.J.'s grades improved; he put on weight. He told his mother he was going out for soccer in the spring semester.

Randy still hectored him, called him filthy names. J.J. ordered a new poster of *Shane* from an online store. He was taping it on his wall when Randy stopped by, lingering and watching from the doorway. His mother was in the kitchen doing dishes.

After supper, his mother came into his bedroom to find him reading another Zane Grey novel, *The Man of the Forest.*

"What the hell did you say to Randy?"

"When?"

"I don't know, when you were taping that cowboy poster up."

"Why?"

"He came into the kitchen and didn't say a word."

"So what?"

"That's not like him. His face was white as a sheet. What did you say to him?"

"I don't remember."

She muttered something and left. He listened to her footfalls down the hallway, knew exactly where she was by the creak of certain floorboards.

"You don't want to know, Mom," J.J. whispered and resumed his reading.

The stand-up mirror in the corner was tilted. J.J. could see himself on the bed. He looked at his reflection, saw a boy who resembled someone else and winked at him.

Just Deserts

Roberta Eaton Cheadle

If walls could talk and tell the world what they saw, humans would behave with more transparency, and crime and corruption would disappear.

We, the walls of the Castle of Good Hope, surveyed him day and night while he lived here. We knew he was a diabolical man. The cruellest and most inhuman despot to have ever governed the beautiful Cape Colony.

His physical body was the canvas that depicted his life of deceit and debauchery. We watched him committing some of the sins and dark deeds that etched heavy lines across his forehead and distorted his once sensuously thick-lipped mouth. Under our all-seeing gaze, he indulged in excessive alcohol, adding to the fine, spider webs of red that crisscrossed his bulbous nose and sagging cheeks. He indulged in the best foods, rich and decadent, and we observed how they thickened and bloated his once lithe body.

He died unexpectedly, his transgressions unrepented. To this day, the late Governor's hideous reflection acts as a reminder of his previous wrongdoings. Fortunately for him, there are no mirrors in his dark, tomb-like residence, only puddles of black water that occasionally catch the light.

We see him every day, wandering in mindless circles in the thick darkness of the prison known as the 'Donker Gat' or 'Dark Hole', wringing his hands, and moaning about his lost ledger. Our numerous eyes recoil at his grotesqueness, and we wonder how we do not crack.

There are several other ghosts who wander the passages and rooms of this castle. They are mostly fools who turned their backs on Heaven's white light for misguided reasons and are now trapped in the Netherworld. He is different though. He is the devil's plaything.

We know his private record of ill-gotten gains is nowhere in the 'Donker Gat'. It's stowed in the small alcove he had installed behind the painting of Governor van der Stel in his old office in this very castle. We watched him putting it there. It's still there, we can feel it pulsing like an evil heart from within our stonework.

That secret died when old Janie Abrahams, the installer, met his unfortunate end. No-one knows about the Governor's hidey hole except us, the all-seeing, all-knowing walls of the Castle of Good Hope. We know everything.

Despite Lucifer's cajoling the Governor into spending eternity pursuing an impossible challenge while entrapped in the damp, windowless black of the 'Donker Gat', we have no pity for him. We know too much about his previous thieving and devious ways. During his short two-year reign as governor, numerous soldiers were incarcerated in this same prison on trumped up charges, to await bogus trails and unfair sentencing. In the extremity of their suffering and anguish, these soldiers talked to each other, or even themselves, about how he embezzled their wages, and arrested them if they attempted to confront him.

In his office, we witnessed the heartless refusal of licenses to trade, withholding renewals of leases, and prevention of trading and elephant-hunting expeditions. These activities and decisions kept the soldiers and general population of the Cape impoverished, while enabling Governor van Noodt to expand his already overflowing coffers.

It was the group hanging that made the Governor famous and signed his death warrant.

There were fourteen soldiers involved in the attempted desertion. Thirteen of them spent time awaiting trial in the 'Donker Gat'. The pathetic Judas who betrayed them to the authorities was spared. He had to live with his conscious – just like the original Judas.

We remember these men well.

"How could he?" The soldier ran his hand through his long, greasy hair. The man's fingers were skeletal, and his face hollow cheeked and drawn. For months, he and his large family had been living on a pittance due to the Governor's theft of the soldiers' wages. They were gradually starving. "How could Adriaan betray us?"

"Fear, Gert," said another man, his pale face a white blur in the inky blackness. "He's just as hungry and desperate as we are. It could only have been fear for his miserable family that guided his decision."

"I hope he rots in hell," Gert muttered hoarsely.

"You mustn't think like that, Gert," said another soldier. "Jesus wants us to forgive those who trespass against us." His large hand clutched the cross hanging from a chain around his neck, seeking reassurance from the moulded metal.

"The Governor wants to hang us all, Hendrik." The speaker, a pale, slender man called Sebastiaan, coughed and hawked.

We felt wet mucus splatter across us.

"Death be upon them. I will take it on me! That's what the Governor said when he heard our plans," Sebastiaan continued, his voice thick and phlegmy. He was sick. Very sick.

"It is in God's hands." The man called Hendrik had a pleasant voice, calm and soothing. "You must believe he knows what's best for you."

SSSSQQQQEEEEAAAAKKKKK!

A key grated in the stiff lock. The heavy wooden door swung open, spilling light into the damp stone cell. Its occupants were temporarily blinded and squinted like new-born rats.

"Food and water," the guard said, setting a plate of course brown bread and a large pitcher of water down, careful not to spill a drop of the precious fluid.

Shoulders slumped, the guard named Renier, turned away. He did not look at any of his previous colleagues. The key turned, the lock's tumblers squealing.

Hendrik shared out the miserable rations and they ate. The pitcher was passed from hand to hand, and each man took a few sips.

Soft scuttling sounds filled the darkness. Several pairs of eyes shone brightly in the miniscule light that crept under the door. Rats!

A soldier kicked out at a pair of eyes. His worn boot connected with the soft furry body, sending is rolling across the floor. It thumped against us in a boneless heap.

The sliver of light under the door turned from white, to grey, to black. The men attempted to find a sufficiently tolerable position on the hardpacked dirt floor for sleep to overtake them. Two leaned heavily against us, their stringy hair absorbing our cold dampness.

Snorts and snores rumbled around the confined space, punctuated by muted plops as drips of water expanded the puddles on the floor. Rats scampered over the prostrate bodies, bold and unchecked, foraging for anything edible.

Sebastiaan coughed. Propped up against us, we felt the warmth of the fever consuming him and heard the chattering of his teeth.

It was midnight when he struck a match and laboriously wrote a message across us. His own blood served as ink which we considered ill-advised in his weakened state. Thirty minutes later, he settled against us and went to sleep. Towards morning, he heaved a sigh. His teeth stopped chattering and his back, resting against us, grew cold. Colder and colder he became, until he was like ice.

Bright morning light eventually crept beneath the stout door. It moved stealthily across the floor and inched up our length, until it finally bathed Sebastiaan's dead face in a golden glow. This was the sight that met the freshly opened eyes of the remaining twelve soldiers.

The sliver of light continued its rotation across the wall and the men saw the message: Do not bargain with the Devil.

"Holy God," Gert exclaimed in horror. "What sort of message is that? What does it mean?"

RATTLE! CREAK!

The great door swung open.

"It's time for your trial, friends," Wilhelm, the Captain of the Guards, announced in a deep, guttural voice. "My God be with you all."

The prisoners marched the short distance to the Governor's Residence and lined up in front of the Kat Balcony. The balcony that served the dual purpose of being the entrance to the building and a convenient platform from which announcements and judicial sentences were read to the inhabitants of the Castle. It was beautiful with its fluted pillars, wrought-iron railings, and curved staircases, but the sentences that were handed down to the twelve prisoners from behind its decorative railing, were harsh and unyielding.

Having witnessed the proceedings inside the Governor's Residence, we already knew the outcome. Eight men were sentence to corporal punishment and imprisonment, but the four ringleaders were sentenced to hang by the neck until they died.

Morosely, we observed the condemned men and a contingent of guards quick marching across the open courtyard and out of the main gates. They soon disappeared from our sight down the dusty road.

Shortly afterwards, the Governor also left the Castle, heading for his Summer House in the vast gardens established in 1652 by the first governor of the Cape Colony, Jan van Riebeeck.

It was only much later that day, after the guards had returned, mute with shock and horror, that we learned what happened.

The guards sat on the hard wooden benches; their flagons of ale untouched in front of them. Silence reigned, intensified by the flickering light of the lamps that created patterns of golden light and dark shadows upon us, the rocky walls. We had never witnessed a scene like it since we were laid in 1679.

Finally, a voice disrupted the stillness.

"I've never heard of anything like it," said Wilhelm. Grasping the handle of his flagon, he downed a great gulp of beer. "The Governor found dead from a massive heart attack on the same day four executions are carried out under his orders."

A faint murmur of agreement ran around the room.

"I heard he was already stiff and cold when they found him," said Johannes, his fingers trembled slightly as he lifted the cup to his lips, drinking deeply. "Sarel, the undertaker's assistant, said his arms were stretched out across the table, the hands stiff-fingered and curled into grotesque cups, as if he was begging for supplication." A shudder wrenched its way up his spine.

"I heard his face was grey like clay, and twisted into an expression of utter terror," added Dawie.

These few words acted like a floodgate and the stoicism of the guards deserted them. They all started to speak together, sharing what they'd seen and heard.

"It serves him right," said Wilhelm. "I hope he's burning in the fires of hell."

"He will be," said Dawie. "He specifically took responsibility for the deaths of our friends. Twice he said "Death be upon them. I will take it on me". I heard him say it. His death is divine justice."

"I was also in the room when the Governor passed judgement and uttered those words. He wanted to hang them all. It was only the protests and requests for leniency by the Members of the Council that spared the lives of eight of our friends."

"He didn't give in easily, Wilhelm," said Dawie. The debate was long and heated before the Governor capitulated. He agreed to lessor sentences for the eight who were spared, but insisted on the death sentence by hanging for the four ringleaders."

"It is incredible that the Governor died on the same day as the hangings," Johannes said, "Especially since he took personal responsibility for the men's death. I don't believe in divine justice; life doesn't work like that. It's just a lucky coincidence; lucky for us as we are now free of the Governor's tyranny."

"Oh, but it wasn't just a lucky coincidence, Johannes," said Wilhelm, a smile of smug satisfaction on his face. He liked being one up on his colleagues.

Wilhelm was slow to share what he knew about the Governor's death. If we'd had feet, we would have kicked him. Instead, we waited impatiently while Wilhelm called for more ale and the serving girl, Nina, topped everyone up.

We knew that the Governor was dead, that much was clear, but we didn't understand how it connected with the hanging of the four soldiers. The guards' fearful reaction to the news of his death seemed excessive. After all, this was not the first time they'd witnessed colleagues hanging by the neck on the orders of the dead tyrant.

"Come on, Wilhelm," said Dawie, after Nina left the room. "Why do you say the death of the Governor wasn't just a coincidence?"

Wilhelm was a good storyteller with a flair for the dramatic.

"I marched with the four condemned men to the gallows at Justitie Plaats. The Governor elected not to accompany us and watch the sentences being carried out. He preferred to stay at his Summer House and continue working."

"It just shows you how insignificance the deaths of our friends were to him," muttered Renier darkly. It was the first time the heavy-set man had spoken since the death of his good friend, Gert, earlier that day.

"At Justitie Plaats citizens had gathered to watch the executions. They were not happy. Undercurrents of anger at this injustice rippled through the crowd.

"Our friends were hung, one by one. Hendrick was last, stepping up to the rope after watching his three dead friends being cut down. As you know, Hendrick was a theology student, and many people believed he walked in the presence of God.

""Governor Van Noodt," he shouted, before stepping off the platform, the rope about his neck, "I challenge you at this very moment, before the judgement of the Almighty God, to answer for my soul and those of my friends!

"Hendrick's neck did not break when he fell, and he dangled from the end of the rope like a rat on a string."

Wilhelm stopped speaking and took a swig of his ale.

"Come on, Wilhelm," Dawid said. "What happened next?"

"As I watched, the shadow of the gallows on the flagstones trembled and changed, forming into a wicked face topped by horns. The mouth of the Shadow Devil moved. It was speaking, but I heard no sound except the whispering of the leaves on the tree.

"The dangling man at the end of the rope reacted. He gathered the last of his strength and the words "I agree," seeped from between his dark blue lips. He shuddered, spittle oozing from the corners of his mouth, and he died.

"God answered Hendrick's final request," Dawid said, his voice filled with reverence. "The Governor's death must have happened just after. It is divine retribution!"

CCCCRRREEEEAAAAAKKKKKK!

Several of the men visibly jumped.

The heavy wooden door opened, admitting a gust of wind that swirled around the room, making the flames dance inside the glass bowls of the lamps. The shadowy patterns decorating us contorted into a twisted, horned devil, jumping and cavorting. We could feel malevolence leeching into our stonework.

The Shadow Devil held out its elongated arms and slowly unfurled its long, claw-tipped hands. Diminutive shadows burst out of the blackness of its palms. They grew, rippling and swirling until they took on familiar forms.

A sign of fear rippled through the room.

Wilhelm and Jacob crossed themselves as they recognised the silhouettes of their dead friends: Sebastiaan, willowy and tall, Hendrik and Tobie, their clerical collars stiff around their necks, Gert, large and roughly hewn like a log, and Pieter, older and slightly bent.

The Shadow Devil danced, twisting, and turning in bizarre celebration, the hand adorned with the silhouettes held out before him. The tiny shapes huddled together, shaking and shuddering, their mouths opening and closing in silent screams of anguish.

The Shadow Devil stopped its wild gyrations. Pulling its dark length up, it stood straight, and over seven feet tall.

"Divine justice you say." Its shadowy mouth opened, and the words burst forth from within its black contours. "There is no divine justice in this world or the next. The need for justice is self-serving and not an act of forgiveness. All justice is thus my justice. Your friend, Hendrik, sought justice. Wanted it enough to make a bargain with me, not only for himself, but for his deceased friends. His desire penetrated the Waiting Room, the place inhabited by the souls of sinners who are making reparations for their sins before going to Heaven and sucked their spirits back from beyond the veil. Now, their souls are beyond redemption, and they will reside in one of my nine circles of hell."

SSSSWWWOOOSHHHH!!!!

The wind roared through the room. It gusted fiercely over the outstretched hand of Lucifer, sweeping the shadowy figures away and swirling them across the room. They hovered above the oil lantern on the table in front of Wilhelm.

Its flame split, the two sides opening like the parting of the Red Sea. The wind, hopped, depositing the shadowy remnants of the five men into the gap. The flame closed over them. The guards watched, mesmerized, as the dark shapes writhed in agony as the flame consumed them.

"Hahaha!" shrieked the Shadow Devil. "What tremendous fun. And that's not all, dear friends. I have another treat in store for you."

Opening his great maw, he exhaled, blowing out a plume of white steam. The steam ran like wax, forming itself into the bloated figure of Governor van Noodt.

"Hello, Governor," said the devil, his mouth forming into the outline of a toothy grin. "I have a wonderful deal for you, Governor," he continued. "Would you like to hear it?"

The steamy Governor nodded his head.

"I'm offering you a challenge, Governor. I've hidden your ledger, the one that reveals all your secrets. If you can find the ledger and ensure its contents are revealed to the world, I will grant you passage to the Waiting Room, where you can work your way towards eternal salvation. Does that sound good, Governor?"

Again, the nod.

"There's one small catch, Governor. You will not be able to move further than five metres from the place called the 'Donker Gat' until you find the ledger. Do you agree to this condition?"

Unhesitatingly, the head bobbed up and down.

WWWWHHHHOOOOOSSSSSHHHH!!!

Again, the wind blasted around the room. It swept up the steam, and the Shadow Devil. Within moments both were gone.

Pieter van Noodt was succeeded by Jan de la Fontaine as governor of the Cape Colony. The soldiers' lives improved under the leadership of this fairer man who paid them their wages. They never saw their friends, the Shadow Devil, or the late Governor again.

We see the soul of Governor van Noodt. He has lingered in the 'Donker Gat, for decades. We do not know if the Governor's spirit knows it was tricked. The devil, darkly humorous, tied his soul to the 'Donker Gat', leaving the ledger hidden in the unknown safe in the governor's office, far from his ghostly reach. We agree that Governor Van Noodt never gave much thought to serious decisions, so this outcome was inevitable.

The Shadow Devil occasionally visits. Appearing as a dark silhouette upon us, the walls. He finds it hugely amusing that the only man who knew about the secret alcove, the man who installed it, died at the hand of the Governor who wanted his secret kept at all costs. If the contents of the ledger are ever exposed to the world, Governor Van Noodt will be able to atone.

To this day, its whereabouts has not been discovered, and the Governor's soul remains the property of Lucifer.

We see, we know; if the humans could only hear us talk, so could they.

The Snow Globe

Chris Barili

The cold December drizzle glazed the grave markers and made the soft earth smell musty and dank. Iron clouds formed a coffin-lid on the world that trapped everything inside, even the pallid daylight trying to slip away for the night.

Larry walked among the mounds. His steps were long and heavy, and though he tried to go gingerly, he often left deep prints in the rain-softened soil. He always worried he'd step on one of the mounds and leave a footprint on the dead. So, he placed his feet carefully, very carefully, as he made his rounds.

The rain whispered against his poncho as he bent his massive frame to pick up a plastic cup that had blown to rest against a headstone. His thick fingers pinched the lip of the cup as if it was toxic and he dropped it silently into a black trash bag in his other hand.

Larry didn't like the rain. It was two days before Christmas, and it should have been snowing. Christmas needed snow to have its magic, and the rain made it seem more like Halloween instead. Especially in the graveyard.

The sound of voices made him pause and glance around. A few yards to his right, two young women knelt beside a grave under a majestic spruce tree. The tree's branches shielded them from the rain, reaching down to embrace them through the gloom. Larry remembered them. They'd buried their mother a week earlier. She couldn't have been that old. Her daughters looked like they were just out of high school. He remembered them weeping—gentle sobs that had floated to him on the afternoon breeze.

He moved closer, plucking a discarded candy wrapper from a bouquet of flowers. As he walked, the women's voices became clearer. They didn't notice him. Despite his size and the orange cap that marked him as caretaker, no one ever seemed to notice Larry at the graveyard. They all had other things on their minds.

"She so loved this tree," one of the women said. "I'm glad she's near it now."

"I wish it were snowing," the other said with a nod. "She said this looked like a giant Christmas tree in the snow."

The first girl pulled something from her pocket and set it on the mound of earth. Larry tried to see what it was, but their backs blocked his view.

He walked toward the tree, stealing glances at the girls as he did.

"This was her favorite," the first was saying. She patted the object she'd set on the ground. Larry still couldn't see it. "When I was a girl, she told me this was the most beautiful thing in the world."

The second nodded with a sniffle. "Now, she can look at it whenever she wants."

Larry stopped on the other side of the tree and squatted to pick up a piece of paper. He couldn't see the women anymore, but he heard rustling and knew they were standing up. An umbrella popped open. Both girls sobbed goodbyes, then walked away.

Larry stayed behind the tree, hidden, until he heard a car drive off. Then he moved slowly, careful not to step on a nearby grave, to the other side.

The women had tied a pink ribbon to their mother's grave marker, and it billowed in the slight breeze, but that wasn't what he was looking for. There, nestled at the base of the headstone, was a glass ball on a shiny silver base. It gleamed in the drizzle as he knelt beside the grave, dropping the trash bag at his side. Inside the globe, tiny figures of a man and a woman skated on make-believe ice. Pellets of artificial snow settled around them.

It was indeed the most beautiful thing in the world. Snow for Christmas. So much prettier than the rain.

Larry picked up the snow globe. He shook it, watching again as the fat flakes fell around the skaters. He smiled, remembering when he'd skated in a scene just like it. Snowflakes had glistened in his daughter's hair then, and her giggles had been like Christmas bells in his ears. It was the most beautiful memory he had.

He started to set the globe down, then paused.

His treasure room. The globe would be perfect in his treasure room, where things sparkled and shone all the time. It was wasted here. The dead had no use for snow globes. No use at all.

The wind whipped suddenly, and Larry jumped to his feet. He glanced around, but the graveyard was empty. He stuffed the globe in his pocket and turned away.

The next day, Larry was back at work. It was Christmas Eve, and the drizzle hadn't stopped. The sky was the same leaden gray it had been the day before. The wind, if anything, was stiffer, whipping the plastic trash bag against his leg.

Many people came to the cemetery to visit loved ones before the holiday. Larry worked silently, watching them all. He wanted the place to look as nice as possible for them, especially today. But he hoped the two young women wouldn't come. He didn't want them to notice the snow globe was missing. They might have seen him from a distance. They'd know who took it.

They didn't come, and finally, with the grim daylight waning, Larry headed toward the caretaker's shed. The rain ran off his poncho—it was coming down heavier than it had the day before—and made the chill temperature eat through his layered clothes underneath.

He shivered as he neared the woman's grave, just out of the shadow of the spruce tree. He felt like someone was watching him. He glanced around, but the graveyard was empty.

He stopped and looked at the woman's grave, half expecting to see a decayed hand reaching for him. The grave was still, but for the waving of the ribbon.

The wind kicked up again, driving the rain against his face. He didn't want his prints leading away from the grave, so he tried to step even more softly than usual.

Again, he stopped. Someone was watching him. He could feel it. He scanned the cemetery, but saw no one. This time, the wind howled and threatened to tear the trash bag from his hand. He thought for just a moment there was a voice in the wind, carried from far away. No, not just a voice—a cry, filled with agony and sorrow.

Larry shook himself and started walking again.

This time, though, his pace was quicker, his steps not as cautious. He wanted to reach the shed. To go home.

A gust of wind buffeted him, and he staggered sideways. His foot squished into the soft side of a grave mound. Larry gasped and jumped away. He stared at his footprint in the grassy side of the mound and heard again the wailing on the wind.

Larry ran. He paid no mind to his footprints now, though he still placed his steps to avoid the mounds when he could. The rain whipped at his face and the wind fought him, howling.

When he reached the shed, he practically threw the trash bag inside, slammed the door, and clasped the padlock. He sprinted from the shed through the gate in the cemetery's stonewall. His keys were in his hand before he knew he had reached for them. Again, the wind screamed at him, flapping his poncho like it was alive.

When he reached his tiny car, Larry's heart was pounding in his chest. He yanked open the door, folded himself into the front seat, and slammed it closed.

Silence. The wind railed at the metal and glass, but it couldn't reach him here. He was safe.

He thought briefly of the snow globe. It had fit perfectly in the treasure room. He'd found the perfect spot for it, in plain sight, lit by the pale-yellow beam from a reading light. It was on a pedestal. A treasure among treasures.

The rain worsened as he drove home, coming down in sheets that curtained his windshield. He almost lost control on one turn, narrowly missing a light pole.

The wind rocked the little car as he drove, and he wished he'd been able to afford a big SUV instead of his sardine can on wheels.

Rain clouded his windshield again, and when the wipers cleared it, a body was careening toward him. Larry slammed on the brakes and swerved to the right. The body streaked past on his left, no more than a blur. He stopped just inches from the guardrail. When he looked back, there was no sign of the body. He rubbed his eyes, but still saw nothing. Taking a deep breath, he forced himself to drive again. It must have been his imagination.

He focused on the road, but the body reappeared. It was a woman, with long hair streaming behind her in the wind. She floated above the road a hundred feet or so ahead of him. This time, Larry hit the gas instead of the brakes. The woman flew at him, her face twisted and grotesque, her mouth open wide in a howl. As she hit his windshield, her scream pierced his ears for a heartbeat.

Then she was gone. And his windshield was intact, not even a crack or a scratch where it should have been shattered.

Larry was shaking now, having trouble controlling the car. He slowed down, keeping his eyes open for the woman. He knew *what* she was—that much was clear. He had an idea *who* she was. And what she wanted.

Yet that knowledge made him quake even harder.

He made it home without seeing her again, but as he climbed the slick, stone steps to the front door of his apartment building, the wind wailed at him. He froze. Glanced around. A woman—a normal one this time—passed on the street, giving him a strange stare. Other than that, he was alone.

Shaking his head, Larry went inside.

He was in the hallway, unlocking the door to his apartment, when he heard it again. The wind carried the sounds of wailing to his ears. This time it made the hair on his neck stand up.

Larry turned toward the sound, back toward the stairs that led to the first floor. The woman floated there, her mouth still open in mid-scream, her form misty and transparent. A gash in her head spilled smoke-like blood across her face, and with one mangled hand, she pointed at Larry.

He worked the lock frantically, but it was jammed. When he looked at the ghost again, she was flying toward him. The deadbolt finally clicked open just before she reached him.

Larry dashed inside and slammed the door. He leaned his head against the wood, panting.

Behind him, someone gasped.

He whirled and saw his next-door neighbor, Mrs. Martinez, standing by the couch. Her rumpled blouse and flattened gray hair said she'd been sleeping. She grabbed her glasses from the table and put them on.

"Oh, Larry," she said, her hand over her heart, "you startled me."

If Mrs. Martinez hadn't seen the ghost, Larry wasn't about to mention it. Instead, he apologized for startling her. The last thing he needed was someone thinking he was losing his mind.

"She's asleep," Mrs. Martinez said, pointing at a door on the back wall of the apartment. She took her purse from the coffee table and headed toward him. "Woke up once today but went right back to sleep. I checked her vitals thirty minutes ago. They were stable."

Larry stepped out of her way, then cringed as she opened the door. He expected the ghost to be waiting there, ready to fly into the room.

The hallway was empty. He breathed a sigh of relief. When Mrs. Martinez closed the door behind her, Larry stood in silence, staring at it for a full minute. He didn't hear the wailing wind. He didn't see anything unusual.

He scolded himself for letting his imagination run away with him. He went to the door and rested his hand on the knob. If it was all in his mind, why did his stomach twist in knots just thinking about opening the door? With a sigh, he turned the knob, slowly at first. Then, as his courage rose, he jerked the door open.

The wailing hit him like a gale-force wind, making him sway. The ghost flew at him again, and Larry staggered backward into his apartment. He tripped over a coffee table and landed on his back, staring at the ceiling.

The ghost swirled around the room like a banshee, moaning. Books flew off shelves, plates shattered on the floor. Pictures fell from their nails and papers formed cyclones in the air wherever she passed. Around the room she flew, screaming as she went.

Larry jumped to his feet. His knees felt like jelly, and he wanted to throw up, but he had to do something.

The ghost saw him and shot straight at him. He dived to one side, but not fast enough. Where she brushed against his shoulder, his flesh went cold and lost feeling. When she passed, so did the sensation, but it was enough to terrify him even more. Screaming, Larry ran for the treasure room. He had to give her what she wanted. That would make her go away.

He fumbled with the knob, his hands shaking. Finally, he yanked the door open, slipped inside, and jerked it closed before the ghost could follow.

His back against the door, Larry took a deep breath and looked around. The room was just as he'd left it. Dimly lit by a reading light in one corner, the treasures around the room were hard to see, but he knew each one by heart. The painting on one wall. The skates hung on a peg. The shelves lined with porcelain dolls and stuffed animals and figurines. All this and more he had gathered here for one reason. The same reason he'd taken the snow globe.

He looked where the beam of the reading light fell on a small end table. The snow globe wasn't where he'd left it, but he knew where it was.

There, in one corner, was the bed. His daughter's form was still and silent. Even from the door he could see how pale and thin she was. Her skin had shone like snow once, back when they would skate on the ice at the park. And her laughter had been enough to lift his spirits on the worst of days. She never laughed now and rarely smiled. Her cheeks were sunken, and her hair nearly gone.

"Tesora." He said her name, though he knew she would not respond. "Tess."

Beside her bed, an IV rack stood, dripping pain medication through a tube. Mrs. Martinez had done her job and kept it flowing. It was all they could do to ease her pain.

Larry stepped closer to the bed. Tess's frame looked frail beneath the sheets. At one spot, a round bulge stood out. She clutched the object protectively against her with both hands around its base.

The snow globe.

Larry knelt by her side. Gently, he eased the sheet off the globe, then stopped. He looked at his daughter's face. One corner of her mouth was curled up in a smile, the first one he'd seen in months. At least the snow globe had given her that.

Behind him, the door rattled, then shook violently.

He reached for the globe, but the door burst open before he could take it, and the ghost shot through the opening. She darted around, sweeping across all the treasures. The picture tilted on the wall. A porcelain doll fell and shattered. And the skates dropped to the carpet at the foot of the bed.

Through it all, Tesora, his treasure, never stirred.

Larry cowered beside the bed, covering his daughter's eyes with one forearm. He feared what might happen if she saw the ghost, feared that it might hasten her departure. She had so little time already.

The ghost flew straight at him, her eyes filled with anger and hatred, her mouth still open, wailing. He squeezed his eyes closed, ready for his heart to stop for good, and said a silent prayer for his daughter. If he was going to die, he wanted her to live on.

Nothing happened.

Slowly, Larry opened his eyes. The ghost hovered, inches from his face. Waves of cold slithered across his skin, like air tumbling from an open freezer, but the ghost didn't move. She just floated, staring.

Staring at Tess.

Larry stood and studied the ghost's face. Her mouth still stretched wide, but the anger and hate were gone from her eyes. Her expression was almost placid as she gazed upon his most valuable treasure.

One ethereal hand stretched out toward the snow globe, but stopped just short, as if the ghost knew that touching his daughter would take her from the world too soon.

The ghost turned to him then, and he noticed something on her cheek. Just under one eye, where the blood had not stained, a tear shimmered.

The ghost watched him for a moment longer, then floated away. Larry watched as she dissolved from sight before reaching the door.

Larry knelt beside the mound of freshly packed earth. The cold soaked through the knees of his jeans and into his bones, and his tears froze on his cheeks. Overhead, the sky was the color of smoke except for a white patch where the sun burned behind the clouds.

She'd fought hard, but in the end her sickness had been too much. Larry had buried many of the treasures with her: the skates, a favorite book, a porcelain doll. The grave marker had a simple inscription: "My Treasure." It needed no more, not even her name.

One item he hadn't sent with her, though. The snow globe had given her joy while she lived, but now it was time to return it to its owner.

Larry kissed his fingertips, touched them to the marker, and rose. To his left, the spruce tree's boughs nearly touched the ground, but hung still in the cold winter air.

He walked to the grave of the woman, intentionally diverting his eyes from the gravestone. He didn't want to know her name.

Her daughters had been there earlier—he'd watched them while he raked the other side of the grounds. They'd left only a few minutes ago, and had placed a bouquet of flowers on their mother's grave.

He knelt again and gingerly placed the snow globe in its original position. The daughters would probably figure it out the next time they visited, but that didn't matter. Larry had given his two weeks' notice, and this was his last day. By the time they figured out he'd taken the snow globe, he'd be long gone.

"Thank you," he whispered. "It made her smile."

He rose, fresh tears turning to ice on his cheeks. As he turned to leave the cemetery, the snow began to fall.

The Whistling

Paul Kane

Hello there.

It's Dodge once again. Dodgson, if you want the full name. Painter and decorator by trade, but part-time chronicler of the adventures of my good friend Tom (if I don't do it, he'll never bother himself). And by Tom, I mean Thomas... Thomas Carnacki.

Maybe you've heard of him, but chances are, unless you've had a run-in with something otherworldly, you might not. Count yourself lucky, if half of what he tells us at our get-togethers are anything to go by. Oh, these are just my notes, transcriptions and what have you from those occasions – whenever he calls us all together for a lock-in at my mate Lumley's pub, *The Crow*.

We all knew each other back in the day, y'see? College days that is. None of us realised what old Tom had been up to since we last saw him though, not till he returned and we began attending these 'soirées'. Me, Hartley, Bierce, Chambers, Dee Nesbit and Lizzy Asquith. All pretty normal folk, or we were until Tom came waltzing back into our lives with his stories. Tales of his own trade, which is quite a bit more exciting than emulsioning a wall, I can tell you. Very generous with his time, is Tom, given he's such a busy guy – but I think he also gets a lot out of the meet-ups.

You catch me as I'm getting down the latest of his exploits, not that anyone will be hearing or reading about these until Tom's too old to care, or he doesn't make it back from a gig. Let's hope it's the former, even if it means I'm an old fart, too. I've grown quite fond of him again, I have to admit, same as I did before when I was younger. And the world's a much safer place with him in it, trust me. He's one of those folk holding the darkness at bay, who finds the ghosts and lays them to rest... usually.

It's more than *he* does, rest that is. In fact, he's been looking quite knackered lately whenever we've seen him, a consequence of taking on several jobs at once. This last time he was in the middle of two, a few hours away from each other. On the west coast, both within sight of Ireland – somewhere he was very familiar with due to his experiences at Laurel House.

"I'm only going to tell you about one of them in detail tonight, however," he explained after we'd eaten (*The Crow* does a rather nice Shepherd's Pie, it has to be said) and were settled down with our drinks, doors firmly bolted and lights turned down low; whether that was for atmosphere, or so the police didn't cotton on to Lumley's lock-ins, you'd have to ask him. "The problem a certain Mr. Sam Tassoc was having with a house he'd bought, and was renovating with an aim to moving in there with his wife to be, a Miss Hailey Donnehue..."

"Lucky so and so," muttered Lizzy at this point, who was probably wishing that was her and Tom judging from the glances. She's got a bit of a thing for him, which she hides well – not. The others rolled their eyes, but Tom simply offered a weary smile. That's the best way I can think of describing him in general actually: weary.

"It was going cheap," our friend carried on, "but nevertheless cost Tassoc all of his savings just to put down a deposit and for the mortgage on the place."

"Usually a sign of trouble that," broke in Bierce, ever the estate agent.

"What is?" asked Dee, who was more familiar with doing up cars than houses.

"Something going cheap, usually things wrong with a building, if that's the case."

"Birds nesting in the roof probably," joked Chambers with a wink. Thinks he's funny does Chambers.

"You should go on stage with that act," I told him, sarcastically.

Tom gave a small laugh himself. "Well, I can't argue with you there. About the problems, not going on stage. Although..." He paused briefly, and for a moment I thought he might nod off, then he continued with the narration. "But no, the main reason Tassoc purchased it was because of the location. His fiancée comes from that area, he met her when he was on a stag do at the coast, apparently."

"Are we talking a *Hangover* type situation here?" Hartley asked, film fan that he is.

"Is that even relevant?" Lizzy said with a huff.

"Depends on what happened on the do," he replied, shrugging. "Look at the shenanigans they got up to."

"He didn't say," Tom offered, again quite wearily, I thought. "I gather there was some bad feeling in the neighbourhood about someone who wasn't local dating Miss Donnehue, but we'll come to that. I do know he loves Hailey very much and just wants to make her happy. In fact, he wishes to surprise her with it when it's all finished and looking nice – so she's staying away until then."

Lizzy clutched her hands to her chest at that and said, "Aww." Chambers poked his finger into his throat, making gagging sounds until she hit him on the arm.

Ignoring the usual banter that inevitably happens, Tom ploughed on. "He'd got in touch because I'd helped a friend of his sister, Theresa..." Sometimes it happened like that, other times it was an official referral; he's worked for famous names, royalty, the lot, has Tom... but he's more interested, really, in just helping your average bloke in a house down the street. Not that this sounded like an average street, or house for that matter. "'Something to do with some buzzing?' Tassoc said when I agreed to meet up with him at the property."

"Buzzing?" I asked.

"Surely I mentioned that previous case, didn't I?" Tom looked puzzled then, but not as confused as I was. "The one with the bees?"

I shook my head. He throws these out a lot, and actually he mentioned a number on this night – I always make a note to circle back and ask about them. *This* one I definitely would. *Bees?* Am I right?

He flapped a hand. "Doesn't matter. It's not important. What *is* important is what he told me when I arrived at the place, your standard ex-council house, three up, two down sort of thing. Looked okay to me from the outside, I certainly wasn't getting any strange feelings about it either way. Just that it required a fair amount of TLC, was definitely in need of some repairs – the garage down the side, for example, was on its last legs, but still being used for storage. I could see an old ladder sticking out through one broken window. Might even have smashed the glass in the first place, for all I knew. We didn't hang around though, as it had started drizzling.

"I saw more of the state of disrepair when he led me inside, Theresa joining us not long afterwards, dressed in dungarees and ready for more manual labour. They've been working on the house off and on for a little while now, even sleeping there overnight sometimes as the sleeping bags and mattresses I spotted indicated. Looked for all the world like they had squatters."

"Well, if they're ever in the market for a lick of paint or whatever," I said, cheekily setting out my stall.

Tom just nodded at that. "Unfortunately work had ground to a halt because of their particular problem. 'It's hard to describe really,' Tassoc confessed, giving me a quick guided tour around the sparsely furnished interior. 'Began not long after we got the keys and started figuring out what repairs were needed, didn't it Tess? The noise.'

"'Ah yes, the noise. There was some mention of a whistling sound,' I said, as that's what I'd been told."

"Whistling?" asked Dee, and Tom held up a hand to say he was getting to the explanation.

"Tassoc shrugged. 'Now, I know what you're thinking,' he said. 'It's the wind coming in through the rafters or something, and I admit there are some gaps up there. Definitely a few holes that need fixing, and it could do with some cladding up there.' I would indeed have been thinking along those lines, as nine times out of ten things like this are down to ordinary, everyday occurrences, apart from the fact I'd been assured it was something *unusual* this time. 'But it's nothing like that, Mr. Carnacki.' He frowned, rubbing his chin. 'At first we thought it might have been the locals playing tricks. You know, because of Hailey. Maybe trying to drive us away. Only it's the feeling you get when you hear it. I can't... It's probably best that you see for yourself, which you almost certainly will if you spend any great amount of time here.'

"'And where did you hear this... whistling exactly?' I asked him.

"'We thought it was coming from upstairs originally,' Theresa – Tess – chipped in. 'We were still working in the kitchen even though it had got dark, sorting out the plumbing – which is a bit of a mess, honestly – when it started up. Softly, quiet like. Then building, louder and louder.'

"'We followed it up the stairs, but couldn't work out which bedroom it was coming from,' Tassoc said, picking up the thread. 'And it was only when it got much, much louder, that we turned to each other and realised: it was coming from everywhere at once.'

"'Everywhere and nowhere,' the sister added, a bit theatrically I thought."

Like Tom can talk, he can lay it on thick when he wants to – though to be fair, he usually has us in the palm of his hand when he's in full flow.

"'It was such a racket, dear God!' Tassoc said. 'We put our hands over our ears, but it didn't seem to help at all. Like it was getting inside your head somehow, worming its way in. We carried on checking the rooms up there, but in the end had to go downstairs to get away from it – and even then it continued. Followed us down there, like the... like the Devil himself was at your back! Do you know what that feels like, Mr. Carnacki?'

"I had to tell him that I did, because it's true. I know *exactly* what that's like, I wish that I didn't. But I gestured for him to continue.

"'All throughout the house that whistling... When it died down, we checked everywhere else in the property – and even outside.' Tassoc shook his head. 'We couldn't find anything, could we Tess?'

"'Not a sausage,' she confirmed. 'No sign of where it might be coming from at all. Not that we expected to, and definitely not after we'd heard it a few times. It's just not something natural, Mr. C.'

"'Tom, please,' I told her, yet she insisted on calling me that the whole time I was there. Which turned out to be a little while, as I wanted to observe this strange phenomenon myself. I'd already done my due diligence, as usual, getting Fitz to check out the house and its history. It was built back in the early '60s, like so many of them on that estate, and although it had seen its fair share of ups and downs – including a small fire, and being used to sell drugs when a young couple lived there in the 1990s – there had been no fatalities in the place itself. The closest was a heart attack in 1987, but the occupant later died in hospital."

"Hold on, hold on. A fire?" asked Lizzy.

Tom cocked his head. "Yes. Back in the 1970s, while the property was empty. Luckily it was spotted and put out fairly quickly, before it did any structural damage, and the council 'spruced' the place up again before the next person on the list was ferried in. They blamed the local kids for it, in much the same way Tassoc did for the whistling when he and his sister first heard it. The more things change, the more they stay the same, it would appear."

"But nothing else suspicious?" Hartley pressed.

"Not that I was aware of," said Tom with a slight shake of his head. "So anyway, I began unpacking my gear to set it up around the place. Sensors, cameras, audio recorders – I figured EVP might well come into play with this one, seeing as it dealt with sound.

"'We've organised a camp bed in the back bedroom,' Tassoc informed me, so I would use that as a base of operations. 'And we'll just carry on sleeping down here.'

"I thought about arguing that perhaps they should just leave me to it, but then again I could understand wanting to keep an eye on everything with a stranger in the house – regardless of the fact they'd brought me in, and I came with recommendations. They didn't really know me and this was a peculiar situation all round."

"They usually are," Bierce pointed out.

Tom gave a tip of his head. "Quite so. Anyway, my hosts ordered in a takeaway and we spent quite a pleasant evening talking about this and that as the rain lashed down harder outside. Small talk to begin with, like where Tassoc was planning on taking his fiancée on honeymoon, although it soon came around to asking about my previous cases. I was more than happy to tell them about a few. The incident with the Grey Dog for example, or the Yellow Finger experiment."

Neither of which he'd ever told us about, I should add. See what I mean?

"'What do you think we're dealing with here, Mr. C?' Tess asked me when I'd finished.

"'Hard to say,' I answered. 'Maybe the herald of a semi-materialisation? Oh, something trying to break through into our reality,' I explained when they both looked confused. 'I suspect we'll know more in due course.'

"They had some cans of lager, but I was happy with just a coke or two. I definitely passed on the nips of whiskey, from a bottle that looked like it had seen a pounding already. I like to keep my wits about me when I'm on a job, as you know. Eventually, I retired upstairs and left the siblings to it – checking on the feeds when I got to the bedroom they'd given me. Once I was satisfied nothing was happening, I read for a little while – though I soon found my eyelids drooping.

"I'd nodded off only for a short time when I heard the noise they'd described. It was indeed an odd whistling, which reached me in that room. Sounding, as Tess had said, like it was coming from everywhere and nowhere at once. I got up and ran to the door, almost bumping into the Tassocs on the landing.

"'Do you hear that?' said the brother.

"'Can't really miss it, can you,' I replied with a frown, looking about me at the same time. 'Here,' I said, passing them each an item I'd brought with me and had meant to give them earlier. 'Put those on.'

"Tassoc held his up, bewildered. 'What is it?'

"'A protection bracelet,' I said, holding up my own wrist and showing him mine. I had them made not long before taking this job on, each bead containing garlic inside – a terrific counter to the kind of Aeiirii forms of semi-manifestation we might encounter. In the time it had taken to do that, the whistling had increased in both volume and strength. Almost to the point of a scream. Not only that, but the whole corridor felt like it was vibrating. Then shaking, the floor especially, pitching us into the wall at one point.

"'Jesus!' shouted Tess. If I'd had time I would've explained that the standard religious icons very rarely offer any kind of defence in situations like these.

"There was a rocking and a creaking, a build up to something – I could tell. 'Get away!' I called back to them. 'Quickly!' But it was too late.

"We were all three of us hit by a blast of something, as if a huge maw had opened – the mouth of a vast pit – and unleashed its fetid breath. It was accompanied by a loud crack of thunder and lightning from outside, at least I think that's where it was coming from.

"We were driven back and half-fell, half-stumbled down the staircase. Back onto the lower level of the house. It wasn't much more pleasant down there, the noise stalking us and the walls and floors shaking accordingly. It felt like an earthquake was going to tear the entire building apart.

"Then as suddenly as it had all started, it stopped. We looked at each other, survivors of this strange event. Worse perhaps, because I had been on site? Or just an escalation that would have happened anyway? In any event, once the excitement was over I said, 'Perhaps I will have that drink of whiskey after all.'"

Lumley gave a small chuckle at that. "Good man."

"Purely medicinal, I assure you," said Tom with a smirk. "Nothing happened the rest of that night, and when I checked all the video and audio recordings, I found an odd distortion during that time period which had prevented them from picking anything up.

"It was at that point I insisted they leave me there on my own. 'Someone will get hurt otherwise, I can feel it,' I told them. Tassoc was as reluctant as I knew he would be, but in the end agreed. I was the expert after all, and if it meant that I could perhaps get rid of whatever was causing this, then...

"So, I was left alone in the house for several days, where I held a vigil. I spread salt across any entranceways, taping them to make sure this wasn't some kind of prank – if it was, then at this point I would have been amazed. And yes, I admit, I have been fooled once or twice in the past – that incident at Laurel House most recently – but it's never usually for very long. Plus, there *was* supernatural activity on those particular grounds when all was said and done..."

Now this one I did get down, and quite the read it makes too! It taught me that Tom isn't mad keen on jokers and *really* doesn't like to be pranked.

"The more time I spent in this location, however, the more convinced I became of my conviction. The bizarre whistling came back a few times, and though I wore earplugs I could still hear its shrieking – a mocking, grotesque parody of a human whistle. It delivered the exact opposite effect; not joy, but a chilling unease. You'd find yourself falling into a sickening depression, hot but cold at the same time. It wasn't even as if I could use an electric pentacle this time, nor any other protective circle – because it was impossible to pinpoint exactly where the noise was originating from. Thus I had to rely on the bracelets – two, plural, one on each wrist – topped up with a loop of the garlic beads around my neck.

"I'm not sure which was worse, the incidents or the quiet between them. A sort of 'purposeful silence' similar to the kind I experienced in the case of the Silent Garden. As if you were waiting for the other foot to fall, which it inevitably did – reminding me of both the cases of the Grunting Man and the Nodding Door."

Come on, Tom! Three in one go I haven't chronicled yet. But I will, don't you worry about that. You can't drop a Nodding Door into the conversation and expect everyone to just forget about it, can you?

"I was also getting nowhere in narrowing down what might be causing this malevolent whistling sound, in spite of consulting many online sources – including Harzan's Monograph on Astral and Astarral Co-ordination and Interference – and being reminded of the Sigsand mannnuscropt by the whole Nodding Door affair. In that, it states quite clearly: 'Theyr be noe sayfetie to be gained bye gayrds of holieness when the monyster hath pow'r to speak throe woode and stoene'. In other words, how do you stop a creature that's using an entire house to conjure up such harmful noises?

"Before I could even embark on a series of tests to work out the best approach, I was called away on an emergency. Ironically also involving sound, the other case I was working on; a particularly troublesome banshee I thought I'd calmed down for the time being had resurfaced, and was putting people's lives in jeopardy. I had to leave temporarily, but assured Tassoc on the phone that I'd be back soon, and made him promise not to set foot inside that house until I did."

Two cases at once, as he'd mentioned. I wonder how often Tom does that, or even juggles more? I know he's the best at what he does, and is in demand and everything, but it explains why he looks so exhausted all the time. Okay, okay... got it. Back to the story.

"As it happened, the banshee business did give me one or two ideas as to how I might handle the whistle plaguing Tassoc's home. The use of sonics against that beast made me consider whether that was the way to expel whatever was causing havoc and preventing Tassoc from living happily ever after with his wife to be."

"I'm not sure I'd want to live in that place *at all* after what you've told us," Lizzy said next, pulling a face. "Even if you managed to get rid of the blasted thing!"

Tom gave another weak smile. "Houses are just houses, Lizzy. Once such problems have been addressed, there's no reason why two people shouldn't go on to be perfectly happy in a home like that one." She didn't look convinced, I have to say. But Tom wasn't to be distracted at this point. "Now, where was I? Oh yes, the banshee. Fight fire with fire, as it were. Or sound with sound. That was my intention upon returning, but it didn't get that far down the line.

"A taxi dropped me off back at the house that evening, and as soon as I got out I felt there was something very wrong indeed. I checked the video feed on my phone, as I'd been doing for days

– seeing nothing untoward, not even the strange distortion that always occurred whenever the whistling piped up. Only now it was going haywire, interference on every camera – but also something else. In-between, flashes of Tess' terrified face. What the hell was she doing inside there? I asked myself. I'd been specific enough! Maybe she just couldn't wait to get started back on the repairs, and had gone behind Tassoc's back?

"Whatever the reasoning behind it, I knew when I heard that cursed whistling – mixed with a scream now – that she was in trouble. I dashed up to the front door, tugging on the handle. It was locked. I rummaged around in my pockets for the spare key Tassoc had given me, finding it at the precise moment a huge yell came from inside. I looked up, gritting my teeth, then got on with fumbling the key in the lock. I tried turning it and—

"It wouldn't budge. No matter how much I twisted it, as hard as I could – fearing I might even snap it off inside the lock itself – I couldn't get it to open. I began banging on the door. 'Let me in! Tess, it's Tom Carnacki, let me inside!' Nothing – other than more whistles and screams.

"Acting fast, I skirted the house – thinking maybe I could smash a window with a rock and gain entrance. But there was no need. A window was open a crack in an upstairs bedroom. I didn't remember doing that, but then again I was in a rush to head off and tackle that banshee, so it was possible, I supposed; there was nothing much to steal inside anyway, aside from all my equipment. But I was glad of my forgetfulness, as it meant I could reach Tess. All I needed was to get up to that window.

"It was then I remembered the ladder in the garage, the one I'd spotted when I first got there. I rushed to grab it, sliding it out through the broken window there and placing it against the side of the house. It was a rickety old wooden affair, and I was concerned it might not hold my weight, but I had to try. I climbed up several rungs before one gave way, almost pitching me back to the ground. But I held on, making it up to the top finally.

"When I got there and looked inside the room, I saw what could only be described as pandemonium. Tools were being flung around; bits of wood, plaster and panelling had been wrenched from the walls and were whirling about as if a poltergeist might be to blame. I could feel the vibrations, the shaking, from the outside – the ladder juddering against the wall as I struggled to stay upright. All the while that infernal whistling and screaming persisted.

"And there, in the middle of it all – the outline of Tess. It snapped me out of my reverie and I yanked the window open wider, clambering through it and tumbling to the floor. I called out the woman's name, hoping she'd call back, 'Mr C!!'; all the time shielding my eyes from the onslaught of wind – that foul breath-like wind I talked about earlier on – and detritus. Only now I was in there, I could see no sign of Tassoc's sister at all.

"I staggered to my feet, making my way across the room like an explorer in a blizzard. The whistling was growing louder again, filling me with dread. The screeching sounds were intensifying, but in amongst it, I could also hear laughter. Whoever was doing this was enjoying it! And still I couldn't see Tess, let alone do anything to help her...

"It was at that moment I became aware of the wall on my right bowing inwards, bellying and forming some kind of shape. I gaped at it, watching as a pair of thick, black, gargantuan lips appeared. Like the Devil's own. They were puckered, surely the source of all the whistling and the sounds that were shaking the structure to pieces. Dust was falling from the ceiling, cracks appearing in the other walls as the lips grew larger and larger.

"I lost my footing, then realised why – the floorboards beneath me were giving way, splintering and caving inwards. I turned to try and reach the window, even the window-sill to grab it as a hole appeared under my feet, but there was no time. Instead, I dropped through with the rest of the floor into the living room below."

There was an audible gasp from some of the audience at this one, Lizzy putting a hand to her mouth. Tom looked at each of us in turn, before carrying on.

"I must have blacked out for a second or two—"

"Understandable," said Chambers, but was quickly shushed for trying to steal the limelight.

"—When I came around and gathered my wits, I realised I'd landed on one of the mattresses the Tassocs had been using, wood and bits of ceiling all around me. Thankfully, nothing seemed to be broken *other than* the roof above, and all was silent once more – but a silence which was building to something once more.

"I remembered Tess, casting around and looking for another body in the room, but spying nothing. Maybe she was underneath some flooring, buried under planks of wood and bits of tattered carpet? The whistling started up again, slowly to begin with and then getting louder and louder, the screaming-laughing accompanying it. I got to my knees, then shakily to my feet, crossing my wrists where I was still wearing those bracelets."

"Like Wonder Woman," whispered Hartley, but was ignored by the group.

"I firmly believe those, and the string of beads around my neck, were all that saved me that night. But I was granted a vision of sorts – intense feelings washing over me, along with the heat. Fire lapping, biting into me. More whistling, but those whistles turning into high-pitched screams and bitter laughter.

"Snapping to, I gave the room another quick scan for Tess; there was still nothing. But as the wind whipped up again, and the house began to shake a final time, I had to give up and head for the door. I felt certain that if I didn't get out of there at that particular moment I'd be a dead man."

More gasps, Lizzy biting her fingernails.

"It was still sticking however, jammed rather than locked. I tugged on it, pulling back with all the strength I had left until the door finally gave on the last effort. I practically fell out into the open air, the sound of sirens reaching me in the distance.

"The emergency services, including the fire brigade and police, had been alerted. Called by the neighbours, probably because it sounded like World War Three was going on in the house. I tried to warn the uniformed figures about venturing inside, but obviously they ignored my ramblings. They did at least confirm that there was nobody else in there, regardless of my insistence that I'd seen Tess.

"Something which couldn't have been possible, as I discovered when Tassoc *and* his sister arrived on the scene – whilst I was being checked over in the back of an ambulance. A few cuts and bruises, nothing major thankfully.

"'What... what happened?' the owner wanted to know, and I couldn't really blame him. Nor did I have any kind of answer to give the man, but as I told him: 'I fully intend to find out.'

"The authorities put it down to a minor isolated earthquake, but of course I knew differently."

"You don't get manifestations of giant lips with those!" Chambers said with a snigger, which was borne more of relief I think than anything.

Tom just sighed and nodded. "I'd been reluctant to involve anyone else in all this, but now I had no choice – and I did at least have a clue."

"The fire," Lizzy said again.

Our friend smiled softly and went on: "At times like these I call on a psychic lady I know called Iris. I've found her to be uncannily accurate in the past, as she was on this occasion, even from a distance – as I didn't want her stepping inside there until we'd figured out what to do.

"I got the whole story from her, of the death on the property anyway... The rest Fitz filled in, once we had a name."

"Death?" spluttered Lizzy. "But you said there hadn't been—"

Tom held up a hand. "Indulge a storyteller some misdirection," he offered by way of an apology, before going into the actual explanation. "It all comes down to the sad tale of a Mr. Manning Frank, also known on the circuit as 'The Jester'. The standup circuit that is, back in the 1970s. As well as telling jokes, he used to whistle little tunes – his most well-known one was a rendition of the so-called 'Song of Fools'."

"Sounds like that guy my nan used to like back in the day, Roger something or other..." said Chambers. "You can find clips of him on MeTube."

Tom just shrugged. "I don't think Mr. Frank ever made it on to TV, in fact his career imploded due to his alcoholism. Something that really ramped up when his wife passed away in childbirth, taking their baby with her. The gigs dried up alongside the laughs, and when he drank a little too much one night and fell asleep with a lit cigarette dangling from his mouth..."

"So it was *him* that caused the fire," said Lizzy, pursuing her line of enquiry. "If he once lived there, then how come your man Fitz didn't flag it when he did the research?"

"Ah, now here's the part that foxed us all," Tom replied. "Mr. Frank never technically lived in Tassoc's home. When everything went sideways for him, he ended up on the streets – ended up breaking into that empty house, between tenants, one fateful night for shelter. That's when the accident happened, when the fire was spotted. And if Iris is to be believed, he woke up when he was already ablaze – doused in spirits, so he was going up like a bonfire – but instead of screaming, he whistled... to begin with anyway.

"Bloody hell," said Bierce. "But didn't they find his remains?"

"They found what was left of his corpse, burnt to a crisp – parts of him already in the walls, the ceilings. Because heat, and fire, rises. Nobody was supposed to be living there, he was a John Doe – remember this was in the days before DNA or anything like that – and so the authorities quietly finished the job at the local crematorium. Don't worry, we've reported all this, but it's doubtful that anyone who was responsible is even still around. Nevertheless, the truth is now out there, as they say."

"*The X-Files*," said Chambers, nodding, then whistled the opening theme tune.

Tom pulled a face. "A tragic clown," he said, looking pointedly at the man, drawing a parallel no doubt. "And a part of the house, sleeping until something woke him up..."

"Tassoc's love for his fiancée," stated Lizzy.

"That's right," confirmed Tom. "I daresay the history of that place, with its drug dealers and such, wasn't a particularly happy one until Tassoc came along. When what was left of Frank realised what a happy marriage those two would have, perhaps even a baby or three, that's what kicked everything off. It made him jealous, angry; and all that negative energy had to come out in some way. Easily mistaken for the Devil's work."

"And when you got involved, I don't suppose it took very kindly to that either," I said.

"I don't suppose it did, no. Which was why it tricked me into thinking Tess was inside at the end, because it wanted to stop me once and for all. Didn't work, though. Because I was soon back, with all the tools at *my* disposal."

You can bet your life that had nothing to do with drills and hammers. In fact, as well as the rituals he hinted at, Tom told us that sections of the walls, skirting boards and floors were ripped out and destroyed.

"Literally fighting fire with fire this time," he said finally, "as they were burned, while I chanted over the ashes." Like I said, Tom doesn't care for jokers much – nor pranksters. But there was more to this than that. "It's my dearest wish that we've granted Mr. Frank some peace now. The house is cleansed anyway, I can assure you of that."

"Sounds like it's been gutted," commented Bierce with his estate agent's hat on again.

"Well, yes. But that's being rectified. Don't worry, I'm covering the cost," Tom added. He's loaded, is Tom. "Let's call it a wedding present to the happy couple."

I could see Lizzy swooning at that.

"I've even told them about a terrific painter and decorator I know, who'll be glad of the work." He winked at me, because Tom's not just generous with his time.

With that, we wrapped up the evening and said our goodbyes (I overheard Dee asking if he had Tess' number, and couldn't help smiling). But I also noticed Tom wincing a little as he dished out hugs – those cuts and bruises a bit more serious than he'd been letting on. So, I dawdled behind to talk to Tom personally; not just to thank him once more, but to ask how he was.

"I'm... I'm good, Dodge. Thanks for the concern."

"You take it easy, okay," I said, placing a hand gently on his shoulder. "Get some rest. Take a break."

He nodded. "I will." But you just know he'll be at it again before too long, taking on the next case or cases – plural. We won't find out what those involved until we all meet up again. I can't help worrying, though. Because, I really have grown quite fond of him.

My mate Tom. Thomas, that is... Thomas Carnacki. Maybe you've heard of him, but chances are unless you've had a run-in with something otherworldly you might not. If that's the case then count yourself lucky, right?

Very lucky indeed.

The Vanishing

(Winning Story in the 2025 WordCrafter Short Fiction Contest)

Denise Aparo

Dvita stared at her reflection, disturbed by the image in the mirror. At twenty-two, she still had a baby-face expression when she was in a good mood. But now, the face in the mirror smiled at her with dead eyes.

Get OUT!

She flinched, trying to back away. Unable to turn her head, her arms hung limp by her sides. Helpless. The image in the mirror was speaking, but there was no sound.

Cheeks wet with tears. Her head jerked back in silent laughter. Hysteria overtook her body, shaking in a frenzy. Wild-eyed, she forced her own words, "STOP!" As she punched the mirror with her right fist, blood spewed from torn knuckles as she fled the bathroom.

The morning sun sliced through the slats of the bedroom window shades as Dvita woke from a night of fitful sleep. Clear band-aids covered two knuckles on her right hand. She examined the dressings. "How did I get these injuries? Another crazy dream?" Her hands ached, and when she peeled back the bandages, she could see that a few knuckles were scabbing over.

"Lost time again?" She couldn't remember. These episodes seemed to happen whenever she was tired. The events were disturbing. It took days to recover. The stress of not knowing what she did during these blackouts was exhausting.

Dvita vividly recalled taking her medicine. She took her pills daily, but the count didn't seem to decrease by much. She had lost track of the days. Doctors diagnosed her with dissociative disorder when she was only seven. She took medication to combat the symptoms when they surfaced. These psychotic episodes had been a constant struggle, off and on, her entire life.

Lucky, if you could call it that, she had a job with flexible work hours and peace of mind doing the accounting for a small local factory. She was never missed at work when a random episode occurred. At least she had this small comfort.

The shrill of her phone broke the silence with the *Reflection* melody ringtone, interrupting her thoughts.

"Hello?"

"Hello, Ms. Twyne. I am Joe Banks. As your grandmother's attorney, I set up a meeting with the realtor of your grandmother's estate. Your appointment is Friday, ah, tomorrow morning, at nine AM."

"Thank you."

"Since you are the only beneficiary of her estate, there's no rush. We can discuss the rest of your grandmother's will when you return. Have a good day."

Dvita clicked off the phone she held in her bandaged hand. She stared at the dark image on the screen, trying to recall the last conversation with Gran at the house in Maine. Her grandmother had asked her to do something.

"What was it?" Dvita sighed as she watched her cat, Twyla, slink across the top of her living room couch. Memory loss was the worst side effect.

The one thing she could never forget was her guilt over her mother's death. Dvita's mom died, giving birth to her. She had been carrying twins, but only Dvita survived. Her mom was so distraught with the loss that she could barely carry Dvita to term. She gave birth a month early and died before she would lay eyes on Dvita. Wallowing in the moment, she felt the weight of grief, anger, and pain wash through her. Her limbs felt heavy and weak. It was so unfair. Gran was the only family she knew—all she had in the world, and now she was gone. Guilt, loss, and pain were the consequences of her life. Poor memory was her only consolation.

"Okay, Twyla. Let's pack. We need to drive to Maine tonight. I need to meet the realtor in the morning." She crooned to her tabby and scratched behind her ears.

She texted work that she would be out tomorrow and a few days next week, then packed a small bag and put a light dinner in a cooler bag for Twyla and herself.

Twyla napped in her crate, buckled to the backseat as Dvita drove along the familiar back roads to Maine, humming to the country station. She enjoyed the evening's peaceful time of reflection. A few trucks flashed headlights as they passed, but the road became vacant as the sun sank below the horizon. It was the best time to view the wildlife that drifted near the thoroughfare. Dvita spotted a mother doe and two babies grazing between the high grasses.

Suddenly, something spooked a fawn. It took off, leaping through the grass and springing across Dvita's path.

"Damn!" As she slammed her foot on the brakes, the overnight bag and small cooler flew onto the floor mats. Twyla yowled. Dvita felt gooseflesh travel the length of her arms and spine. The two remaining deer promptly followed their mother as Dvita sat too stunned to move.

HONK-HONK! A large truck suddenly appeared from behind, vibrating its heavy woofers. It quickly swerved around her and then took a rapid left to turn down the adjacent road.

Puffing out a loud exhale, Dvita pressed down hard on the gas pedal. She turned off the music, deciding to ride in silence. "Ugh! Sorry, Twyla! Are you okay back there?"

"Rarrrr-sisssss." Twyla paced inside her crate.

"Almost there." Dvita waved her right hand, trying to soothe the miffed cat from the front seat, then focused back on the road. Gran's long driveway was just ahead. Thinking of the last time she was here with her grandmother, Dvita tried to recall what she had told her. They discuss their family tree, literally. An old black alder tree stood alone at the end of the property.

"Dvita, you need to understand. You must come live here someday when I am gone."

"Gran, don't talk like that. You will live a long time."

"I hope so, but what I must tell you is very important. It's your duty."

Dvita always had a difficult time whenever her grandmother talked about family duty. It was ironic since there were no living relatives. Gran was all she had since her parents had died in a car crash when she was only seven years old.

"Gran, there's no one left. I am only accountable to you and me."

"That's what you need to know. I should have told you years ago!" Gran was visibly upset. Her voice had trembled, almost in fear.

That was all Dvita could recall. Occasionally, the blackouts caused memory lapses, and her memories became muddled. She just had to rest and concentrate, and it would return to her, eventually. Rest always helped her remember.

Finally, pulling onto the long driveway with only the car headlights and the bright full moon to guide her, Dvita parked on the lawn next to the front door. Gran's house was dark, and the nearest neighbors were at least three acres away.

Stepping through the door of her grandmother's oversized farmhouse, Dvita smelled the familiar sweet, earthy, and herbaceous aromas of essential oils mixed with the heady and refreshing minty scent of eucalyptus. It smelled like home. Once in the kitchen, the large pantry radiated multiple savory and earthy tangs with a musty hint of dried spices and jars of roots.

Dvita put her overnight bag in the room Gran had set up for her years ago. The bed had a white headboard and a white comforter with muted pastel throw pillows. A plain white dresser sat in the corner with watercolor floral paintings on the wall.

Twyla jumped up onto the queen-sized bed and snuggled under the throw pillows. "Not so fast, Kitty. Move over." Dvita chuckled, pulling down the bed linens and slid under the covers then turned off the bedside lamp. She lay next to Twyla, letting her bones sink into the comfort of sleep.

The morning sky brought a downpour that howled through the old gutters, making sputtering protests as it hit the muddy ground. Through the torrent, the doorbell chimed several times in quick secessions.

"Sorry! Dvita yelled over the rapping rain." The door overhang, amongst other items, was tidily placed in the backyard shed, still awaiting repair. "Coming!"

The man had water dripping from his soaked hair and ruddy face, and his coat quickly left a small puddle on the indoor mat. He wiped his feet. "Sorry for the mess." He shrugged. "I'm your realtor, Byron Mallory." He extended a plump, damp hand.

"Yes. Come in. Don't worry about the water." Dvita gestured toward the parlor with a band-aid drooping off one finger. She smoothed down the bandage, trying to hide her minor embarrassment. "Please, sit down. I made coffee if you'd like?"

"Thank you. That sounds excellent right now."

Twyla paced the couch, scowling at the soggy man and making low growling sounds.

Dvita returned with two steamy mugs and set them on the coffee table.

"Thanks." Mallory gripped the hot cup and sipped the rich brew gratefully.

"Do you have a buyer yet?" Dvita was anxious to sell the old home despite her grandmother's wishes to keep it. There were too many memories, and she knew it wouldn't be the same without Gran here.

"Nothing concrete, but there are two interested. One is a company looking to build a shipping warehouse, and the other is an older couple needing space for a family member."

"Oh. I wouldn't want this house torn down to be a warehouse." Dvita frowned. "Gran would hate that. Tell me more about the couple."

"Yes. Oh, but before I forget, I need you to sign this paper saying you'll allow me to pursue buyers for you."

Dvita took his offered pen, with her band aid securely in place, and quickly signed.

"Thanks."

"You're welcome," he smiled back at her. "The couple are in their sixties and care for a parent who lives with them. They liked the addition to the house with its full on-suite. It's a perfect living space."

You're not selling this house! Dvita shook her head. Why was she thinking this?

I won't let you do this to me or Gran! Dvita stood up, feeling that familiar sensation of terror wash over her body. "Oh no! NOT NOW!" She could feel one of her episodes approaching. It was terrible timing.

Twyla nudged Dvita and circled her head. She continued to rub against her face, purring and whining loudly.

"I'm up. I'm up." Dvita protested to Twyla. Her head ached. She tried to turn in the bed, but something blocked her. She sat up and then slowly held out her hands. They felt sticky.

"Oh, my GOD! Blood? What is happening? She scanned the room and realized she was not in the bedroom. Why am I in the basement?" She shouted as her entire body shook. She looked down at her feet. "Where are my shoes? I don't think it's my blood. Oh God, whose blood is this, and where did all this mud come from?"

Twyla circled her, growling and whining.

Dvita tried to stand, pushing against something hard. Something metal. "A shovel? What is that doing here?" Confused dread filled her chest.

Finally, upright, she swayed as she tried to gain her balance. Gran's old chest was open with scattered flecks of mud and blood. She searched the dim basement and then staggered to the stairs. Taking one step at a time to the main floor, she tried to remember.

Daylight shone through the living room windows. It was morning, and the rain had stopped. She searched the room for Mr. Mallory. She dreaded the thought of him leaving and not wanting to sell her grandmother's house. "What happened?" Fear felt like ice through her veins.

After a much-needed shower, Dvita dressed and went back to the basement. She had called and left a message with the realtor to call her.

Twyla circled the hatchway door. Dvita understood and opened the hatch. She stepped outside and promptly followed Twyla toward the back property. The cat mewed, stopping to look at Dvita, ensuring she was behind.

"What's wrong, girl?" Twyla mewed several times and kept going.

She trailed the cat to the large black alder tree on the back property. The sodden grass glistened as the morning sun reflected off the long blades.

Twyla circled again. This time over a large mound of dirt under the old tree.

"What is it, Twyla?" Dvita's voice quivered. Fear rose in her chest, and she felt the anguish rise in her throat. "No," she whispered, fearing what lay beneath the saturated earth.

Dvita backed away and then ran to the basement. Sprinting the hatchway stairs, she reached the bottom and eyed the dirt-crusted shovel. She swiftly snatched the handle and ran back to the old tree.

Standing in front of the mounded soil, she stared. Her right hand shook as she carefully lifted the dirt a little at a time. On pulling away the third scoop, a muddy hand flopped back down onto the earth.

Dvita heard the distant sound of a scream. "Where was that coming from? Who is screaming?" The place was cold and dark. The darkness bound her, and she could not move or see. Fear seemed an afterthought or a distant plea.

"Where am I?"

You know.

"I do?"

Yes, Dvita. You have always known.

"Who are you?"

You know that, too.

"Where am I?"

You never left.

Fear gripped Dvita, feeling the chilling, familiar words seep into her skin.

You cannot leave this place. Gran tried to cast a spell, but I had to stop her.

"No!" Dvita turned in circles within the dark space.

But, yes! The dark voice mocked her.

Dvita pictured her grandmother swaying from the old alder. She had joined the rest of her people who hung for their crime of witchcraft. When they took her down from the noose, they buried the charmed rope beneath the tree. The demon in her head laughed.

"Oh, no! Gran."

She can't help you. I stopped the spell. It's my turn.

Dvita quickly caught a glimpse of her wavering reflection in the murky puddle next to the old tree.

"GET OUT!" Dvita screamed.

That won't work on me. I took Gran's grimoire and bound you.

Dvita struggled to think of what to do, but her thoughts were clouded by a murky madness. She had to regain control of this chaos. "This can't be real. Is it?" Dvita struggled to focus. "GET OUT!" Struggling with her thoughts, Dvita used all the strength she could pull from inside her mind. All she could see, and feel was darkness.

Light flickered through Dvita's heavy eyelids. She heard talking. "Was someone calling out to her?" It seemed so far away. It was an effort to use her voice. Her throat hurt as she strained to speak. She tried to open her eyes.

"Hello? Try to look at me." The low voice called again, gently.

Finding a way through the haze, she croaked in a muffled tone. "Wh-ah... where am I?"

"I'm Doctor Twila Gataki. You had a nasty fall and hit your head. Do you know your name?"

"I'm Del—Dvita. Dvita."

Dr. Gataki smiled at her. "Good. Now rest. I will return later."

Dvita fluttered her heavy eyelids and drifted.

The next time Dvita opened her eyes, she could see she was in a white room with a monitor beeping soundlessly. Was she in a hospital bed? The lingering scent of a disinfectant solution clung to the space.

On closer examination, she noticed she was in a twin bed in a solitary room with a television mounted in the corner and a painting of wildflowers intentionally placed on the wall. They were the only items other than a noiseless monitor with zig-zags dancing across the screen.

Dvita tried to raise her right arm. She noticed an IV line inserted there and connected to the soundless machine.

"Hello?" she croaked, barely audible.

"Yes? Be right there." A distant voice echoed from the nurse pager at her side.

A slender young woman entered, wearing blue scrubs. "How are you this morning, Ms. Twyne?"

"Where am I, and what day is it?"

"It's Sunday. Doctor Gataki will be here to see you shortly. She will talk to you and answer all your questions."

The woman set a tray of food on a side table, positioning it in front of Dvita. She then checked the monitor, pressing a few buttons, then moved Dvita's IV and checked the fluids. She tapped on the bag and smiled. "Everything is fine. The doctor will be here shortly." She glided out the door with a nod.

A short while later, Dvita heard a voice say, "Good morning," and looked up to see Doctor Gataki again. This time, she held a clipboard and pen. She pulled a chair closer to the bed and sat down.

"How do you feel this morning? Do you know your name?"

"I'm okay, I guess. Of course, I know my name. I don't think I hit my head that hard. Where am I? I want to go home?"

"I need to check your eyes. Head injuries can be unpredictable. You're at Maine Medical Center, and I need to assess you before I release you from my care."

Dvita tried to sit up.

"Here." Doctor Gataki reached behind, adjusted Dvita's pillow, and pulled her food tray closer. "Your meal is hot. I can run through my assessment while you're eating."

Dvita nodded. She tried to pick up the fork, but the IV line hindered her from movement. After making some effort, pushing her food around her plate, she asked, "Can you take this out? I'm right-handed."

The doctor wrote a few things on her clipboard, then looked up at Dvita with a closed smile. "Oh, sorry. Just do the best you can."

Dvita took a bite of eggs with her shaky left hand. She felt her staring, outwardly searching her face for what? "This feels strange. You're staring at me. I could never do much with my left hand." Dvita frowned.

The doctor shook her head, "No. I'm sorry. It's a hazard of the job. I'm just checking your eyes for dilation. You had a hard fall, so we must watch you for a while.

Dvita didn't believe her, but she took a small bite.

"So, tell me what you remember about yesterday?"

Dvita dropped her hands, staring down at them as she spoke. "My grandmother's lawyer called to tell me to meet the realtor, Mr. Mallory, on Friday at my Gran's house in Maine. I drove there with Twyla, and the next morning, Mr. Mallory arrived in the pouring rain. I gave him a cup of coffee, and that's all I remember."

"Do you remember the next day?"

Eyes wide, Dvita leaned forward. "Twyla! Where is my cat, Twyla?"

"Oh. Don't worry. I'm—your cat is fine. I have an officer checking in on her and feeding her." Dr. Gataki shook her head with a smile. "Sorry, let me check my notes. Oh, here. Officer Dan Gatto. Now, do you remember anything about the realtor, Mr. Mallory?"

Dvita returned to staring at her hands. "No. Not much. I don't remember seeing him again." Her memory was spotty. She could not piece anything rational together.

"I see. Well, we can come back to that. Do you remember what you spoke about when you gave Mr. Mallory coffee?"

"He mentioned having two interested buyers. One was a business, and the other was a family. I told him my grandmother would hate having her home transformed into a business. He said he would draw up the paperwork. I—I don't recall anything after that. I must have passed out."

"I see." Dr. Gataki wrote on her clipboard.

"What are you writing?"

"Just a few notes. I'm trying to help the police locate Mr. Mallory. He's missing. Your information is helpful to their investigation.

Dvita studied her hands again. "Okay."

Doctor Gataki's phone buzzed. "Hello? Yes. Yes. I understand." As the doctor ended her call, she looked at Dvita. "Dvita, I need to stop right here. I hope you don't mind, but I must go to my office and verify some information. We can discuss this tomorrow."

"Oh, okay," Dvita stared back at the doctor, confused but tired. "I guess I'll see you tomorrow, then."

Dr. Gataki quickly gathered her belongings, avoiding eye contact as she approached the door. She looked back at Dvita and said, "You'll be fine." With a reassuring smile, she walked out, closing the door behind her.

The following morning, Dvita woke up with a headache. She had asked the aide for a pain reliever. After dozing off, she noticed the aide had left a couple of tablets on her tray when she woke up again. She quickly took the tablets with the cup of water placed beside them.

Moments later, a knock sounded, and the door promptly opened. An elegant, gray-haired woman entered, wearing a crisp white lab coat and badge. "Hello, Dvita," she smiled broadly.

"It's nice to meet you. I'm Doctor Dillion Lucian." She extended a slender hand to Dvita.

Dvita reluctantly responded with the one free from the IV. "Where is Dr. Gataki?"

"I'm going to be covering for her this week. Unfortunately, she had a family emergency." Dr. Lucian gave her a close smile. "I've reviewed your history and believe I am up to speed. I have a few questions regarding Mr. Mallory."

"I told Dr. Gataki everything I know. I want to go home." Dvita lifted her right arm, pointing to the IV. "And I want this off," she said, frowning.

"Yes, all in good time. But, first, we need to discuss Mr. Mallory."

Dvita's eyes darkened, "You're not the police. Why would you care? I want to go home now." She suddenly flashed her eyes to the doctor, "I want to leave, NOW!" Dvita's face suddenly curled into a broad smile. "You think you are clever, don't you?"

"No. I don't judge. I'm just getting facts straight to help you deal with this dilemma. I'm trying to figure out what happened to Mr. Mallory because you were the last one with him. Since you blacked out after you spoke to him, I need to help you remember. It's for your mental health."

"Maybe he's home."

"No. Mr. Mallory is still missing. He never checked back into his office, and his wife said he never came home."

Dvita's shoulders shrugged as she lifted both palms and dropped her hands.

"I think you know more than you are saying." Dr. Lucian shook her head.

"She's an idiot!" The dark voice rose from within Dvita.

"Who's an idiot?" Dr. Lucian calmly asked.

"Humpf."

The doctor sat motionless, watching Dvita's face. "So, who's an idiot?"

"You look familiar."

"Oh? I must have that sort of face?" said Dr. Lucian.

"You can't discuss my private information."

"No. I cannot," said Dr. Lucian.

A broad smile widened across Dvita's face. "I'm Delaney."

"I see," Dr. Lucian replied with no hesitation.

"Gran tried to cast me out, but I stopped her."

Dr. Lucian continued to watch Dvita's face. "How?"

"I possessed Dvita on her last visit to Gran. I watched them both, and then I took Gran's grimoire, tied her to the tree, and bound Dvita."

"Why did you do that?" asked Dr. Lucian.

"The old woman was going to tell her about me. She planned to reveal how to cast me out. She had to die."

"I see."

"No, you don't! Not yet!"

Dr. Lucian nodded. "Then tell me."

"I know you from somewhere. Where?"

"Probably because I admitted Dvita when she first arrived."

"Maybe."

Dr. Lucian continued to observe. "Tell me what I do not know."

A smile broadened across Dvita's tired face. She flung her head back against the pillow and laughed. When she stopped, she clenched her fists. "I'm not leaving."

"Agreed. I am not releasing you until I have made my assessment."

"What? No! You can't keep me here!"

"Yes, you cannot go until I complete my task." Dr. Lucian stood and pulled a large book from a sack by her feet.

Dvita's eyes widened in shock. "No! How did you..."

"I am a practitioner in your grandmother's Emperor's Coven. I am her High Priestess. I am the Plague Doctor." Her eyes darkened as she swiped the tray from the table. It crashed to the floor. She replaced it with the large grimoire.

"You can't unbind her. It's an unbreakable curse!" Delaney flinched as the Plague Doctor leaned closer.

"But I can." Raising the old book, she began to murmur ancient words as a slow mist rose from the floor.

The young woman tried to move, but an old rope emerged and threaded itself around her, deliberately coiling her like a snake. "Let go!"

The doctor chanted low, slowly increasing her pace.

Buzzing filled her head as Dvita's body shook and jerked back against the pillow. A gray mist filled the room as she trembled with every word, bed knocking against the stark white wall.

The chanting became a chaos of lyrics that pulsed through the room as the small frame shook. Her dark eyes rolled up—replaced by white pupils.

An eerie cry erupted from the thrashing body, filling the room with a cacophony of dual screams—one high and one low.

The sound persisted for several minutes. Until, finally, silence.

The gray mist that filled the room slowly settled, vanishing as swiftly as it arrived.

The doctor stood silently, watching the young woman.

Sweat soaked her petite frame. Blood leaked from her pale nose. Dr. Lucian remained still, waiting.

Several minutes passed. The young woman stirred in the bed. The rope still confined her limbs as she moved her head from left to right. Finally, her eyes flashed open. Unshed tears trickled down her cheeks. "What?" Confused, she began again. "What's happening?"

Dr. Lucian waved her hand over her limp body, and the ropes evaporated. "How are you feeling?"

"Tired. What am I doing here?" She said, eyes scanning the room and bed. "Wh—where's my cat, Twyla?"

"She's safe. Can you tell me your name?" Dr. Lucian asked.

"Dvita." She closed her eyes, attempting to touch her forehead with her right hand, then dropped it. She then lifted her left hand to touch the IV stuck in the right one. "Why do I have this?"

"I can remove the IV now. I know having it in your right hand had to be difficult to perform any task," she told Dvita as she pulled the wrappings off and glided the needle from her hand. "There. You can move now."

"Thank you."

"You had fallen and hit your head, but you can go home today. Your head seems better. No signs of concussion." She smiled, lifting a large sack with her clipboard.

"I'll get the aide to help you dress and gather your things for discharge," she said, leaving the room.

The aide entered, holding the door for the doctor. "All set. I have your things."

"Is the doctor returning?" Dvita asked, looking at the bag in the aide's hand.

"Once dressed, you can see the doctor for a last check so she can sign your discharge papers."

Dvita's legs felt shaky as she swung them over the bedside. She stood barefoot against the cold tile. "I can dress myself," she told the aide.

"Okay. Here are your items." She handed her a clear plastic bag filled with her clothes and then walked to the door, pausing before she left. "Doctor will be in shortly."

After ten minutes, Dr. Lucian entered the room. Dvita's hands rested patiently on her lap as she sat in the side chair, fully dressed and ready to leave.

With a clipboard against her arm, the doctor scribbled something on the board and looked at Dvita. "Tell me how you are feeling now. Do you remember anything about your visit with your realtor, Mr. Mallory?"

"Ah. I guess. We spoke at my Gran's house. He said he has a buyer, a family interested in buying my grandmother's house, but I need more information. I will wait to see the police findings." She shrugged, then released her limbs, drooping slightly.

"Yes, well, you've had a hectic time. I've changed your meds according to your bloodwork. Dvita, you need to know that when your mom was pregnant, she had twins. You have been suffering from the effects of that twin's genetic makeup in your system. It's called the Vanishing Twin Syndrome. You carry the DNA of both you and your lost twin. Your body absorbed your twin inside the womb. I gave you an infusion to help combat the foreign proteins in your system. Your body was fighting the cells like an infection. But you should not have any more problems. We can discuss it at your follow-up visit next week."

Dvita stood with her belongings and walked to the door. She nodded. "Okay, wow. Thank you. I can't believe that all I had was an infection. I would like more information about it at my follow-up appointment."

"Get some rest, and I'll see you again in a week."

Dvita turned and opened the door with her left hand. For a brief moment, the whites of her eyes flashed black before returning to white. She turned back toward the doctor and smiled slowly. "I guess I'll see you in a week."

About the Authors

Mario Acevedo – "Villa's Gold"

Mario Acevedo is the author of *The Nymphos of Rocky Flats* in the national bestselling Felix Gomez detective-vampire series, the YA humor thriller, *University of Doom;* and co-authored the Western novel, *Luther, Wyoming*. His work has won an International Latino Book Award, a Colorado Book Award, and has appeared in numerous anthologies to include *Midnight Roost; Denver Noir; ¡El Porvenir, Ya!;*and *Shadow Atlas*. Mario was a faculty member in the Regis University Mile-High MFA program and Lighthouse Writers Workshops and was the editor of *Ramas y Raíces: the Best of CALMA*, an anthology from the Colorado Alliance of Latino Mentors and Authors.

Mario is a contributor to Ask the *Authors 2022: Writing Reference Anthology* and has been a presenter and panelist for WordCrafter virtual writing conferences. In addition, his story,

"Immediate Intervention" is featured in *Midnight Garden: Where Dark Tales Grow* (volume 2, Midnight Anthology Series, 2024).

Joseph Carrabis – "Jeremiah", "The Boy Who Loved Horses", & "Them Doore Girls"

Joseph Carrabis is a master storyteller with a sharp sense of humor and deep linguistic expertise. Hailing from New Hampshire, USA, his passion for writing began at the age of seven while washing dishes with his older sister, Sandra. She'd read 'Mission to the Heart Stars' for a book report and shared her fascination and excitement over the story. Joseph, a plate in one hand and a dish towel in the other decided, "I want to give that joy in the written word to people." With a career deeply embedded in evolving technologies, Joseph served as Chief Research Officer, Chief Neuroscience Officer, and Senior Research Fellow at several institutions and agencies while earning numerous awards for his journalism and trade technical writing.

Joseph refers to himself as boring - something loudly debunked by his readers and peers - and weaves wildly imaginative stories that dance on the boundary of the known and unknown sciences where natural, preternatural and supernatural intersect. Fans' comments regularly mention Carrabis' ability to bring together advanced mathematics, quantum physics, cybernetics, and neuroscience with believable multi-dimensional characters and spellbinding future technology.

Joseph has been nominated for the Pushcart Prize, recommended for a Nebula Award, and received an honorable mention in 'Writers of the Future'.

Joseph's story, "Marianne", is featured in the 2022 *Visions* anthology, and his stories, "The Beach" and "Blood Magic" are featured in *Midnight Roost:Weird and Creepy Stories* (volume 1, Midnight Anthology Series, 2023); and his stories, "The Last Drop", "Grande Ture", "The Exchange", "The Tomb", and "Striders" are featured in *Midnight Garden: Where Dark Tales Grow* (volume 2, Midnight Anthology Series, 2024); his story "Mercy" is featured in *Tales From the Hanging Tree: Imprints of Tragedy* (2024), and his stories, "It's a Man's World" & "Grafton's Ghost-Child" are featured in *Curses: Chronicles of Darkness* (2025), all from *WordCrafter Press.*

Jon Shannon – "The Stairs"

Jon Shannon and his wife, Lori have been married since 1995 and have two adult sons. They all live in Saco, Maine.

For over 20 years, Jon has been a morning show host on the top country radio station in the state of Maine. Tune in to 101.9 WPOR any weekday morning for the fun with Jon, Joe and Courtney. Jon is also a Maine Broadcasting Hall of Fame inductee, and was named one of the Top 30 Country Program Directors in America by *Radio Ink Magazine*.

Jon also hosts the popular Maine People Podcast, featuring notable guests from all over the state. Jon's first novel, *The Longest Summer*, (National #2 Hot New Release as chosen by Amazon), is available at many bookstores as well as Amazon, Kindle, and as an audiobook from Audible and Apple Books.

Jon's story, "Stitch", is featured in *Midnight Garden: Where Dark Tales Grow* (volume 2, Midnight Anthology Series, 2024), from *WordCrafter Press*.

Rebecca M. Senese – "The Price of Beauty"

Rebecca M. Senese weaves words of horror, mystery, contemporary fantasy, and science fiction in Toronto, Ontario. She is the author of the contemporary fantasy series, the Noel Kringle Chronicles featuring the son of Santa Claus working as a private detective in Toronto. She garnered an Honorable Mention in "The Year's Best Science Fiction" and has been nominated for numerous Aurora Awards. Her work has appeared in *Bitter Mountain Moonlight: A Cave Creek Anthology*, *Promise in the Gold: A Cave Creek Anthology*, *Pulphouse Fiction Magazine*, *Home for the Howlidays*, the *Obsessions Anthology*, *Fiction River: Superpowers*, *Fiction River: Visions of the Apocalypse*, *Fiction River: Sparks*, *Fiction River: Recycled Pulp*, Tesser acts 16: Parnassus Unbound, Imaginarium 2012, Tesseracts 15: A Case of Quite Curious Tales, Ride the Moon, *Hungar Magazine*, *On*

Spec, *TransVersions*, *Future Syndicate*, and *Storyteller*, amongst others. Find her at http://www.RebeccaSenese.com

Rebecca's story, "The Mirror Slacked" is featured in the 2022 *Once Upon An Ever After* anthology and her story, "Take Two", is featured in *Midnight Roost: Weird and Creepy Stories* (volume 1, Midnight Anthology Series, 2023), both from *WordCrafter Press*.

DL Mullan – "The Initiation"

A writer at heart, Undawnted's own creative spark, DL Mullan, began writing short stories and poetry before adolescence. Over the years, Ms. Mullan has showcased her literary talents by self-publishing several collections of her poetry. She also writes novels, designs apparel, and creates digital art. Ms. Mullan's creative writing is available in digital and print collections, from academia to commercial anthologies. As an independent publisher, she produces her own book cover designs as well as maintains her own websites. She is an award-winning digital artist and poet.

Currently, she has embarked on writing her multi-book Legacy Universe, Supernatural Superhero Series, as well as creating original soundtracks for her publications and independent electronic music albums, featured on SoundCloud and YouTube.

DL Mullan holds a Master of Arts in Teaching and Learning with Technology, and is a syndicated columnist, writing Undawntech monthly.

For news and updates, subscribe to the Undawntable Newsletter. Find DL on Amazon, Facebook, LinkedIn, and YouTube. As always: Like, Comment, Follow/Subscribe!

DL Mullan's story, "The Reality Hackers" is featured in the *Visions* anthology (2022), her story, "Mangled", is featured in *Midnight Roost: Weird and Creepy Stories* (volume 1, Midnight Anthology Series, 2023), her story, "Kurst", is featured in *Midnight Garden: Where Dark Tales Grow* (volume 2, Midnight Anthology Series, 2024), and her story, "Twelve Angry Dead", is featured in *Tales From the Hanging Tree: Imprints of Tragedy* (2024), all from *WordCrafter Press.*

Zack Ellafy – "Darkness Tolls"

Zack Ellafy is a writer of short stories, novels, and comics. He left a career as a small business co-owner of a comic store to pursue his dream of writing full time. His favorite genres include science fiction, fantasy, horror, and crime. He is currently working on his second novel and revising his first. Follow him on his Twitter@ZackE89 and look out for his self-named website coming soon! He lives in the suburbs of Denver, Colorado with his wife, Erica Ellafy, and their three dogs and cat.

Zack's story, "At the Mountains, Majesty" is featured in the 2022 *Visions* anthology and his story, "House on the Plains" is featured in *Midnight Roost: Weird and Creepy Stories* (volume 1, Midnight Anthology Series, 2023), and his story "Self-Mutiny" is featured in *Midnight Garden: Where Dark Tales Grow* (volume 2, Midnight Anthology Series, 2024), all from *WordCrafter Press.*

Christa Planko – "Such a Time as This"

Christa Planko, MA, is a professional writer with a passion for creative expression. She has had her poetry and short stories featured in several publications, including *Tanka/Haiku Journal, Poetry Quarterly, Every Day Fiction*, and several *WordCrafter Press* anthologies. Her story, "The Olde-Tyme Village," won the *2021 WordCrafter Short Fiction Contest.*

Following a battle with leukemia in 2024, she wrote a story about her cancer experience entitled, "Joyful in Hope," which won the 2025 Christian Writer's Awards writing contest.

Christa is currently in remission and resides in South Jersey with her feline muses. For her bio and list of published works, visit christascorner.godaddysites.com[1].

Christa contributed the winning story, "Olde Tyme-Village", in the *2021 WordCrafter Short Fiction Contest* and *Where Spirits Linger*

1. http://christascorner.godaddysites.com/

(Narrating the Paranormal Anthology Series, 2021), her story, "The Vanishing Tattoo" is featured in the 2022 *Visions* anthology, and her story, "The Easterville Glass Ghost", is featured in *Midnight Roost: Weird and Creepy Stories* (volume 1, Midnight Anthology Series, 2023), all from *WordCrafter Press*.

C.R. Johansson – "Inside Out"

C.R. Johansson writes gripping thriller, science fiction, fantasy, and even horror stories with a genetic twist. Her characters explore universes where the unknown prevails and the impossible is possible akin to her life with congenital heart disease. She works and plays in the Pacific Northwest with her husband. When not writing, she enjoys listening to the nearby river and communing with nature and the world around her. You can find her on Facebook and GoodReads.

C.R. Johansson's story, "Her Beholder" is featured in the *Visions* anthology (2022), her story, "She Shed Galleria", is featured in *Midnight Roost: Weird and Creepy Stories* (volume 1, Midnight Anthology Series, 2023), and her story, "Therion's Heart" is featured in *Tales From the Hanging Tree: Imprints of Tragedy* (2024), and her story, "Road Kill" is featured in *Curses: Chronicles of Darkness* (2025), all from *WordCrafter Press*.

Kaye Lynne Booth – "Sangoma, Zombie Elephants, and Tokoloshe, Oh My!"

For Kaye Lynne Booth, writing is a passion. Kaye Lynne is an author with published short fiction and poetry, both online and in print, including her short story collection, *Last Call and Other Short Fiction*; and her paranormal mystery novella, *Hidden Secrets*; Books 1 & 2 of her Women in the West adventure series, *Delilah and Sarah*, and book 1 in her Time-Travel Adventure series, *The Rock Star & The Outlaw,* as well as her poetry collection, *Small Wonders* and *The D.I.Y. Author* writing resource.

Kaye holds a dual M.F.A. degree in Creative Writing with emphasis in genre fiction and screenwriting, and an M.A. in publishing. Kaye Lynne is the founder of *WordCrafter Quality Writing & Author Services* and *WordCrafter Press*. She also maintains an authors' blog and website, *Writing to be Read*, where she publishes content of interest in the literary world.

Kaye is the founder and executive editor of WordCrafter Press with short stories in all the WordCrafter Short Fiction Anthologies: *Whispers of the Past* (2019), "The Woman in the Water"; *Spirits of the West* (2020), "Don't Eat the Pickled Eggs"; *Where Spirits Linger* (2021), "The People Upstairs"; Once Upon an Ever After (2022), "The Story Witch"; *Refracted Reflections:Twisted Tales of Duality & Deception* (2022), "The Not So Perfect Prince" & "The Devil Made Her Do It"; *Visions* (2022), "If You're Happy and You Know It"; *Midnight Roost: Weird and Creepy Stories* (2023), "Melina"; *Midnight Garden: Where Dark Tales Grow* (2024), "The Puppet Men"; *Tales From the Hanging Tree: Imprints of Tragedy* (2024), "The Legend of Cottonwood Hollow" & "One That Got Away", and *Curses: Chronicles of Darkness* (2025), "Caverna del Oro (Cave of Gold)" & The Death Clock".

Robert White – “Cattails”

Robb White lives in Northeastern Ohio. He is a Derringer-nominated author of genre fiction and three series detectives: Thomas Haftmann, Raimo Jarvi, and Jade Hui. *Betray Me Not* was selected for distinction by the Independent Fiction Alliance in 2022. His 2024 publications include a collection of noir tales: *Fade to Black: Noir Stories of Grifters, Drifters, and Unlovable Losers.* A new thriller is *Jersey Girl* from Close to the Bone Publishing, U.K.

Robert’s story, “Fire Sale at the Burdock Family Business” is featured in *Midnight Garden: Where Dark Tales Grow* (volume 2, Midnight Anthology Series, 2024), and his story “The Longspeth’s Curse” is featured in *Curses: Chronicles of Darkness* (2025) from *WordCrafter Press*.

Roberta Eaton Cheadle – "Just Deserts"

Roberta Eaton Cheadle, is a South African writer and poet specialising in historical, paranormal, and horror novels and short stories. She is an avid reader in these genres and her writing has been influenced by famous authors including Bram Stoker, Edgar Allan Poe, Amor Towles, Stephen Crane, Enrich Maria Remarque, George Orwell, Stephen King, and Colleen McCullough.

Roberta has two published novels and a collection of short stories and has horror, paranormal, and fantasy short stories included in several anthologies. She is also a contributor to *Ask the Authors 2022* (WordCrafter Writing Reference series).

Roberta is also the author and illustrator of sixteen children's books, illustrator to a further three children's books, and the author and illustrator of four poetry books published under the name of

Robbie Cheadle, and has poems and short stories featured in several anthologies under this name.

Roberta Eaton Cheadle is a contributor to many short fiction anthologies from *WordCrafter Press*, as well as co-editor for the Poetry Treasures Anthology Series, volumes 1-5. She contributed the winning story, "The Bite", in the *2022 WordCrafter Short Fiction Contest* and *Visions* anthology, as well as contributing to the following *WordCrafter Press* anthologies: *Whispers of the Past* (volume 1, Narrating the Paranormal Series, 2019): "The Last of the Lavendar" & "Missed Signs"; *Spirits of the West* (volume 2, Narrating the Paranormal Series, 2020): "The Thirstyland Journey" & "The Ghost in the Mound"; *Where Spirits Linger* (volume 3, Narrating the Paranormal Series, 2021): "Listen to Instructions"; *Once Upon an Ever After* (2022): "The War Babies"; *Midnight Roost* (volume 1, Midnight Anthology Series, 2023): "The Behemoth's Rage"; and Midnight Garden (volume 2, Midnight Anthology Series, 2024): "Amahle's Demon".

Chris Barili – "The Snow Globe"

Chris Barili will retire later this year after forty-two years in the US Intelligence Community, so he can write full-time. He writes all kinds of stories, and has published fantasy, science fiction, horror, western, paranormal romance, and crime. He is author of the weird western Hell's Butcher series, and also writes under the pen names B.T. Clearwater (Supernatural romance) and T.C. Barlow (western). Chris holds a degree in English from the University of Nebraska at Omaha, and a Master of Fine Arts in Creative Writing (Genre Fiction) from Western State Colorado University.

Chris is also a contributor to the *WordCrafter Press* Ask the Authors series: *Ask The Authors* and *Ask the Authors 2022* and served as presenter and panelist for the 2020 Stay in Place Virtual Writing Conference and the 2021 New Beginnings Virtual

Writing Conference, hosted by WordCrafter Press. His story, "Shaken", is featured in *Midnight Roost: Weird and Creepy Stories* (volume 1, Midnight Anthology Series, 2023), from *WordCrafter Press*.

Paul Kane – "The Whistling"

Paul Kane is the award-winning (including the British Fantasy Society's Legends of FantasyCon Award 2022), bestselling author and editor of over a hundred and sixty books – such as the *Arrowhead* trilogy (gathered together in the sellout *Hooded Man* omnibus, revolving around a post-apocalyptic version of Robin Hood), *The Butterfly Man and Other Stories*, *Hellbound Hearts*, *Wonderland* (a Shirley Jackson Award finalist) and *Pain Cages* (an Amazon #1 bestseller). His non-fiction books include *The Hellraiser Films and Their Legacy* and *Voices in the Dark*, and his genre journalism has appeared in the likes of *SFX*, *Rue Morgue* and *DeathRay*.

He has been a Guest at many conventions over the years, as well as being a panellist at FantasyCon and the World Fantasy Convention, and a fiction judge at the Sci-Fi London festival. A former British Fantasy Society Special Publications Editor, he has also served as co-chair for the UK chapter of The Horror Writers Association and co-chaired ChillerCon UK in May 2022.

His work has been optioned and adapted for the big and small screen, including for US network primetime television, and his novelette 'Men of the Cloth' was turned into a feature by Loose Canon/Hydra Films, starring Barbara Crampton (*Re-Animator*, *You're Next*): *Sacrifice*, released by Epic Pictures/101 Films. Paul was also asked to pitch, along with a co-writer, for the remake of *Hellraiser* in the late 2010s. In 2023 HorrorCon screened a retrospective of his Film & TV adaptations, and interviewed Paul in front of the live audience. His audio work includes the full cast drama adaptation of *The Hellbound Heart* for Bafflegab, starring Tom Meeten (*The Ghoul*), Neve McIntosh (*Doctor Who*) and Alice Lowe (*Prevenge*), and the *Robin of Sherwood* adventure *The Red Lord* for Spiteful Puppet/ITV narrated by Ian Ogilvy (*Return of the Saint*), plus his plays have been performed at FantasyCon and by Hideout Theatre in London.

He has also contributed to the Warhammer 40k universe for Games Workshop and has been asked to pitch on projects for both DC/Warner Bros. and Marvel. Paul's latest novels are *Lunar* (set to be turned into a feature film), the YA story *The Rainbow Man* (as PB Kane), the sequels to *RED* – *Blood RED* & *Deep RED*, all collected in an omnibus edition – the award-winning hit *Sherlock Holmes & the Servants of Hell*, *Before* (an Amazon Top 5 dark fantasy bestseller), *Arcana* and *The Storm*. In addition he writes thrillers for HQ/HarperCollins as PL Kane, the first of which, *Her Last Secret* and *Her Husband's Grave* (a sellout on Waterstones.com and at The Works) came out in 2020, with *The Family Lie* released the following year (*all* three novels were Amazon sellouts). His books have been translated into many languages, including French, German, Spanish, Ukrainian, Turkish, Czech, Bulgarian and Polish. Paul lives in

Derbyshire, UK, with his wife Marie O'Regan. Find out more at his site **www.shadow-writer.co.uk**[2] which has featured Guest Writers such as Stephen King, Charlaine Harris, Robert Kirkman, Catriona Ward, Dean Koontz, Olivie Blake and Guillermo del Toro.

Paul sat on panel discussions and presented the Keynote speech for 2021 WordCrafter New Beginnings Virtual Writing Conference and is a contributor to the *Ask the Authors 2022: Writing Reference Anthology* from *WordCrafter Press.*

His story, "The White Lady" is featured in *Midnight Roost: Weird and Creepy Stories* (volume 1, Midnight Anthology Series, 2023), his story, "Drip Feed", is featured in *Midnight Garden: Where Dark Tales Grow* (volume 2, Midnight Anthology Series, 2024), his story "The Hanging Men" is featured in *Tales From the Hanging Tree: Imprints of Tragedy* (2024), and his story, "The Weeping Man", is featured in *Curses: Chronicles of Darkness*, all from *WordCrafter Press.*

2. **http://www.shadow-writer.co.uk/**

Denise Aparo – "The Vanishing"

Denise Aparo is an author with four published short stories in the horror/supernatural genre in the WordCrafter Midnight Anthologies. Her *Curses* and Midnight Series stories are written under Denise Aparo and are edited by Kaye Lynne Booth, through *WordCrafter Press*.

As a native New Englander, she lives with her husband Joe, spending much of her time writing, reading, gardening, making crocheted blankets, and crafting with her grandchildren. She loves the paranormal historical fiction genre and has recently completed edits on her first novel, a historical fiction titled *Crossbows*, which will be self-published in the near future.

She has a Master's Degree in English - Fine Arts/Creative Writing with concentration in Fiction from Southern New Hampshire University (SNHU). And a member of five honor societies with leadership recognition. She is published in several newspapers and magazines—special interest articles, along with poems and short stories that have been published in print and digital format. She is a member of the Connecticut Authors and Publishers Association (CAPA) and the author of a WordPress writing blog, The Write Voice.

Denise has three short stories in the horror/supernatural genre in the Midnight Anthology Series, through *WordCrafter Press*. These short stories are published under Denise Aparo. A short story published in another *WordCrafter Press* anthology, ***Curses: Chronicles of the Darkness***, is titled, "Mohawk Monster: The Curse of the Herkimer Diamond," a horror/supernatural genre based on curses. This anthology is also edited by Kaye Lynne Booth.

Midnight Roost: Weird and Creepy Stories: 20 authors created 23 paranormal stories of horror. Creepy tales that give you goosebumps!

https://books2read.com/MidnightRoost Her short story is "The Pines."

***Midnight Garden: Where Dark Tales Grow*:** 17 authors crafted 21 eerie horror stories. https://books2read.com/MidnightGardenAnthology[3]. Her short story is "Jack Moon and the Vanishing Book."

Midnight Oil: Stories to Fuel Your Nightmares: Chilling stories that steal into your thoughts! Her short story, "The Vanishing" was chosen as the winning story in the *2025 WordCrafter Dark Fiction Contest*.

3. https://books2read.com/MidnightGardenAnthology%20%20

Thank You for Reading Midnight Oil: Stories to Fuel Your Nightmares

If you liked it, please leave a review for the complete anthology or for any of the individual stories. Show your support for the wonderful authors whose stories are featured here.

It's okay to post a review that's only about the stories that you read.

You may also like these other anthologies from WordCrafter Press

Midnight Roost: Weird and Creepy Stories: https://books2read.com/MidnightRoost

Midnight Garden: Where Dark Tales Grow: https://books2read.com/MidnightGardennthology

Whispers of the Past: https://books2read.com/WhispersPast

Spirits of the West: https://books2read.com/SpiritsoftheWest

Where Sprits Linger: https://books2read.com/WhereSpiritsLinger1

About the Publisher

WordCrafter Press publishes quality books and anthologies. Learn more about ***WordCrafter*** and keep updated on current online book events, writing contests, up coming book blog tours and new releases on the ***Writing to be Read*** authors' blog: https://writingtoberead.com/